Critica

RUBY SILVER

"A bloody showdown . . . Old West style."

—Ken Hodgson, award-winning author

"He [Trace Brandon] may be the focal point in terms of rich character development, but the other foils and players, including Coffee, who I particularly enjoyed, were also well crafted and memorable. I think that's the best way to describe this book—completely memorable."

—John J. Staughton

"Reneau has created a character in Trace Brandon as raw and heroic as the types from Ian Fleming's James Bond to James Patterson's Alex Cross or Tom Clancy's Jack Ryan."

—Gary Harp, Hall of Fame Reviewer

DIAMOND FIELDS

"*Diamond Fields* is a rare find; one of the best adventure tales this side of *Treasure Island.* If Robert Louis Stevenson was from Texas, his name would be Randall Reneau."

—Kinky Friedman, *New York Times* bestselling author

"*Diamond Fields* is a timely page-turner in the style of Clive Cussler or the late Robert B. Parker. Immensely entertaining."

—Ken Hodgson, award-winning author of
The Man Who Killed Shakespeare

"Diamond Fields is highly recommended, and compelling to the very last page."

—*Midwest Book Review*

DEADLY LODE

"*Deadly Lode* is a great fiction novel and a very easy, enjoyable and quick read."

—*Reader Views*

"Catapults the reader into a well-told story with all the excitement of a big-budget blockbuster."

— *Spokane Coeur d'Alene Living Magazine*

"*Deadly Lode* is a wonderfully entertaining book with an intricate plot."

—*Freebooksy*

"The pace is fast, the dialogue snappy, and deception lurks at every turn."

—Sheldon Russell, award-winning author of
Dead Man's Tunnel

"Wraps up tidily in a satisfying, action-packed conclusion."

—*The US Review of Books*

Acknowledgment

A very special thank you to Jenny Meadows for her excellent editing, insightful comments, and good humor . . .

By the Same Author

Diamond Fields

Deadly Lode

Ruby Silver

Randall Reneau

south of good

This book is a work of fiction. Names, characters, places, and incidents either are products of the author's imagination or are used fictitiously. Any resemblance to actual events or locales or persons, living or dead, is entirely coincidental.

First paperback edition September 2014

For additional information, please visit our website at: http://randall-reneau.com

Cover design by Jerry Reneau - www.reneaugraphics.com

Manufactured in the United States of America

10 9 8 7 6 5 4 3 2 1

ISBN: 978-1497342477

ISBN: 1497342473 (e-book)

This Book is for Clyde Yancey, fellow mineral mercenary, fisherman, graduate of the Evelyn Wood Academy, and all-around good guy . . .

Chapter 1

When you stop and consider it, most of us are pretty much just hanging on by our fingernails. Think about those folks sitting at their desks having a morning coffee, and looking up to see, very briefly, the nose of a Boeing 767. Or the rogue cell in your pancreas that decides to heed the call and "go forth and multiply." Five billion offspring later, a shadow shows up on your x-ray.

Beneath the *Ozzie and Harriet* veneer, the world is in a constant flux of good versus evil. And in 2010, Cameron County, Texas—was way south of good.

In ten more days I'd be forty-six. I shook my head in disbelief and propped my dusty cowboy boots on a desk that'd been in the Cameron County Sheriff's office for as long as anyone could remember. I fired up my last Nicaraguan cigar, took a deep pull and let my mind wander back to what I considered the beginning—Texas A&M and the Corps of Cadets.

I'd graduated with a degree in Criminal Justice and a minor in chemistry. Hell, I'd have made a better drug dealer than most of the cretins I was currently locking up.

After college, I was commissioned as a "butter-bar" second lieutenant and was obliged to give *Uncle Sugar* four years of my life. He conveniently arranged to extend my tour long enough so I could participate in the first Gulf War.

After discharge from the Army came twenty years as a DEA agent, two wives, two divorces, a drinking problem, but no children, which, all things considered, was probably a blessing.

In three more months, I'd have served a full year as the duly elected Sheriff of Cameron County—what used to be a sleepy South Texas border county.

Thanks to America's insatiable appetite for Columbia's *white lady*, the cocaine drug-gates had opened and the border area of Cameron County had become a war zone.

I still cannot comprehend an America where so many people feel their lives are so hopeless that the only way they can get through the day is by snorting lines of pharmaceuticals.

But maybe that's always been our nature. Before drugs flooded our culture, we were awash in a sea of booze. I watched alcohol kill my father, and by extension my mother. And it has its delicious tentacles firmly entwined in my gray matter.

My best friend from high school, Wesley Stoddard, was up to his nose in drugs. Not that he used the white powder; he didn't. Wes liked pot and hated cocaine and the people behind it. But he was in the trade and once you're in, it's usually for life—however short.

Wes had attended UT-Austin for a couple of years, studying aeronautical engineering. His major accomplishment during his brief stay in Austin was obtaining his pilot's license. Turned out Wes was a natural pilot, and before long he was ferrying bundles of marijuana in an old, beat-up, Cessna 210. It was good money, the authorities tended to look the other way, everybody got high, and nobody got killed.

When I was with the DEA, I'd heard rumors about Wes's little smuggling operation. Fortunately, I worked the Eastern Caribbean, and Wes never strayed from the Texas-Mexico border area.

I took another drag on my cigar and blew a perfect smoke ring. Smoking was prohibited in county-owned facilities, but the powers that be cut me a little slack. I knocked the ash from the end of my cigar into the wastepaper can and answered my cell phone, which was vibrating like some kind of dildo in my shirt pocket.

"Sheriff Hardin Steel."

"Stainless, it's Buck. How about lunch?"

I laughed. Only a few of my oldest friends remembered my high school nickname. "Sounds good. Where are you?"

"I'm in downtown Brownsville. How about Mexican at Lupe's?"

"Perfect. I'll see you in ten."

Buck "bite 'em in the butt" Bateman and I had been friends since grade school in Harlingen. He got the "bite 'em in the butt" handle from our high school football days. Woe be the ball carrier at the bottom of the pile if he was within chomping range of Buck. Our team recovered more than one bite-induced fumble.

Buck was a licensed PI and worked out of a small office on the second floor of a partially restored historic building on the corner of Adams and Eleventh Street in downtown Brownsville.

He was waiting in front of Lupe's Café when I pulled up in a sheriff's cruiser. As I parked, I noticed a few of the local panhandlers scurrying off like so many cockroaches.

Buck was smiling when I walked up and shook hands. "Boy, you sure cleared out the local winos."

I looked around. "Yeah, I guess I did at that."

Buck was two inches taller than me, at six-foot-four, and, at 250, outweighed me by fifty pounds—if you caught him before lunch. He wore his reddish hair in a close-cropped crew cut under an omnipresent Aggie baseball cap. Buck favored pastel T-shirts tucked into khaki slacks, and cordovan penny loafers.

Back in my serious drinking days, we'd put away a prodigious amount of liquor. And we both had a few busted capillaries in our cheeks to prove it.

Buck grabbed one of the double doors in his huge hand. "Let's get some chow. I'm about to faint from hunger. And I've got some info you may be interested in."

We took a booth at the back of the small restaurant and ordered cheese enchiladas, guacamole salads, a large bowl of queso, chips, and iced tea.

I knew Lupe's cooks probably didn't have their green cards, but that was a problem for Immigration. All I was interested in was a good enchilada.

Buck dipped a tortilla chip into the artery-clogging bowl of queso and spooned on a large dollop of guacamole. He managed to get most of it in his mouth. When he finished chewing he looked around the café and then leaned forward.

"Word on the street is our old teammate, Wes Stoddard, has a planeload of shit coming across the border in two or three days."

I leaned back in my chair, took a long drink of my iced tea, and set my glass on the table. "Any idea where the drop is going to take place?"

"Word is Wes is using the old airstrips on Roughton Ranch. You might mention it to Rory, next time you see her."

I nodded and worked on my enchiladas. "I'm having supper with Rory on the island tonight. I'll pass it on."

Buck took a drink of his iced tea and shook his head. "You know, Wes is not a bad guy. Hell, he started out flying in a few kilos of weed and just kind of got sucked in. And he's never been convicted of trafficking."

"I know," I replied. "I think there's a part of him that wants out. But I suspect that's no easy thing."

Buck snorted. "Not when you're transporting coke for Frederick Ochoa."

I looked at Buck. "Do you know the story on Ochoa?"

Buck shook his head. "Not really. I just know he's a brutal son of a bitch."

I dipped a chip into the queso. "His father was a Nazi, and a bad one. He fled to Argentina after the war and eventually worked his way to Durango, Mexico. He married into the Ochoa family and took their name. Toward the end of his life, the old man managed to knock up one of the Ochoa women."

Buck chuckled. "Those old Nazis were hard to the bitter end."

I snorted and nodded. "I guess so. Anyway, the old man died shortly after Frederick was spawned. And the rest, as they say, is history. The DEA's been trying to punch FreddieO's ticket for years. But he's too well protected in Mexico."

Buck finished his enchiladas and pushed his empty plate away. "I'll bet."

I nodded and pointed my fork at Buck. "It's not only his drug money and connections, the Ochoas made millions in silver mining, and old Frederick controls that money, too."

Buck shook his head. "Jesus, how much is enough?"

I chuckled. "More." I paused for a second. "How do you know Wes is using the old airstrips on the Roughton place?"

Buck wiped his mouth with his napkin. "I know the ranch foreman. He said his cowhands have seen a big twin-engine doing touch-and-goes from some of the old dirt strips. Wes is smart. He doesn't stop, just touches down long enough to have a helper kick the dope out the back door."

"Was it a King Air?" I asked.

Buck nodded. "Could've been."

I put my knife and fork on my now-empty plate. "Wes flies a King Air 350."

Chapter 2

Later that evening, I met my on-again-off-again girlfriend, Rory Lee Roughton, at her condo on South Padre Island. We tended to be "on" when I moderated my drinking, and "off" when I didn't.

Rory's condo was on the bayside of the narrow barrier-bar island. It was one of six in a small development midway up the island. Each condo was two-story with a balcony off the upper level and a private patio off the downstairs living area. Steps led from the patio to a private pier jutting into the shallow waters of Laguna Madre.

Rory was the only child of Robert Lee Roughton, rancher, oilman, and proud son of the Confederacy. She had the looks, body, and money to cruise through life, but she chose to work and was a very successful real estate broker and investor. She'd made millions investing in South Texas real estate. Rory was a prime example of the rich getting richer.

We'd been dating since I'd returned to Brownsville, after having been asked to retire from the DEA. And since my election as Cameron County Sheriff.

I poured Rory a glass of chardonnay and fixed myself a diet Coke with a slice of fresh lime. We sipped our drinks and watched the sun sink into the bay.

The tide was coming in, and schools of redfish were chasing baitfish into the shallows. The waters of Laguna Madre looked like liquid fire with the last rays of red-and-gold sunlight hitting the surface.

Rory kicked off her flip-flops and started to peel off her shorts and halter top. I watched her as she got down to her panties and bra.

She laughed and opened the sliding glass doors that gave onto the patio. "Hot tub?"

She didn't have to ask me twice. I got naked—quick—and followed her out on the patio.

Rory glanced at my rather robust erection and laughed. "Babe, hang a towel on that thing 'till we get in."

I wiggled my eyebrows. "Does that mean I get to get in?"

She laughed and tossed me a towel as she shrugged out of her flimsy bra, kicked off her panties and stepped into the hot tub. "If you're going to get in, Hardin, get in."

Afterward, I walked to the end of the dock and dove into the bay. The cool water felt good after thrashing around in the hot tub.

Rory sat on the end of the dock with a towel around her waist and watched me doing a lazy backstroke. "You know, they caught an eight-foot bull shark in the channel just behind you," she paused and chuckled, "and I hear they're nocturnal feeders."

Thus ended the swimming for the night. We got dressed and headed out for a late supper.

We ended up at Bluebeards, just up-island from Rory's condo. Over fresh-caught Mahi-mahi, I mentioned what Buck had told me at lunch.

"Babe, Buck thinks Wes Stoddard may be using some of the old smugglers' strips on your ranch. People have seen a twin-engine flying in and out. It could be Wes's King Air. You might want to mention it to Robert Lee."

Rory finished a bite of the grilled Mahi-mahi and took a sip of Pinot Grigio. "I'll tell Dad. But you need to find Wes and tell him to cool it. If Pops catches him offloading drugs anywhere on the ranch, there'll be shooting."

I nodded and looked out at the surf breaking behind the open-air restaurant. The moonlight was dancing on the crests of the swells as they rolled in and broke on the sandbars. "I'll set up a meeting with Wes in Matamoros and give him a heads-up."

Rory looked at me. "You still like him, don't you?"

I swirled the wine around in my glass. "Yeah, I guess I do. Hell, he's hard not to like."

*****

Two days later, I put on some civvies, jumped in my Jeep Laredo, and headed for Matamoros.

Wes was supposedly in the produce transport business and kept an office and condo in Brownsville, but he was seldom there. He felt more comfortable south of the river. He'd bought a walled compound from a dead drug dealer's wife in an upscale, or as upscale as one could find in a war zone, part of Matamoros. And he pretty much stayed put, except for his smuggling forays.

When I crossed the International Bridge into Matamoros, I was pretty sure I saw the late Rod Serling leaning against a lamppost, smoking a cigarette. As I passed by he smiled, took a deep drag, and flipped the butt into the Rio Grande. And then he was gone.

Wes was waiting for me on the other side of the bridge. He got out of his white Ford Explorer and waved. I pulled in and parked as near to the Mexican Immigration office as possible. I really liked my Jeep and hoped parking near Immigration would keep it safe.

As an extra precaution, I paid a kid five bucks to keep an eye on it. Then I walked over to Wes's SUV.

Wes was about six feet tall with straight brown hair, piercing blue eyes, and a perpetual tan.

"Stainless," Wes said, extending his hand. "Welcome to Dodge City."

I smiled and looked around. "I don't see many Yankees," I said, shaking hands.

Wes frowned and looked at the nearly empty border crossing. "Yeah, things are a bit out of hand down here, I'm sorry to say."

"Ochoa?" I asked, keeping my voice low.

Wes nodded. "Yeah. FreddieO has definitely upped the ante," he said, opening the driver-side rear door of his Explorer. A large Mexican wearing khakis and a white Guayabera shirt was driving. A second, slightly smaller man, dressed in jeans and a crisp white shirt, was riding shotgun. Except he had an AK-47 across his lap.

I glanced over at Wes. "Expecting trouble?"

Wes shrugged. "Nowadays, you never know. How about a little lunch? I know a place with great *cabrito*, and only sporadic gunfire."

I nodded and rolled my eyes. "Sounds good."

Wes gave me a wink, leaned forward and spoke to the driver in Spanish. "*Los Cuatros Amigos.*" He turned back to me. "Best damned grilled goat in town."

Wes was right. The cabrito was some of the best I'd ever had. And evidently a lunch cease-fire had been declared. So far, no one but the goat had been killed.

As I was off-duty, unarmed, and in a foreign county, I decided to have a Dos Equis with lunch. The amber-brown bottle was ice cold. Condensation ran down its sides and pooled on the table. I drank about half the beer before I set the bottle back on the table.

Wes watched me inhale my beer as he finished a bite of cabrito. "Jesus, Hardin. Long cruise?"

I nodded. "Yeah. I have to watch myself or I slide back into very bad habits."

Wes laughed. "Hell, you'll fit right in down here. We got us a passel of bad habits in *mañana-ville*."

I finished my beer and motioned to the waiter for another. "That's why I asked for this meet, Wes. You're skating, or flying, on thin ice north of the river. My old DEA contacts tell me the Agency is foaming at the mouth to bust your ass."

Wes tossed back a shot of Cuervo Gold and chased it with a healthy swallow of Dos Equis. "Hell, Hardin, if I was flying shit in, and I'm not saying I am, those pukes at the DEA couldn't catch me if they tried."

I took a sip of my newly arrived replacement beer and looked across the table at Wes. "Well, the thing is, pard, they're going to try. And try real hard."

Wes twisted his head around, stretching his neck muscles. "That's what you came over here to tell me?"

I leaned my elbows on the table and laced my fingers together. "That, and to ask you to quit while you're ahead. If you get out now, Wes, you'll skate. I'll guarantee it."

Wes leaned back in his chair and rolled the neck of his Dos Equis bottle between his fingers. "I can't, Stainless. I'm in too damned deep."

I started to say something, but saw Wes quickly cut his eyes toward his two bodyguards sitting at a nearby table. He got their attention and then tilted his head toward the front door. The lunch cease-fire was about to end.

Three rough-looking men in jeans, straw cowboy hats, and snap-buttoned western shirts with the tails left out walked into the restaurant. It took a minute for the men's eyes to adjust from the searing sunlight to the soft light of the eatery. In that minute, Wes's men cut loose with .45 autos they had tucked into the waistband of their pants.

Wes flipped our table on its side, sending plates and drinks flying, and the few other customers in the joint scurrying for cover.

In the next second, he was blazing away using the table as a shield. As I dove behind the table, brass shell casings from Wes's 9mm automatic rained down on me.

The three men entering the restaurant were cut down before they ever saw their assailants.

Wes looked over at his two companions and motioned toward the door with his pistol. Then he looked at me. "Time to go, Stainless," he said, tossing two $100 bills on a nearby table.

On our way out, one of the downed men moaned. Wes put a round between his eyes without breaking stride. He looked over at me and grimaced. "Head for the truck—now!"

Safely in the Explorer, I looked over at Wes and started to say something. He cut me off.

"Those were three of Ochoa's men," Wes said, and then paused for a moment. "I may have forgotten to mention—I'm having a few problems with the cartel."

Chapter 3

Wes dropped me at my Jeep and told me to stay out of Matamoros for a while.

I stared at Wes. "You think?"

Wes just smiled. "Sorry, pal. But occasionally it gets pretty western on this side of the ditch."

I nodded and unlocked my Jeep. "Think about what I said, Wes. There's still time to pull out."

Wes smiled and waved as he and his *pistoleros* hauled ass for safer environs.

The shooting I'd just witnessed was a problem for Wesley Stoddard and the Ochoa Cartel. Last I'd looked, Matamoros was not in my jurisdiction.

I got in my Jeep and drove across the International Bridge. Once clear of the border, I pulled over and used my cell phone to call my office. Everything was copacetic, so I headed to my place just west of Port Isabel—on the low-rent side of the bay. I stopped at Fred's drive-through liquor store and bought a bottle of tequila. I needed a drink.

*****

At eight the next morning my cell phone went off. I could hear the damn thing, but fumbled around for a minute before I found it.

"Sheriff Steel." I said, trying to get enough saliva generated to talk.

"Hardin, it's Rory. Did you meet with Wes?"

I paused for a moment, trying to clear the tequila cobwebs from my brain. "Yes, I saw him."

"Well, how did it go?"

"Before or after the shooting started?"

"What?"

"Never mind, I'll tell you about it later."

"Uh-huh. You sound used up, Hardin. Have you been drinking?"

"Just a beer or two with Wes," I lied.

Rory paused for a long moment. "I hope that's all."

"I'm fine. How about supper?"

"Can't, have to run up to Corpus for a closing. I sold a house in Port Aransas."

"Okay, call me when you get back and I'll fill you in on Wes."

"How'd he look?" Rory asked.

"Tan."

The line went dead. Sometimes Rory didn't have much of a sense of humor.

I showered, put on a uniform and choked down a couple of poached eggs and some toast. I was just about to head for the office when I heard an outboard. It sounded like whoever it was intended to tie up at my dock.

I went out on the back deck of my small bay-front cottage and walked down the half-dozen weather-beaten wood steps to my private dock. I recognized the 22-foot Boston Whaler. It belonged to another of my high school buddies, Dennis Deleon.

Dennis was a professional fishing guide who worked out of Rick's Pier over on the island. We were about the same age, but decades on the saltwater had left him weathered and looking older than his years. On his right calf he carried a four-inch angry-looking scar, a reminder from a stingray to shuffle your feet when wade-fishing.

I caught the line Dennis threw me and tied off the Whaler. "Morning, Dennis. How's the fishing?" I asked, grabbing his right hand and helping him step onto my dock.

"Fishin' is damned good, if you can stay out of the way of the druggies."

"Smugglers?" I asked.

Dennis looked around at a number of boats racing up and down the Intercoastal Waterway. "Used to be a few potheads, but now it's cocaine and AK-47s."

"That why you stopped by this morning?"

"Yeah, Hardin, it is. The damned smugglers are running up the Mexican coast and dropping their loads near Boca Chica, or coming through Lighthouse Pass and heading up the bay to Corpus. It's just a matter of time before some unlucky *turista* stumbles onto a drop and gets turned into chum."

I nodded and looked across the bay at the rows of million-dollar condos. I wondered how many had been bought with laundered drug money.

"Well, Double D, there's not too much I can do. I can put a few more deputies on the water, and I'll notify the Coast Guard of the increased activity."

Dennis nodded. "I'd appreciate it."

"You want to come in for a cup of coffee?"

"Thanks, Hardin, but I have a charter going out of Rick's in about thirty minutes."

"Okay. I'll do what I can. Watch yourself out there."

Dennis slipped the bow line off the dock piling and stepped into the Boston Whaler. "Just so you know, Hardin, from now on I'm packing heat on my boat."

"I don't have a problem with a man protecting himself. Just one thing, Dennis…."

He pushed the boat away from my dock with the end of an oar. "What's that, Sheriff?"

"If you carry a concealed handgun, make sure you have a permit."

Dennis smiled. "It's in my wallet, right behind my fishing license."

I nodded. "Keep me posted."

He winked and turned the ignition key, firing up the 200-horsepower outboard. "Will do, Sheriff." He paused and laughed. "Stay clear of the prop wash."

He gunned the six-cylinder outboard and headed across the bay toward Rick's Pier and a $500-a-day charter.

I watched until Dennis's boat was just a speck in front of a white wake. I shook my head and glanced at my watch. *Drugs—by land or sea or air—*what *a friggin' mess.*

Chapter 4

Frederick Ochoa didn't give a rat's ass about losing three men in Matamoros. Life was cheap in his chosen profession. But he did give a rat's ass about Wes Stoddard's airdrops cutting into his profits.

In the old days, Stoddard had flown tons of marijuana across the river for him. But the introduction of cocaine had soured their relationship.

Ochoa lit a Cuban cigar and shook his head. *A drug runner with a conscience, an oxymoron if ever there was one.*

Leaning back in his overstuffed leather chair, he gazed out the open window of his second-story study and watched the waves breaking on the rocky beach below. He refused to call the stunning body of saltwater the Gulf of California, preferring the Spanish name—*Mar de Cortez*.

Ochoa picked up the phone on his desk and punched one of the eight buttons. Two minutes later his driver brought the bulletproof CL-Class Mercedes around to the front of the compound.

The driver bowed his head slightly as Ochoa strode past the open rear door and slid into the big Mercedes. Like most of the people who worked for Ochoa, he was terrified of his boss.

Frederick Ochoa was a hybrid: half German, half Castilian-Mexican. He was blond and dark-skinned, with cobalt-blue eyes that would have made him a poster child for Nazi Germany.

The skin on his hands and forearms had been badly burned and scarred during an explosion and fire at a jungle cocaine lab. In public, even in the hottest weather, he wore thin lambskin driving gloves and finely tailored long-sleeved shirts.

At five-seven, 150 pounds, he was short and slight compared to his tall, aristocratic father. In the sewer that was Ochoa's subconscious, he harbored a special hatred for men of height. And he took great pleasure in cutting them down to his size.

His father, Baron Frederick Beck, had been a young SS Major during the war. His reputation for brutality had served him well in the Nazi regime. However, the Allies had also become aware of Beck's penchant for torture and had penciled him in for a date with the hangman. With help from ODESSA, Major Beck had escaped to Argentina shortly after Berlin fell.

Other than his height, Ochoa hadn't fallen far from the Baron's genetic tree. His appetite for torture and sadomasochistic pleasures was well known by his enemies, and by the whores in local brothels.

Ochoa glanced up at the driver holding his door. "Café Allegro."

The driver nodded, waited until Ochoa was properly seated, and gently shut the rear door of the Mercedes. He then executed a smart half-turn, took a step, and slid in behind the wheel. The driver knew Café Allegro well; it was one of Ochoa's favorite watering holes.

The swank café was located in the historic district of Mazatlán, but close enough to the beach and the trendy hotels to lure a good supply of female tourists. Ochoa considered it prime hunting grounds.

Ochoa glanced at his 1930s vintage *Rolex-Standart*. His father's name and rank had been engraved into the back of the chromed steel case. Below his name and rank was the double-S symbol of the *Schutzstaffel*.

Ochoa sighed and shook his head. There would be no time to lure a foreign beauty to his lair. Today was set aside for business.

His villa was only twenty miles up the coast from Mazatlán. But with city and tourist traffic, it would take about forty-five minutes to get to the café. And he didn't want to be late. The gentleman he was meeting had come all the way from Buenos Aires, Argentina.

The shooting in Matamoros didn't even make the Brownsville news. So many Mexicans had been killed in the drug war, it wasn't a big deal anymore. If an unlucky or stupid tourist, down from Kansas to get cheap dentures, wandered into a gunfight and got massacred, check page three of the *Brownsville Sentinel.*

It was simple, really. Kill enough people and the rest of the world goes numb. Hitler knew it, so do the current pissant third-world dictators, and so do the leaders of the drug cartels.

The secret to getting by with mass murder is to correctly pick one's targets. In World War II, nobody gave a damn about the Jews, and Hitler slaughtered them by the millions.

Flash forward to today, and nobody gives a second thought to a pile of dead drug dealers. The only time these killings even get a mention is when there's significant collateral damage.

God forbid we should legalize and control drugs to stop a decades-long war that has cost thousands of lives, not to mention billions of U.S. taxpayer's dollars. For what? For nothing.

I finished out the week with normal sheriff's duties: clean-ups after knife fights in Hispanic bars, rousting hookers on the island, and putting a lid on drunken or stoned beach revelers.

By Friday afternoon, I was ready for a break. I called Rory, but she was still tied up with clients in Corpus.

I left the sheriff's office at five and headed to my place. Along the way, I called Buck.

"Buck, it's Hardin. What're you doing in the morning?"

"Stainless . . . I heard there was a little shoot-out across the river. And I heard Wesley might have been involved."

"Could be, pard. It *is* the friggin' *Twilight Zone* over there," I said, leaving out the part about seeing the late Rod Serling smoking a cigarette on the International Bridge.

"Uh-huh. So what about in the *mañana*?"

I stopped at a red light and watched some idiot with California plates scoot through the intersection just as the light changed. I reached down and hit the lights on my cruiser. The driver hit his brakes and pulled over. "Hang on a sec, Buck."

I turned and drove thought the intersection and pulled up next to the driver's side of the SUV. I rolled down my passenger window and motioned for the driver to roll his window down. Then I leaned over and explained how traffic lights worked in Texas. I let him go after the verbal warning.

Buck was chuckling when I got back on the phone. "I loved the lecture. Let me guess . . . California plates."

I laughed. "You got it."

"You asked me what I was doing in the morning," Buck said, dragging me back on point.

"Yeah, if you're not busy, how about taking me fishing in my custom bay boat?"

Buck laughed. "You mean the boat I bought clandestinely through a third party so you could send half the proceeds from a—sort of—arms-length transaction to your ex-wife Margaret?"

"Yeah, that'd be the one."

I'd been married and divorced twice. First to June, who'd since remarried and moved to Charleston, South Carolina and totally out of my life. Followed by Margaret, who was the antithesis of Mary Magdalene.

I'd tried to marry gals who were named after '50s TV wives, like *June Cleaver* or *Margaret Anderson.* Good-looking women who cooked and vacuumed while wearing dresses, pearls, and heels.

At the time, through a whiskey haze, it seemed like a helluva good plan. But in retrospect, there may have been a couple of minor flaws.

Chapter 5

I drove over to the island at seven the next morning and met Buck at Rick's Pier. He already had my, or rather, his boat fueled and in the water.

I grabbed my tackle and a backpack containing my Sheriff's badge and ID, my Glock 9mm, and a pair of army surplus binoculars.

"Morning, Stainless," Buck said, grinning from ear to ear. "Come aboard. There's breakfast tacos in the brown paper bag," he said, pointing to a bag on the console. "Help yourself, but mind you don't spill any hot sauce on my boat."

I nodded, gave him the finger, and helped myself to a bacon, egg, and cheese taco.

Buck laughed, cast off the lines, and fired up the big Evinrude outboard. He eased the boat in reverse away from the dock, gently brought the bow around, and headed for the Intercoastal Waterway.

The Intercoastal was a manmade channel, 12 feet deep and 138 feet wide, that ran up Laguna Madre between the barrier-bar islands and the mainland.

Buck eased into the channel and idled the outboard. "Where to, Stainless?"

"Run up the bay a ways," I replied, pointing more or less north. "I want to get a feel for the local boat traffic. See who's fishing and who has other things on their minds."

"Roger that," Buck said, easing the throttle ahead, putting the boat on plane.

My jurisdiction ended just past Arroyo City, a small unincorporated town about twenty-five miles up Laguna Madre. As I watched the coastline pass by, I could see hundreds of small bays, islands, and inlets. It was, and had always been, a smuggler's paradise.

About ten miles up the bay, a 30- or 35-foot, light-blue "go fast" boat blew by us doing about 50 knots.

I looked over at Buck.

"No way, Hardin. He can probably hit 80 knots flat out."

I grabbed the binocs out of my backpack, but the "cigarette" boat was too far away by the time I got a look-see. I eased up next to Buck so he could hear me over the outboard. "If he pulls in before we get to the county line, I'd like to say howdy."

Buck nodded and pointed to a bunch of birds feeding at eleven o'clock. "Interested in catching some fish?"

I watched the gulls and pelicans feeding. Something was pushing the baitfish to the surface, and the birds were chowing down.

Buck eased the boat within casting distance of the feeding frenzy. We rigged up and cast weedless silver spoons into the melee. We both had big redfish on in seconds. Minutes later, lunch was in the livewell. We caught and released several more reds and then it was over. But we'd get four big fillets from the two reds we'd kept.

We'd just fired up the outboard when Buck tapped me on the shoulder and pointed up the bay.

"He's back," Buck said, powering up.

This time I was ready. I grabbed the binocs off the console and got the boat registration number and name—*HavanaNiceDay*.

"Notice anything, Buck?"

"Yeah, he's going faster than when he passed us before."

"Yep, and he's riding higher in the water. He dropped of someone, or something, up the coast.

"You going to call it in?" Buck asked, gunning the engine and running parallel with the go-fast boat for a few seconds.

"Nope. He's empty. But I'll find out who owns her and have a little talk with them."

"Ochoa?"

I watched the boat and the driver disappear down the bay. "He probably paid for it, but it'll be registered to someone down the line."

Buck nodded and backed off the throttles. "Maybe somebody at Rick's Pier will know the boat. There aren't too many like that around."

"Could be. Maybe we'll get lucky."

"Hell, Hardin, we already did. We got two fine reds in the livewell."

*****

Ochoa's driver let his boss off in front of the Café Allegro and drove off to park the Mercedes. The manager greeted Ochoa as he walked into the bar area.

"Señor Ochoa, so very nice to see you again. Your party is waiting on the balcony. Please follow me."

"That won't be necessary. I see my guest."

"As you wish, señor. Enjoy your meal."

Ochoa waved the maître d' away like he was flicking a piece of lint from his sleeve.

As Ochoa approached the table, his guest stood up, almost as if at attention. Ochoa smiled and nodded, but did not offer his gloved hand. The nerve damage from the burns still caused pain if his hands were squeezed.

Ochoa took a seat and switched to flawless German. "Good to see you, Ludwig. How are things in Buenos Aires?"

Ludwig Duerr was in his seventies, but lean and hard as the organization he headed. He had prominent Nordic features, although his blond hair had long ago gone gray. He was dressed in a finely tailored dark suit. Ochoa noted the small gold lapel pin with a black onyx swastika intricately set in a red ruby.

"Very good, Frederick," Ludwig replied and then paused, "but we are losing the last of the great ones."

"Yes, I would imagine so. The war has been over for a long time."

Ludwig nodded. "In some ways that is true; in other ways, it continues."

Ochoa smiled. “Indeed. And that requires continued funding, does it not?” he said, sliding a plain envelope across the table.

Duerr glanced around the café as he deftly picked up the envelope and tucked it into the inside pocket of his suit coat. “Indeed it does.”

“The envelope contains a check drawn against one of my Cayman Island accounts. You should have no trouble depositing it.”

Duerr returned the smile. “Your generosity will not go unmentioned . . . to the unmentionables.”

Ochoa nodded and then cut his eyes to a stunning young blonde who had just walked into the café. The woman was wearing a white blouse, tied in a knot just below her magnificent breasts, and a flimsy cover-up over a bikini bottom.

If only I had the time, I’d introduce you to the dark side of pleasure.

Chapter 6

You need any help putting the boat up?" I asked Buck as we pulled in to Rick's Pier.

"Nope, I'm good to go. I've got a kid who washes the boat down after I get her in the lift. She'll be cleaned, fueled, and ready for sea in about twenty minutes."

I nodded and jumped onto the dock. "Okay, pard. I'm going to shag it up to Rick's office and see if he knows anything about the go-fast boat."

Buck nodded and moved off slowly toward the floating marina.

I walked down the pier and up a flight of stairs to the main marina office.

"Afternoon, ma'am," I said, touching the bill of my maroon Aggie ball cap. "I'm Sheriff Steel. Is Rick about?"

The very cute gal manning the front desk smiled and nodded. "Yes, sir, he's in back. I'll fetch him."

"Thanks," I said, glancing out the window at a group of fishermen pulling up to the dock.

"Howdy, Sheriff," Rick said, walking into the front office, trailing his assistant. "Long time, no see. You fishin', or is this business?"

Rick Moore was a retired merchant marine four-striper. He was about five-ten, 200 pounds, with a beer keg for a chest. His salt-and-pepper hair was close-cropped, and he sported a tattoo on each of his Popeye-sized forearms. One was an anchor and the other was a heart with the word "Mom" inside it. Occasionally, an idiot would poke fun at "Mom", but usually only once.

"A bit of both, Rick," I replied. "Buck and I caught some nice reds up the bay, before we were nearly run down by *Suck My Wake.*"

Rick laughed. "No shit, that was the boat's name?"

I smiled and shook my head. "No, that's from an old John Candy movie. This boat was named *HavanaNiceDay.*"

"Cute," Rick said. "Smugglers?"

"I suspect she's one of Ochoa's go-fast boats. Have you seen it around?"

"Never close enough to get the name. But, yeah, I've seen her a few times, running up the Intercoastal. She's hard to miss."

I nodded. "She ever put in here for fuel or supplies?"

"Nope. She runs hard up the bay and then a couple hours later back down, and evidently out the pass to the Gulf."

I nodded. "Thanks, Rick," I said, handing him one of my cards. "If the boat ever puts in here, give me a call. In the meantime, I'll run the registration by the Coast Guard and see who owns that fast mama-jama."

"Good luck with that. I'll bet you a sawbuck she's registered to an offshore company."

I smiled. "I don't think I'll take that bet. Thanks for your time, Rick."

I met Buck in the parking lot.

"Any luck?" he asked.

"Not much," I said, walking with him toward my Jeep. "Rick's seen the boat hauling ass up and down the Intercoastal. One trip up, one trip back. No stops that he knows of. He figures them for smugglers."

Buck snorted. "Yeah, no great surprise there. Pretty hard to troll for reds at Mach 1 with your hair on fire."

I chuckled. "Got time for some soft-shells and a beer?"

"Bluebeards?"

"The one and only."

"Since we used *my* boat and fuel, I guess you're buying?"

I punched Buck in his massive shoulder. "Guess I am."

Back in my office on Monday morning, I ran the go-fast boat registration numbers through the Coast Guard computer registry. Just as Rick had predicted, *HavanaNiceDay* was owned by an offshore company registered in the Caymans.

I still had a contact in the Coast Guard from my DEA days, and I figured the go-fast boat was worth a phone call. I walked out of my office and down the hall to the dispatcher's desk. "Betty, get me Commander Wilson at the Coast Guard station, will you?"

"Right away, Sheriff."

I took a cigar from my shirt pocket, but when Betty frowned I put it back. "I know: No smoking 'till I quit the building."

"The Commander is on line two, Sheriff."

"Thanks, Betty. I'll take it in my office."

I walked back to my office, closed my door, opened a window, and fired up my cigar.

"Jim, it's Hardin Steel. Have you got a minute?"

"I'll be damned. The DEA's former finest. Sure, Hardin, I always have time for a brother-in-arms. What's up?"

"You got anything that can catch a go-fast boat?"

"A cigarette boat?"

"Yeah. This one's about 30- or 35-feet long and fast, Jim. Very fast."

"The short answer is—no. I've got an 87-foot cutter and a 41-foot utility boat. Neither has the speed to run down what you're talking about. But we could probably interdict them."

"Probably?"

"Yeah, Hardin, if they can operate in shallow water, we can't follow. Our utility boats are pretty much tied to running in the Intercoastal."

"What about air?"

"I have an H-65 Dolphin helicopter that'll do 175 knots."

"Armed?" I asked.

"One 7.62mm machine gun," Jim paused. "What about the Sheriff's department? Don't you have some marine assets?"

"Yes, basically bay boats with 200-horse Merc outboards. But like you, we don't have the speed if the bad guys make a run for it."

Jim was silent for a long moment.

"Got an idea, Commander?" I asked.

"When do you want to stop them?"

"You mean what day?"

"No, Sheriff, I mean ingressing or egressing the bay?"

"The boat is riding low in the water when it comes through Lighthouse Pass, and they're riding high on the return trip," I replied.

"Okay, so we'll take 'em as they enter Laguna Madre. Once they're in the bay, I'll block the pass with our cutter, and we'll use our utility boat and your outboards to stop them."

"What about air?" I asked.

"I'll have the H-65 on station."

I thought for a moment. Our plan had a chance. It just depended on how rough the skipper of the go-fast boat wanted to play. "Okay, Jim. I'll work on it from my end and y'all do the same. First one with some good intel . . . wins. Just one thing, Jim."

"Yes?"

"If the bad guys decide to go down in a blaze of glory, we only return fire from the chopper. I can't have rounds from our boats going into Port Isabel or shooting up the tourists on the island."

"Roger that. I'll put a sharpshooter with a .50 caliber sniper rifle on board the chopper. If the skipper makes a run for it, we'll put him down."

Chapter 7

Undeterred by our little conversation or the shooting at *Los Cuatros Amigos*, Wes was prepping his King Air 350 for a low-level "boot and scoot." He had 450 kilos, about 1000 pounds, of marijuana stashed and ready to load whenever the call came. The only problem was the load hadn't been sanctioned by the Ochoa Cartel.

Wes was taking a hell of a chance. I'd warned him in Matamoros that the Sheriff's Department was aware of his landing sites on the Roughton Ranch. And anything my office knew, the DEA knew.

Even worse, once Frederick Ochoa learned that Wes was back freelancing for the competition, even if it was only pot, his wings would get clipped—permanently.

I couldn't be in two places at once. And I really didn't want to be there when one of my best friends got busted or shot up. So I decided to send one of my deputies to hang with the DEA. I wanted to make damn sure Wes got a chance to surrender. The DEA had a nasty habit of shooting first and asking questions later. In the meantime, I kept two deputies on standby for the go-fast interdiction, if it happened.

The following Saturday, it happened. Evidently, the skipper of the cigarette boat figured there would be more boating traffic on the weekends. Normally a good plan. But a 30-footer clipping along at 50 knots is hard to miss, even on a busy boating day.

The Coast Guard H-65 chopper spotted the light blue cigarette boat about eight miles offshore and heading north at a high rate of speed.

I got the call minutes later. "Hardin, it's Jim Wilson. Your boat is inbound, riding low and moving fast. We're monitoring him from a chopper, high and on his six."

"Roger that. I'll scramble my deputies and we'll meet your utility boat on the west side of the causeway. We'll take the cigarette boat when he makes his turn to head up Laguna Madre."

"Understood. Once the target has cleared Lighthouse Pass, I'll move my cutter into a blocking position."

I grabbed my gear and Deputies Alex Rodriquez and Tom Allen and headed for the pier where we kept our patrol boats.

I took the helm of one of the sheriff department's patrol boats, and Deputy Allen skippered the second boat. As we headed out into the bay, I keyed my radio. “Remember, Tom. If there’s trouble, let the Coast Guard chopper do the shooting. No lateral fire. Roger that?”

“Roger, wilco, Sheriff,” Tom replied.

The Coast Guard 41-foot utility boat was already on station on the west side of the bay and just north of the causeway connecting Port Isabel with South Padre Island.

Tom and I pulled our 22-foot bay boats into position on the port side of the Coast Guard utility boat and switched our marine VHF radios to channel 16.

“Steel to Coast Guard. Radio check. How do you read me? Over.”

“This is Coast Guard Cutter *Bluefish*. We read you five-by-five. Over.”

“This is Coast Guard boat 41-400 on your starboard beam. We read you five-by-five. Over.”

We bobbed in the gentle waves of the bay for twenty minutes and maintained radio silence.

“This is Coast Guard Cutter *Bluefish*. Target has cleared Lighthouse Pass. We are moving to block the channel. You should have a visual in five-zero minutes. Over.”

I keyed my radio. “Roger that, *Bluefish*. Standing by. Over.”

Tom and I and the Coast Guard utility boat had been turning just enough RPMs to hold our positions against the incoming tide. I scanned the lower bay and spotted the go-fast boat. I signaled to Tom, who nodded, and keyed my radio. “Coast Guard 41-400, target in sight. Off your starboard bow, range 2000 yards and closing fast.”

“Roger that, sir. We will take up a blocking position to the stern of the target, once he clears the causeway.”

I scanned the sky and could see the H-65 at about 1500 feet and closing on the stern of the target.

I looked over at Tom, gave him a wind-’em-up signal, and pushed the big Merc’s throttle open.

The go-fast boat had just made a turn to starboard and was heading for the main channel. I got across the channel and turned hard to starboard and chopped the throttle. Tom was opposite me on the west edge of the channel.

The Coast Guard utility boat was now in position about 300 yards astern of the target. I looked up just as the H-65 cleared the causeway and hovered at about 300 feet above the bay.

I grabbed the bullhorn and ordered *HavanaNiceDay* to stop and be boarded. And that’s when the shooting started. The skipper of the cigarette boat jammed the throttles full ahead and the sleek boat leaped forward. Two men in the stern had opened fire with AK-47s—the preferred weapon of slime-balls worldwide.

Rounds tore through the water in front of my boat. I looked over at Tom and could see pieces of fiberglass flying off his bow. I gunned my boat and headed directly at the bow of the oncoming go-fast boat. Tom saw my strategy and did likewise.

I keyed my radio with my free hand and yelled for the chopper to return fire. The H-65 swung hard to starboard, giving the sniper, positioned on the port side, a clear field of fire. I couldn't hear the report over the 200 horses of my Merc outboard, but I saw the skipper of *HavanaNiceDay* slump and the nose of the boat fall off plane.

I keyed my radio and yelled, "Cease fire!" The two shooters in the stern tossed their weapons into the bay and held up their hands.

The Coast Guard utility boat came up astern of the cigarette boat and trained an M-60 machine gun on the two idiots who had fire on us. Tom and I eased our boats up on either side of the now dead-in-the-water go-fast boat and tied off.

I nodded to Deputy Rodriguez. "Take the helm."

I jumped aboard *HavanaNiceDay* and handcuffed the two shooters to tie-down cleats at the stern of the boat, and then went forward to check on the downed skipper.

The guy who'd been driving the boat had a hole the size of a quarter through the back of his life vest. I rolled him over and checked the exit wound. His life vest was open in the front; the exit wound was about the size of an orange. The kind of wound a .50 caliber round makes. Very ugly and very lethal.

A large piece of the boat's steering wheel was missing and the front windshield was shattered. The .50 caliber round had evidently exited the boat driver, ricocheted off the steering wheel and shattered the windshield. Which was lucky for us; otherwise, there would have been a very large hole in the hull of the go-fast boat.

The dead guy had a kill-switch lanyard attached to his life vest. When he went down and fell away from the throttles, the lanyard pulled the key and killed the two massive engines. A pretty handy safety device if you happen to fall overboard at 50 knots. And, in this case, a bit of luck for the good guys.

I yelled for Tom to call the *Bluefish* and tell them the mission was complete. Then I went astern to talk to the two shooters. "*¿Habla usted inglés?*"

The moron I'd handcuffed to a metal cleat on the port side of the boat nodded. "*Sí,* I speak English."

I dropped down on one knee and got in the man's face. "Okay, pardner, you may as well tell me where the dope is, otherwise we're going to tear this boat apart."

The man looked past me at his partner and said something in Spanish. The other man shrugged and nodded.

"The drugs are in the bags of coffee beans in the bow," the shooter said and paused. "But you have made a very bad mistake, señor."

I laughed. "No, I believe it's you boys who are *chinga'd.*"

The man cut a quick glance at his partner. I could see the fear in both men's eyes.

"Okay, *hombre*, let's have it," I said.

"The man you have killed is Adolph Ochoa. He's one of Señor Ochoa's bastards."

I arched my eyebrows and looked over at Tom to see if he'd heard. He nodded and grinned.

"So the coke on board is Ochoa's?" I asked.

The man shook his head. "I say no more."

As the interdiction had taken place in the Intercoastal Waterway, and as the Coast Guard had done the shooting, I ceded any jurisdiction I might have to them. They towed the cigarette boat and the occupants to Station South Padre Island and notified the DEA.

A couple of days later, Commander Wilson called me.

"Hardin, Jim Wilson. I have an update for you."

"Mornin' Jim. Fire when ready."

Jim snorted. "Well, *HavanaNiceDay* was one hell of a boat. Would've made the late, great Don Aronow proud."

"Wow, now there's a name I haven't heard in years," I said.

Don Aronow had developed and raced cigarette boats until he was gunned down in a drive-by shooting in Miami. Aronow had been good friends with then-Vice President George Bush, who owned one of Aronow's boats.

"Yeah, I think it was 1987 when he bought it," Jim said.

"A bit before my time with the DEA," I replied. "So what did you find on the boat?"

Jim snickered. "About 500 pounds of the best Columbian coffee beans you ever put in a grinder. And hidden in the coffee beans, 23 kilos of extremely pure cocaine."

I did a quick calculation in my head. "Damn, that's about 50 pounds of coke."

"Yep, worth about 62 bucks a gram."

I punched 23,000 into my desk calculator, times 62. "Jesus, that's like a million and a half bucks."

"Make you think, doesn't it?" Jim said.

"Yeah, makes me think we're never going to win the war on drugs," I said. "What about the guy your sniper tapped? Any ID?"

"Nothing on him or the other two. But I can tell you, the two shooters are scared shitless."

"So maybe they're telling the truth, and the boat driver was one of old man Ochoa's bastard offspring?"

"Could be, Hardin, but one thing is for sure . . ."

"What?" I asked.

"Whoever he was, he's sure as hell dead."

Chapter 8

Wes turned and looked aft over his right shoulder. Juan Obregon had secured the cargo and was strapped in. He nodded and gave Wes a thumbs-up. Wes returned the gesture and finished his pre-flight. He checked the flaps one more time to be sure they were fully extended, and then slowly pushed the King Air's throttles to full power.

With fuel and nearly a half-ton of weed onboard, the plane was heavy. Wes used nearly all 3500 feet of the dirt strip. At 117 knots, he pulled back on the yoke and the dope-loaded bird lifted off.

He climbed to 500 feet, turned to a heading of 355, and leveled off. Flying time to the Roughton Ranch was about fifteen minutes.

In five minutes, they'd be crossing the Rio Grande. He knew the tethered Aerostat Radar mini-blimps stationed along the river had picked him up as soon as he took off. Their 200-mile-range, low-level, downward-looking radar was nearly impenetrable by aircraft.

Wes's advantage was speed. Even with 1000 pounds of Mexican pot on board, the King Air could make 350 miles an hour. He'd make his drop before the feds or sheriff deputies could get to the remote landing strip.

As Wes approached the Rio Grande, Alexsie Yazov stood in front of his black Land Rover and tracked the King Air with his Soviet-made Strela-2, a shoulder-fired, heat-seeking, ground-to-air missile. Yazov allowed the King Air to pass and then depressed the trigger halfway, allowing the weapon to track and lock on. When he heard the tone, Yazov smiled and fully depressed the trigger.

Wes had the Rio Grande in sight when he caught a glimpse of a small contrail at his eight o'clock-low position. He knew immediately someone had fired a surface-to-air missile at his plane.

He yelled for Juan to hold on and pulled back hard on the yoke, putting the plane into a tight-displacement barrel roll. The maneuver would bring the King Air around, putting them on a head-on course with the rapidly closing missile.

Wes knew his only chance was if the missile was an old version of a heat-seeker, one that needed to engage from the rear of an aircraft.

He pulled out of the tight roll as the Strela-2 flashed by the cockpit at better than 900 miles per hour.

"Jesus, that was close," Wes whispered, turning to see if Juan was okay. A couple of bales of marijuana had shifted and pinned him to the starboard side of the cabin. He looked pretty shaken, but otherwise okay.

Wes dropped the nose, just skimming the tops of the mesquite trees, and headed for home.

With the King Air now nowhere in sight, Yazov muttered a few choice words in Russian and flipped open his disposable cell phone.

When Ochoa answered, Yazov switched to passable German. "Sir, the pilot took some rather remarkable evasive action and returned, I'm assuming, to his base."

"So the delivery was not completed?" Ochoa asked in fluent German.

"No, sir."

Ochoa snuffled. "Well, sometimes a harsh lesson is as good as a kill. And I'd hate to lose a pilot with Mr. Stoddard's skills."

I got two personal calls Friday morning. The first was from Rory, asking me to take her to dinner at around seven. Not a problem. The second call was from Wes, and it was a problem.

"Hardin, I just found out the old man knows you snuffed one of his offspring."

"The old man?"

"Very funny, Stainless. You know exactly who I mean."

"Okay, maybe I do. But it wasn't me or my deputies. The Coast Guard took the shot."

"It doesn't matter who did the shooting, it was your operation."

"And you're concerned because . . . ?"

"Because Ochoa doesn't forgive or forget, Hardin. He'll seek retribution."

"I appreciate your concern, Wes. But it goes with the territory. And by the way, speaking of retribution, you'll never guess what old Norm Davis, down on the 'Bar-No-Debt' ranch, found along the river."

Wes paused for a moment. "A Book of Mormon buried in a mesquite grove?"

I cracked up. "Close. Norm found a Russian-made surface-to-air missile. Seems the damned thing landed on his ranch."

"Did it explode?"

"Nope. I got the bomb squad to pick it up and turn it over to the Coast Guard. But funny thing, Norm said he saw a twin-engine plane flying like . . . Let me see, I wrote it down here somewhere. Oh, yeah, 'flying like a goddamned Kammeekazi'—his pronunciation—'with a cattle prod up his ass.' I don't suppose you'd know anything about that?"

Wes paused a couple of seconds. "Russian-made?"

"That's what the Coasties told me. Why? Does that ring some bells?"

"Well, I heard a rumor about Ochoa doing business with the Russian Mafia. Drug deals, money laundering, assassinations. Your normal run-of-the-mill cartel shit."

"Why would they take a shot at you?"

"Who said it was me?"

"Right. Look, Wes, I told you over lunch, your days are numbered. The big dogs in the DEA have got a major hard-on for you. *¿Comprende?*"

There was a long pause.

"Look, pal," I said, breaking the silence, "I'm having supper on the island tonight with Rory. Why don't you grab Lacey and meet us at Bluebeards, around seven?"

"Okay, Stainless. I could use a change of scenery, and company. We'll be there at seven.

"Wes, just one more thing."

"Yeah?"

"Leave the plane in the hanger."

I went home, grabbed a shower, and changed into khaki slacks, cordovan tasseled loafers, and a black silk Tommy Bahama polo shirt. I downed a quick shot of Cuervo Gold so I'd be ultra-suave, and jumped in my Jeep. I stuck my badge, ID, and a Sig Sauer .380 auto in the console. There was always the chance Wes might be right about Mr. Ochoa.

Traffic on the causeway was light for a Friday evening. I pulled into Rory's condo about half past six. I had a key to her place most of the time, depending on my behavior.

I opened the door and stuck my head in. "Rory, it's Hardin. I'm coming in. Don't shoot," I said, thinking I was pretty witty, or maybe it was just the Cuervo?

Rory stepped out on the top of the staircase. She was drying her hair with a big green bath towel. And she was naked. "I'm drying my hair. Fix yourself a drink, I'll be down in a minute." She paused. "I said *a* drink, Hardin, as in one."

I smiled and headed for her well-stocked bar. "You need any help up there?"

"Not if you want to be at Bluebeards on time."

She had me there. Quickies were not in my repertoire and never would be. "No, babe, I'll catch you later."

Rory laughed. "Getting pretty cocky, aren't you, Hardin. Or should I say hard-on?"

I ignored the jab, put some ice in a glass and poured two inches of Cuervo Gold over the top. Booze or broads, I don't like to change partners in the middle of a soirée. I took a sip and felt the soft warmth of a south-of-the-border evening spreading from my innards to my outards.

I glanced up in the direction of Rory's bedroom. "Very funny. By the way, I invited Wes Stoddard and Lacey to join us for supper."

Roy came out of her bedroom and looked down at me. She was dressed a cream-colored blouse, navy shorts and sandals. "Damn, Hardin. Wes is a drug runner. Do I need to bring my Beretta?"

I took another sip of tequila and shook my head. I knew that my inviting Wes would raise a few hackles. "No. He's promised to be on his best behavior, and he's coming by car. I think he said he left the King Air on one of your dad's strips, so he can get an early start in the morning."

Rory shot me a *look* and came down the steps to the living area. She glanced at her gold Rolex. "Very funny, Hardin. Fix me a short one, will you? I like to be slightly gassed before I have dinner with the Cartel's chief pilot."

I stepped over to the bar and fixed her a Jack Daniels and water. Rory preferred bourbon to tequila, whereas I generally stuck with Cuervo Gold. I handed her her drink. "You look great, kiddo."

Rory smiled and blushed just a tad. She knew she was a knock-out, but she had the class not to flaunt it. "Thanks, babe," she replied, taking a sip of Mr. Daniels. "You look pretty good your own self. Kinda preppy for an Aggie."

I knocked the ice around in my glass and drank about half of the remaining tequila. "Yep, no socks and tasseled loafers. I figured I'd kick it up a notch, seeing's how we're having supper with a legendary South Texas smuggler."

Rory punched me in the shoulder. At five-nine, 120 pounds, she could hit pretty good. I laughed and rubbed my shoulder. "Hey, ask Wes about his close encounter with Strela."

"Who the hell is Strela?"

I kissed her lightly on the lips. "I'll let Wes tell you. Come on, kiddo. I don't want to be late."

Wes and his mostly full-time girlfriend, Lacey Harris, were just getting out of Wes's midnight-blue Corvette when Rory and I pulled in to Bluebeards.

"Evening, Wes, Lacey," I said, walking around my Jeep to open Rory's door. Woe be the man who forgot or hadn't acquired any social graces. "Y'all know Rory."

Wes looked at me and rolled his eyes. "Only since grade school. And you both know Lacey Harris."

Lacey had grown up in Brownsville and we'd all gone to school together, through high school. She was a couple inches shorter than Rory, with a slighter build, but gorgeous with short golden-brown hair and brown eyes.

Lacey had gone on to UT and now taught fourth grade in Brownsville. She and Wes dated off and on when the dashing Mr. Stoddard was on the north side of the ditch. And not dodging the bloodiest cartel leader since Pablo Escobar and the boys from Medellín.

We got a table with a view of the bay and Port Isabel and ordered drinks and a starter of fried calamari. Wes and the girls went with a two-year-old Pinot Grigio. I stuck with Cuervo, gold-tone. Like I said, I don't like to switch horses once I'm in the saddle. And I was riding pretty good with the Cuervo Palomino.

Rory stabbed a piece of calamari and looked over at Wes. "So, Wes, what's the deal with Strela?"

I couldn't help but laugh, and damn near choked on a bite of squid.

Wes looked at me. "It was a Strela?"

I held up my left hand, asking for a moment while I wrestled with the chewy chunk of squid. "So the

Coasties tell me," I said, finally able to swallow and talk.

"Well, that explains why I . . . I mean, why the pilot was able to get away. The Strelas have a number of design flaws, not the least of which is that they're built by the Russians."

Rory looked at Wes. "The Russians were shooting at you?"

Wes lifted his eyebrows. "Somebody shot at an unidentified aircraft with a Russian shoulder-fired surface-to-air, piece-o'-crap, Cold War-era missile."

Lacey put her hand on Wes's arm. "Is that true, Wes? Was it you?"

Wes cringed, looked over at me and scratched the corner of his right eye with the middle finger of his right hand. "No, Lacey, it wasn't me. But a pilot in a plane like mine did have a close encounter with a small surface-to-air missile, or so Stainless here claims."

Lacey looked at Wes with her big browns. "I think it's time you bring your plane back across the river, before," she lowered her voice, "before Ochoa puts one of those Russian rockets right up your exhaust pipe."

Wes grinned and nodded. "I'll work on it, babe. Now can we order dinner . . . and change the subject?"

After supper, Wes and Lacey headed over to Wes's condo in Brownsville, and Rory and I drove back to her place on the island.

“Well, at least Wes is thinking about it,” I said, getting the Jeep door for Rory. “Thanks to Lacey.”

Rory took my hand and stepped out of my Jeep. “Yes, women’s powers are unlimited when it comes to men,” she said, giving me one of those ‘come do me’ smiles. “Come on upstairs and I’ll show you what I mean.”

As she led me to bed, I knew she was right. Wes didn’t have a chance . . . and neither did I.

Chapter 9

Frederick Ochoa sent one of his underlings to claim Adolph's body at the border crossing in Matamoros. The DEA had required an autopsy, and between the .50 caliber round and the medical examiner's cutting and groping around, Adolph was more than ready for interment.

The burial would be in Matamoros, but Frederick Ochoa would not be attending. He seldom ventured far from his compound north of Mazatlán. Even with his power and money, it was dangerous for him to venture outside the State of Chiapas.

Ochoa felt no particular remorse over the loss of Adolph. The boy had been a good earner and reasonably intelligent, but was one of a long list of bastards he'd sired.

What did concern him was a hick county sheriff seizing one of his prized cigarette boats, along with a million and a half in cocaine.

Ochoa decided he needed to know a lot more about Sheriff Hardin Steel.

*****

Buck called me on Monday morning, at just past eleven. “You got a few minutes, Hardin?”

I looked at my watch and heard my stomach growl. “How about we talk over lunch? That growl you heard was my innards.”

Buck laughed. “Usual spot?”

“I think I need some barbeque. How about Red’s place?”

“I’ll be there in fifteen,” Buck replied.

It took me about twenty minutes. I pulled in next to Buck’s black Ford F-150 and parked. My mouth started to water as I stepped out of my Jeep. There’s nothing like brisket cooking over mesquite to get the juices flowing.

I walked into the old BBQ joint and spotted Buck at a table near the back. “Howdy, Buck,” I said, walking over and pulling out a chair.

Buck nodded. “Right back at you, Hardin. And I must say you had yourself one hell of a week.”

I nodded and looked around for the waitress. She caught my glance and came over to our table. “Hi, Sheriff, Buck. What’ll it be, boys?”

We both ordered brisket, sausage, beans, coleslaw, and sweet tea. Hopefully, it would be a slow afternoon at the Sheriff’s office.

“You were saying, Buck?”

Buck looked around Red's and leaned forward. "I was saying you had a hell of a week, even without Wes damned near getting shot down."

I started to reply but our food showed up and I held off while we were served.

"If you boys need anything else, just let me know," the waitress said, leaving us to our meal.

I nodded and then looked across the table at Buck. "You heard about that?"

"Why hell, yes. Every swingin' dick along the river knows about it. Old man Davis has never been known to keep things to himself."

I snorted and took a bite of brisket. "Damn. Red sure knows how to finish a piece of meat."

Buck laughed. "Yeah, and so does Freddy Ochoa. If you're not real careful, Stainless, you're liable to end up on his grill."

"Over Adolph?"

"Who?"

"Adolph Ochoa. The go-fast boat driver the Coasties bagged and tagged."

Buck wagged his fork at me while he chewed on a piece of sausage. "Hardin, Frederick Ochoa was a walkin' sperm bank when he was younger. He don't give two hoots in hell about Adolph." Buck paused and chuckled. "Jesus, was that really the kid's handle?"

I nodded. "That's what one of the other men in the boat told me."

"Why in *the* hell would Ochoa name one of his whelps Adolph?"

I took a drink of sweet tea. "You know, I've been wondering the same thing."

Buck smiled. "You think the old man's got a soft spot for Nazis?"

"Could be, pard. His old man, Baron Frederick Beck, was a major in the SS. He ended up in Argentina after WWII."

"A baron, huh?" Buck said, rolling his eyes.

"According to his German military files."

"We talking ODESSA-assisted resettlement here?"

"That's what some of the professional Nazi hunters claimed," I replied.

Buck snickered. "Damn, this is getting good. Next thing you know we'll see Frederick 'fuckin' Forsyth walking through the door."

I laughed. "I think one Frederick is enough."

Buck chuckled. "I'll damned sure drink to that," he said, downing about half his sweet tea. He set his glass on the table and looked at me. "All kidding aside, you and Wes could be in deep shit."

"Wes is, that's for damned sure," I said. "If he wasn't a hell of a pilot, we'd be pickin' pieces of a Strela-2 out of his dead carcass."

"That's what they shot at him?"

"According to the Coast Guard weapons guys."

"Strela. Sounds Israeli." Buck said.

"Russian."

Buck leaned back and pulled on his lower lip. "Russian?"

"Yeah, that mean something to you?" I asked.

"Maybe. Some of my *clients* have mentioned hearing rumors about Ochoa teaming up with the Russian Mafia."

"That's exactly what Wes said when I told him he'd had a close encounter with a Russian surface-to-air missile."

Buck finished a last bite of brisket and pushed his empty plate toward the center of the table. "Well, Hardin, you'd better be watchin' your six as well. Adolph aside, FreddieO isn't going to take the loss of one of his coke shipments and a go-fast boat lying down."

Chapter 10

Ochoa was reclining in his overstuffed chair, watching the naked masseuse work the nerve pain gel into his hands, wrists, and forearms. Being in the chemical-pharmaceutical trade had certain advantages. His chemists had mixed up a cocktail of Ketamine, Neurontin, Clonidine, and Nifedipine into a gel for topical application.

The exotic mixture eased his pain for a number of hours and he always got an erection during the application process—which came in handy with an already naked masseuse.

When Alexsie Yazov walked in, Ochoa tossed a towel to the masseuse and motioned for her to leave the room.

"How are the hands, comrade?" Yazov asked, watching the very well-built masseuse depart.

"Good for now," Ochoa replied. "But the pain always comes back." He paused and smiled. "But then, so does the young lady. And I remind you,

Alexsie, I am a Nationalist Socialist, not a Communist."

Yazov looked at his diminutive but nonetheless dangerous employer. "Of course. Sorry. It's an old habit, and a necessary one when I'm back in Cuba."

Ochoa shook his head. "Communism was doomed from the start. The Soviet Union has disintegrated and Cuba is now back in the Stone Age."

Yazov pursed his lips and nodded. "Russia went broke trying to keep up with the goddamned American weapons systems. And Fidel turned into just another power-hungry, greedy dictator."

Ochoa flexed his fingers. The masseuse had done a good job. There was very little pain. "Interesting, is it not, that the Americans continue to spend and spend on weapons, even though your country is no longer a serious threat."

A wry smile spread across the Russian's large face. "Yes, and very soon they will suffer the same fate they delivered to us."

Ochoa was quiet for a moment. "Indeed. But I called you here to discuss another matter. I want to send a message to a meddlesome sheriff in Brownsville, Texas. And I want the cocaine he seized when he grabbed my boat."

Wes had a serious problem. The pot he'd been trying to deliver when the Strela interrupted his flight plan was now sitting in his hanger south of Matamoros. And the buyer and seller were both getting antsy. The seller wanted his money and the buyer wanted his pot, and Wes was caught in the middle. Not where you wanted to be in 2010 Matamoros.

There was only one option: Load the marijuana back on the King Air and make another run for the border. Wes contacted both principals and told them he'd make the drop the next night.

By sundown the next day, Wes and Juan had the King Air loaded, fueled, and ready to fly. Wes checked the coordinates for his favorite airstrip on the Roughton Ranch. Once airborne, he'd punch the lat-long into his GPS navigation system. Locating the old dirt strip would be a cinch; the "touch and go" landing, using only light from the buyer's pickups, would be a bit trickier.

Just before takeoff, Wes went to his Explorer and pulled out a hard-plastic case. He walked back to the plane and set the case on the port wing and motioned for Juan to join him.

Wes opened the case and took out a flare gun. "Ever use one of these, Juan?"

Juan shook his head. "No, señor, but it is a flare device, is it not?"

"Yes, it is," Wes said, showing Juan how to break the action open and load a flare shell. "Just as simple as that, amigo. Now you try it."

Juan opened the action and pulled out the shell.

"Very good, Juan. Now reload and fire it up in the air, toward the south."

Juan looked at him. Wes could see the small man was nervous. "It shoots just like a regular handgun,

Juan. Just pull the hammer back, point, and squeeze the trigger."

Juan's hand shook just a bit as he cocked the gun.

"Okay, point south and let her rip," Wes said.

Juan took a double-handed grip on the flare gun and turned his head away as he pulled the trigger. The bright red flare arced across the evening sky.

"See, nothing to it," Wes said, patting Juan on the back. "If we run into any trouble, like the other day, I may tell you to fire a couple of rounds out the door, away from the aircraft. Do you understand?"

Juan opened the action of the flare gun, pulled out the empty shell, and tossed it aside. "Sí, señor, I will do as you say."

Wes smiled and took the flare gun from Juan and put it back in its case. "Good. Now help me take the door off the plane. When I touch down, kick the bales out onto the runway as fast as you can. I won't be stopping."

"Sí," Juan replied, working his ratchet on the door bolts.

Wes put his hand on Juan's shoulder. "If I tell you to shoot, be damned sure you stick your arm out the door before you fire the flares. We don't want one going off inside the plane."

Juan smiled. "That would be a bad thing, yes?"

Wes nodded and stowed the case just inside the door of the King Air. *Yep, almost as bad as flying 350 miles per hour at tree-top level, in the dark with a lode of dope, hoping some Russian mercenary doesn't shoot a rocket up your ass.*

Wes signaled for Juan to pull the wheel chocks and get aboard. Two minutes later, he fired up the King Air's two Pratt and Whitney turboprops, watching as the 105-inch propellers began rotating. Combined, the two engines could deliver a maximum of 2100 horsepower. She was one hellacious aircraft and a smuggler's wet dream.

Wes taxied out to his private strip and checked the windsock. Dead calm. He brought up power and released the brakes. Thirty-five hundred feet later he and Juan were wheels up. He set the GPS heading, trimmed the plane, and put the pedal down.

The tethered radar blimps on the U.S. side of the border picked up a blip when the King Air climbed through 200 feet. But Wes was already approaching the Rio Grande. He stayed at 300 feet and watched for vapor trails. But the night was quiet. No sign of surface-to-air ordnance.

Five minutes later, Wes reduced power, dropped the flaps and the landing gear. He turned and looked at Juan. "*¿Listo?*"

Juan nodded and gave him a thumbs-up. Forty-five seconds later pickup trucks at either end of the narrow caliche airstrip flashed on their headlights. Wes gently pushed the nose down, flaring just before the tires bit into the white caliche. Immediately, Juan started kicking the bales of marijuana out the door. Twenty seconds later, Wes pushed the throttles wide open and lifted off, just clearing the small mesquite trees at the end of the primitive runway.

"Jesus, that was close," Wes whispered to himself. He pulled up the gear, got three green lights and brought the plane around low and fast to a reverse heading of 175 degrees.

He'd just crossed the river when he saw it. A grapefruit-sized fireball moving fast off to his left. He dropped the plane down even lower and turned and shouted at Juan. "*Ahora la pistol fuego! Ahora, Juan!*"

Juan opened the plastic case, grabbed the flare gun and two shells. He opened the action, dropped in a shell and closed the breech. Bracing himself, he stuck his arm out the door and pulled the trigger.

The flare arced low in the general direction of the missile. Wes banked hard to starboard and came back on his original course of 355 degrees. He glanced quickly to his right and saw the fireball tracking the flare. A moment later an explosion rocked the aircraft.

Wes turned right to a heading of 090 degrees and beat it for the coast. When he hit the Gulf, he'd turn southwest and fly back to his strip.

Wes rocked the plane gently to port and starboard, looking for more missiles. He didn't see any more grapefruit-sized tracers. Glancing back at Juan, he could just make him out in the pale light of the cabin. Wes gave him a thumbs-up. "Nice shooting, my friend."

Wes pulled back gently on the yoke and took the plane to 1000 feet and increased power to the max cruise rate of 360 miles per hour.

He pulled his lucky blue bandana from his left back pocket and wiped the sweat from his face.

Goddamn, this place is turning into Bagdad West. Maybe Stainless is right; maybe it's time to quit.

Yazov got the call an hour later. He'd stationed one of his Cuban mercenaries along Wes's previous route of flight, just in case the American made another run.

When the Cuban finished his report, Yazov swore under his breath in Russian and closed his cell phone. *That guy is either the luckiest SOB alive, or one hell of a pilot . . . probably a bit of both.*

In any case, Yazov didn't see any necessity in reporting another miss to Ochoa. He had the distinct impression that reporting too many failures to that Nazi-loving pig could be hazardous to one's health.

Chapter 11

A few days later, Wes called me. "Hardin, I'm at Lupe's. Got time for a bite?"

I checked my day-planner and looked at the stack of messages on my desk. "Yeah, I've got nothing here that can't wait 'till after lunch. What are you doing on this side of the ditch?"

"I'll tell you when you get here. Enchilada plate okay for you?"

"Sure. Order it. I'll be there in a few minutes."

Lupe's was on a side street in downtown Brownsville. The joint looked a little rough on the outside but always got high 90s on health inspections, and the TexMex was as good as any in the state.

I walked in and waited a minute for my eyes to adjust to the dimmed lights, a process which had proven fatal for Ochoa's men in Matamoros.

In a moment or two, I saw Wes sitting at a table near the rear of the restaurant. I walked over just as my enchiladas arrived. "Perfect timing," I said, pulling out a chair and sitting down.

"Good choice of words, Hardin."

"Really?"

Wes nodded. "Yep."

"Okay, pard, what's on your mind?"

"Going straight," Wes said, taking a sip of his beer.

I took a bite of my cheese enchiladas and smiled at Wes. "Don't tell me one near miss is going run you off."

"Two."

"You tried another run?"

"Off the record?"

I drank some of my sweet tea, wishing it was a beer, or better yet, a margarita. But I was in uniform and armed. "Yeah, off the record."

"I had to deliver the *cargo* I was unable to deliver the other day," Wes said, looking around the room. "The seller is a pretty bad *hombre* in his own right. Not up there with FreddieO, but I'd be just as dead."

"So what are you telling me?"

"I think it's time to retire from my current occupation, but I need to get my plane stateside," Wes said, pausing for a moment. "I can make a legit living with the King Air. Without the plane, I'm toast."

I nodded. "And you're toast if you don't move on."

"That's about the size of it," Wes said, reaching for his beer and draining about half of it.

"So, what can I do?" I asked.

"Help me get my stuff stateside," Wes said.

"By *stuff*, I take it you mean your possessions in Matamoros and the King Air."

Wes nodded.

I took a tortilla chip, dipped it into my refried beans and took a bite. "You'll have no problem with me, Wes, but I think you're going to have offer up something to the DEA to get their hard-on to recede."

"Something like what?" Wes asked.

"Something like your old boss."

Wes choked on a tortilla chip. "Ochoa?"

I nodded. "I think it would balance out the books."

"Jesus, Hardin, you're talking about the worst of the worst. Do you really have any idea how dangerous that fuckin' degenerate is?"

"Yeah, I have a pretty fair idea," I said. "Look, Wes, you want to skate, you're going to have to help the big dogs nail Ochoa."

Alexsie Yazov left Ochoa's compound two days after the last attempt to shoot down Wes's King Air. He had a clear understanding of what Ochoa wanted, and was already formulating a plan.

In Yazov's leather attaché case was a compete dossier on me. Everything from my days at A&M, my military record and DEA history, to my election as Sheriff of Cameron County. The report stated that I had a drinking problem, two ex-wives, and not much of a net worth. Also noted was my sometimes-relationship with Rory Lee Roughton.

Yazov had circled Rory's information in red pen and written a one-word memo in the right margin. The word was *мишень*, which in Russian meant "target." And he'd underlined it twice.

The rest of my week was taken up with normal sheriff's duties and a little politicking. I was, after all, a duly elected county official, and this was South Texas, home of Archer Parr and the Johnson ballot boxes. There were certain protocols to be observed.

By quitting time Friday, I was more than ready for a rematch with Jose Cuervo and a bit of skinny-dipping in Rory's hot tub. As I pulled up to my low-rent-side-of-the-bay bungalow, I saw Wes's midnight-blue Corvette parked in my driveway.

I parked next to the Vette and walked into my humble abode. Wes had the blender on purée and a George Strait greatest-hits CD playing in the background. Both were music to my ears.

If you're going to have unexpected company, this is the kind to have, I thought, unclipping my holster from my belt.

I laid my pistol and holster on an empty bookshelf and headed for the blender. I could see Wes on the dock behind my house. He was smoking a cigar, had a margarita resting on the rail, and was gazing across the bay. South Padre Island is directly across the bay from my shack. Resplendent with condos, hotels, restaurants, gorgeous women, and lots of money—some clean, some needing a bit of laundering.

Wes had folded a damp towel and laid it beside the blender. I pushed the rim of my glass into the towel and watched a small amount of water ooze up and over the edge. I dipped the damp end of my glass in a saucer covered in salt.

Properly prepped, I decanted a full measure of frozen margarita into my glass and took a long drink. If Wes quit flying dope, he'd make one hell of a bartender. Hell, I might even open up a bar and hire him.

I took my drink and headed out back to see what was up with the rocket-dodger.

"Wes," I said, sidling up beside him, "I think your real future is in mixology rather than pharmaceuticals."

Wes grinned and knocked a half inch of ash from the end of his cigar into the water. A bunch of small minnows appeared and checked out the droppings, then disappeared back under the shadow of the dock.

I frowned. "Is that one of my five dollar cigars?"

"It's one better, Stainless. It's a Cubano, hand-rolled on the thighs of an eighteen-year-old Cuban virgin."

I laughed. "Hell, you and I both know there's no such thing."

"What? No hand-rolled Cuban cigars?"

"No. Eighteen-year-old virgins in Cuba."

Wes snickered. "You want a cigar or not?"

I held out my hand. "Thanks. So, what's the occasion?"

Wes took a deep pull on his cigar, holding the smoke deep in his lungs before slowly exhaling. "I've been working on a plan, and I think I know a way to grab Ochoa."

I took my Swiss Army knife from my pants pocket and trimmed the end of my cigar. Wes watched and then handed me his Zippo.

I fired up the cigar, took a sip of my margarita, and looked at Wes. "I'm listening."

Wes grinned. "You're sure you're ready? You don't need anything else?"

I smiled and nodded. "Positive. Fire away."

"We use the cigarette boat and the coke you grabbed as bait. Hell, the dope alone is worth nearly a mil and a half. And the boat is, say, another quarter mil."

I took a drag and watched a powerboat race by. One of the women in the back of the boat noticed me and stood up. She pulled up her T-shirt, exposing two perfect breasts.

Wes laughed. "Friend of yours?"

"Nope, but I get that a lot when they see the uniform, and I'm on land and they're in a boat."

Wes shook his head. "So what do you think?"

"I think she was a 36D."

Wes snorted. "Not the tits, Stainless, the plan."

I swirled my margarita around and took a drink. "In theory, interesting. In fact, it has a few flaws. Not the least of which is the Coasties have the dope and the go-fast boat."

Wes leaned on the rail and watched a good-sized redfish glide by. "Do you have any pull with those boys?"

I pondered his question and knocked my cigar ashes into the bay. “Maybe.”

Chapter 12

First thing Monday morning, I placed a call to Commander Wilson at the Coast Guard Station.

"Jim, it's Hardin Steel."

"Mornin', Sheriff, got another go-fast boat for us?"

"Funny you should ask, Jim, because I'm calling about the boat we grabbed."

"*HavanaNiceDay*?"

"So far, so good," I replied with a chuckle. "Do you still have the boat?"

Wilson paused for a half-second and digested my attempt at humor. "Yeah, we still have the boat, but not the dope. The DEA jumped on the cocaine like a strung-out junkie."

"Damn. I should have figured that."

"What's up, Hardin? You planning something?"

I wondered how much I should tell Commander Wilson, but I decided to bring him in the loop. You never know, I might need the Coasties' firepower down the road.

"I'm setting up a sting operation."

"Going after some of the local talent?" Wilson asked.

"Frederick Ochoa." I said, waiting for Jim's response. I didn't have to wait long.

"Jesus, Hardin, are you sure the Sheriff's Department can handle that kind of take-down?"

I paused for a moment. "No, I'm not sure, which is one of the reasons I'm calling you."

"I see," Jim replied. "And the other reason is the boat?"

"That's why you wear three stripes, Jim."

"Uh-huh. I'll need the proper chain-of-custody documents . . . before you pick up the boat."

"Not a problem."

"And Sheriff . . ."

"Yes?"

"Keep me informed. We're good at rescuing folks who get in over their heads."

"Thanks, Jim, I'll bear that in mind."

"Anything else the Coast Guard can do for you, Sheriff?"

"Yeah, just one more small item," I said. "Which DEA agent did you turn the dope over to?"

"Lee Fairchild, with the Brownsville field office." Wilson paused. "I take it you know Lee?"

"Oh, yeah. He and I go way back."

"Uh-huh, I gathered that from talking with him. Well, in any case, he's holding the cocaine."

Lee "by the book" Fairchild and I had a bit of history. He'd given me the worst fitness report of my career and had encouraged me to put in my retirement papers—the day I hit my twenty years.

I checked with my deputies and, satisfied everything was working like a well-oiled machine, I headed for the DEA field office on Coffee Road.

In about fifteen minutes, I pulled into the parking lot of a one-story, red-brick building. A small sign in the grass by the front door said "U.S. Drug Enforcement Administration."

A young clean-cut, ivy league-type, male DEA agent was manning the front desk. "Morning, Sheriff. How can I help you?"

"I'd like to speak to Lee Fairchild, if he's got a minute."

"Sure thing, Sheriff. Take a seat and I'll tell Agent Fairchild you're here."

I nodded and took a seat. In about three minutes, the young agent returned. "Follow me, Sheriff. Just step around the metal detector."

"Thanks, Agent . . . ?"

"Bill Johnson," the young man replied, holding out his right hand.

His handshake was firm and dry. "Nice to meet you, Agent Johnson."

"Yes, sir. Same here. Do you know Agent Fairchild?"

I smiled and nodded. "Oh, yeah, we go way back."

Agent Johnson gave me a wry smile. "Okay, Sheriff, go right in . . . and best of luck."

I smiled and winked at Agent Johnson, and stepped into the lion's den.

"Well, I'll be damned. If it isn't 'Lone Wolf McQuade.' You think you might let this office know the next time you're planning to interdict one of Ochoa's drug shipments?"

"Sorry, Lee," I said, taking a seat before I was invited. "We really didn't know what we had for sure. And we had the Coast Guard for backup."

Lee Fairchild was in his late fifties and built like Jake LaMotta in his prime. He was five-seven and 170 pounds with close-cropped, salt-and-pepper hair, and wore gold wire-rimmed spectacles. He had a thin scar running across his left cheek. A souvenir from a drug bust gone bad.

"Uh-huh. Well, next time give us a heads-up. If nothing more than a professional courtesy," Fairchild said in the most condescending voice I'd heard in a long time.

I nodded, but part of me wanted to come around his desk and see if Agent Fairchild could still do the full-fist-on two-step. But I needed his help, so I took a breath and collected myself. "That's why I stopped by, Lee. I'd like to use some of the cocaine the Coast Guard took off the cigarette boat as bait."

Fairchild snorted and shook his head. "Bait? For whom?"

"Frederick Ochoa."

Fairchild laughed. "Ochoa? Are you kidding me? You're a bit out of your league, aren't you, Hardin?"

I could feel the color rising in my cheeks. "I don't think so. I have good contacts on both sides of the border, and I have two things Ochoa would like to have back—his boat and 23 kilos of cocaine."

"If by 'contacts' you mean Wes Stoddard, we're very close to busting him."

Good luck with that, I thought, but I let it pass. "I've developed a number of contacts, Lee. Some probably not on your radar screen."

Fairchild leaned back in his chair and nodded. "Like your PI buddy, Bateman?"

"Yes, for one," I said. "Buck has excellent contacts, on both sides of the border. Some that the DEA would never be able to cultivate."

"I'm sure that's correct. Some of his clients are lower than snake shit."

"Yeah, well, were not talking about busting some frat party for smoking marijuana. We're talking about taking a Nazi-loving, drug-dealing warlord off the board. You going to get off your ass and help—or just sit there and criticize?"

As much as Fairchild hated me, he was still a good cop. And he wanted Ochoa's scalp as badly as I did.

Fairchild clasped his hands together, put his elbows on the table and looked at me for a long minute. "What do you need from me, Hardin?"

"I need enough cocaine to bait the trap."

I watched Fairchild's reaction and knew I needed to sweeten the pot. "And I'll need your help to close the deal."

"A joint operation, with joint credit?" Fairchild looked over the top of his spectacles.

"Agreed," I said, locking him in. "But it's a Sheriff's Department operation. I'll be in command."

Fairchild rubbed his hands together and nodded. "Fair enough, Hardin. By the way, is your drinking under control?"

I signed a DEA chain-of-custody form and took delivery of a kilo of Ochoa's coke. On the way back to my office, I called Wes and Buck and told them to be at my house at six that evening.

I went straight to my office and locked the cocaine in our property-room safe. Driving around a South Texas border town with $62,000 worth of coke, is not a smart idea—Sheriff or not.

Buck said he'd bring some BBQ from Reds, and I promised to have the blender stoked and ready to churn. At six sharp, I heard two vehicles pull into my driveway. I hit purée and was decanting three margaritas when Wes and Buck knocked on my front door.

"Come on in, boys, the door's open," I said, topping off the last margarita.

After we'd chowed down and finished the first round of margaritas, we got down to business.

"I picked up a kilo of coke from the DEA. So we've got the bait. What we don't have is a plan," I said, mixing a fresh batch of margaritas.

I looked at Wes. "You're the expert in this arena, pardner. Any suggestions?"

Wes walked over to the bar and I refilled his glass. “Yeah, I suggest we be goddamned careful, or we’ll all be goddamned dead.”

I looked over at Buck and nodded. “I think we’re all agreed on that. So have you got something in mind?”

Wes looked at me. “How do you feel about becoming a ‘bad’ cop?”

I laughed. “Well, some folks would say that’s not much of a stretch.”

Wes smiled. “That’s good, because I’m going to get word to Ochoa that you have his dope and you’re looking to make a deal. I’ll throw in some shit about you and the DEA having a bit of a history.”

I smiled. “Again, not much of a stretch.”

Wes nodded. “Good, because Ochoa is no fool. He’ll check this out, three ways to Sunday.”

Buck stood up and walked over to the blender for a refill. “What about me? How do I fit in?’

“You’re going to make the delivery,” I said, glancing at Wes, who nodded in agreement.

Buck looked at me and Wes. “Jesus, sorry I asked,” he said, topping off his margarita until it spilled over the sides.

We spent the rest of the evening fine-tuning our plan and tomorrow’s hangovers.

At a bar in Benito Juárez International Airport in Mexico City, Alexsie Yazov sipped his vodka and did likewise.

Chapter 13

It was no small thing to grab an American national, especially one whose father was as rich and well-connected as Rory Lee Roughton's.

Yazov was planning the abduction like a military operation. He'd knocked off or grabbed and ransomed a number of so-called big shots from half a dozen Central and South American countries. And he knew the first twenty-four hours were critical. Past that, his chances of being caught were almost nil.

The hick sheriff would get Ochoa's message loud and clear. And he'd never see his woman again. Yazov would keep her alive as long as she pleased him. When the pleasure wore off, he'd shoot her in the back of the head and feed her carcass to the sharks.

Yazov smiled and shook his head. He'd never understood the lengths and expense the Americans went to to execute a person. A 9mm to the back of the head was quick, efficient, probably painless, and cost less than a dollar.

Yazov's plan, however, did not include returning Ochoa's cocaine. He knew dealers in Havana who'd buy the 23 kilos, no questions asked. They'd cut the dope ten times over, and have it on the streets of Miami in 48 hours.

He'd demand $65 per gram. And he'd get it—Ochoa's dope was the best of the best. Yazov smiled to himself. *A million and a half bucks went a long, long way in Castro's Cuba.*

It took about a week before Wes heard from an Ochoa underling. I got the call a little past five on Friday.

"Hardin, it's Wes. I got a bite."

I took a deep breath. "Really."

"Yeah, one of FreddieO's lieutenants got word to me that the big man is interested in buying his coke back—at a discount."

"Damn. He doesn't miss a trick, does he?"

"Not many, Hardin. That's why the rich get richer and the rest of us stand around scratching our backsides."

"You mean like the Wall Street investment banker who loses his client's money, but still gets a hefty year-end bonus?"

"Yep, just like that," Wes replied.

"Okay, so how does the deal play out?"

"Well, we sell Ochoa his dope back for, say, a flat million, and we throw in the cigarette boat as a token of our good will."

I thought about it for maybe five seconds. "Okay, set it up. One thing, Wes . . . the big man has to be there for the exchange."

"I figured that would be the case. And that's going to be difficult. Hell, Hardin, a million bucks ain't much to a guy like Ochoa. I think the only reason he's even making an offer is to save face."

"Doesn't want the competition seeing him lose a shipment?" I asked.

"Exactly," Wes replied. "It sets a bad precedent. The perception of power is as good as the real deal. And in this business, any perception of weakness is fatal."

"So how do we entice Fred to come to the party?"

"That's easy, we offer him something to sweeten the pot—no pun intended."

"Like what?"

"Like you."

"Me! Are you nuts?"

Wes chuckled. "Don't worry, Stainless. Buck and me, and a few of my associates, will be there to see you get out, more or less in one piece."

"Uh-huh. Thanks, I feel a whole lot better."

"Look, you've seen a couple of my boys in action. They'll stand behind their guns if the shit hits the fan."

I thought about the little altercation in Matamoros. He had a point. "Okay, Wes, set the meet, but it has to be in Matamoros. I'm not going down into the interior of Mexico, where you and me and our little band of immortals get 'disappeared'."

"Don't worry. I'll set the meet somewhere where both parties can fly in. A neutral spot near Matamoros."

"What about the boat?" I asked.

"I'll tell Ochoa's people they can pick it up on the Mexican side of Boca Chica," Wes replied.

I ran over the plan in my mind for a long moment. Offhand, I could think of only a dozen or so things that could go wrong and get me killed. "Okay, Wes, make it happen."

"Not a problem. But there's one more thing, Hardin."

Always is, I thought. "And that would be?"

"You have no authority south of the ditch, and the Mexican police are not in on this." Wes hesitated for a second. "Nobody is going to get arrested. Do you read me, Stainless?"

I paused for a long moment. Wes was right, of course. We'd never get Ochoa out of Mexico to stand trial in the States. And he'd never see the inside of a Mexican prison. "I read you five-by-five," I said and I couldn't help but snicker.

"What's funny?" Wes asked.

"This situation kind of reminds me of a joke a guy told me once about Custer's last words at Little Bighorn."

"What were they?"

"Take no prisoners."

Chapter 14

Someone once said, "A butterfly flaps its wings in China and a hurricane forms on the other side of the world."

It must have been a damned big butterfly flapping its wings in China, because this storm was brewing up to be one for the record books.

The storm was spawned from a small low-pressure system just east of the Leeward Islands. As the low approached the Yucatan, its thunderstorms were topping 40,000 feet. Sustained winds around the eye were clocked at 60 mph, becoming the first named storm of the season—Tropical Storm Adair.

Wes flew his King Air to Valley International Airport, outside of Harlingen. Local customs agents were waiting and gave the plane a good going over, but Wes and the plane were clean.

I pulled into the airport shortly after Wes landed. Driving over to the hanger he'd rented, I passed several customs agents I recognized; they didn't look too damn happy.

I parked my cruiser next to the hanger and walked through the open hanger doors.

Wes waved when he saw me.

I smiled when I shook Wes's hand. "I just passed a bunch of customs agents. They all looked like they'd just bitten into a piece of sour owl shit."

Wes laughed. "Yeah, like I'd be dumb enough to fly dope into this airport. And tell them ahead of time I was coming."

I nodded. "No comment. They are, for better or for worse, my comrades in arms."

Wes shook his head. "No wonder we're losing the war on drugs."

"Yeah, well, I think America's appetite for the white powder has a lot to do with it."

Wes leaned against the sleek fuselage of the King Air. "You do realize, Stainless, we're never going to win the so-called war on drugs."

"Indeed, I do. But it could be managed by legalization."

Wes smiled. "You think?"

I nodded. "Look at Prohibition. People wanted booze; the government, in its infinite wisdom, outlawed it, so the gangsters provided it. It's the same thing with drugs. People want it, they can't have it, so the bad guys, like Ochoa, provide it. Legalize it and we'd have a chance."

Wes laughed. "You should run for office."

I tapped my Sheriff's badge. "I did, pardner. I did."

*****

Alexsie Yazov boarded the three o'clock flight from Mexico City to Havana, Cuba. The plane was a Russian-made Tupolev 204CE. Yazov preferred the European Airbus 300. He may be Russian, but he could read safety reports.

Shortly after take-off the Captain announced that there would be no food or drink service on the flight. There was a tropical system approaching from the south, and heavy turbulence was expected.

Yazov swore inaudibly in Russian and tried to relax by thinking about all the money he'd make if he pulled off his scheme. The mental masturbation worked until the plane dropped violently as they hit the first of the turbulent air. It would be a long two hours and forty-five minutes.

Yazov spent several days in Havana making the necessary arrangements to bring the 23 kilos of cocaine into Cuba. Smuggling in the coke raised few eyebrows in the Havana underworld. Smuggling in a kidnapped American woman raised plenty of eyebrows, and the ante.

From the photos Ochoa had included in the sheriff's dossier, Rory Roughton looked to be worth the extra trouble and expense. Yazov was now re-thinking killing the woman. Maybe he had a *twofer.* He'd steal Ochoa's coke, and he'd ransom the woman. Roughton's family, according to the information Ochoa had provided, was loaded with oil money.

Yazov checked out of the Hotel Nacional, feeling very good about his prospects. He hailed one of a dozen 1950s-era cabs parked in front of the historic Havana hotel and headed to the airport.

The eye of Tropical Storm Adair had crossed the Yucatan and was now in the warm, hospitable waters of the Gulf of Mexico. Her northwest motion has slowed and the pressure in the eye was going down—way down.

The National Hurricane Center in Miami was on full alert. Early projections showed landfall in approximately 96 hours. The cone of uncertainty ranged from south of Corpus Christi to north of Tampico, with a projected bull's-eye on Brownsville.

My cell phone rang as I was parking my Jeep in my assigned spot. Being Sheriff did have a few perks.

"Hardin, it's Wes. Have you seen the weather reports?"

I killed the ignition and leaned back in my seat. "Yeah. Looks like we could get hammered."

"Affirmative, Stainless. And it throws a big monkey wrench into our plans with Señor Fred."

I exhaled and looked out the driver-side window at the clear blue sky. "Well, maybe it will hit further up the coast."

"Maybe. But in any case, I've got to move my plane inland. At least as far as San Antonio."

"Understood, Wes. We'll just have to postpone our little meeting until this damn storm passes."

"Yeah. I doubt the sawed-off Nazi likes hurricanes any more than we do."

I chuckled. "Probably not. Anything else on the radar besides Adair?" I asked.

"Funny you should ask, Hardin," Wes replied. "I got a piece of information from a low-level *drugista* who owed me a favor. He said word in the trenches is Ochoa *is* using a Russian mercenary for some of his more interesting capers."

"Like shooting Strelas at innocent, low-flying, aircraft?"

"Yeah, exactly like that. But there's more, Hardin. Turns out the Ruskie is also into kidnapping. He's grabbed some big-time folks in Mexico and South America."

"You got a name, or a description?" I asked.

"Not really, Hardin. My contact said the fellow is definitely Russian and speaks German, Spanish, and English. He's a big fellow and shaves his head."

"Damn, Wes, that's not much to go on."

"I know," Wes replied. "And there's one more thing, Hardin . . ."

"What?"

"If Ivan shows up at our little meeting, he goes out with the rest of the trash."

Chapter 15

Frederick Ochoa was watching the weather on CNN International. He switched off the TV and poured two fingers of A. de Fussigny cognac into a heavy crystal glass. The glass, one of two, had been given to his father by Hermann Göring. A swastika had been deeply etched into the base of the crystal.

Ochoa held the glass to the light and gently swirled the deep amber liquid. "To the Fatherland, and all who fell defending her," Ochoa whispered. He finished the cognac just as Alexsie Yazov walked into his study. He was carrying the dossier Ochoa had given him.

Ochoa didn't offer the Russian a cognac. Yazov was useful, but Ochoa hated the Russians for what they did to Berlin after WWII. When Yazov was no longer needed, Ochoa had a special termination in mind.

Ochoa set the heavy glass on a coaster and looked at Yazov. "Is everything in order?"

Yazov nodded his large bald head. "It is, sir. Except for the weather." As a courtesy, he spoke in German.

"Yes. I've been monitoring the storm," Ochoa said, taking a seat in one of his leather chairs. He had the chairs specially made by a local artisan. The dimensions had been skillfully reduced so as to not dwarf the diminutive drug lord.

Ochoa motioned for Yazov to sit. The big Russian had to sit at a bit of an angle in the scaled-down chairs, but managed.

"Coffee?" Ochoa offered. "Or perhaps something a bit stronger?"

Yazov knew better than to dull his wits with alcohol when dealing with a psychopath like Ochoa.

"Coffee, please."

Ochoa pressed a button on the underside of a side table, and a servant appeared in less than a minute. "Two coffees," Ochoa said, switching effortlessly from German to Spanish.

When the servant left, Ochoa turned to Yazov. "Storms like this one are very bad for business, Alexsie. Supply lines get disrupted; ships, planes, and people disappear."

"Indeed," Yazov replied. "I've been thinking about just that."

"How so, my Russian friend?"

The servant returned with two cups of dark Columbian coffee. Yazov waited until they'd both been served and the servant had departed.

"The sheriff would be no problem to kill in Matamoros," Yazov said, pausing to take a sip of coffee. "My compliments, Patrón. This coffee is exceptional."

Ochoa came as close to smiling as he ever did, and nodded at Yazov. "One of my Columbian coca growers also grows exceptional coffee. You were saying?"

Yazov set his coffee cup and saucer on a side table. "I was saying that killing the sheriff is not a problem. But I would not expect him to bring all 23 kilos to our first meeting. Maybe a kilo to show good faith."

Ochoa looked at the big Russian over his coffee cup. "Agreed. Continue."

Yazov opened the dossier Ochoa had given him and pulled out a photograph and handed it to Ochoa. "This woman is the key."

After his meeting with Yazov, Ochoa clicked on his computer and went to the U.S. National Hurricane website. He hit the storm-tracking tab and looked at the projections. No change. Brownsville remained in the crosshairs.

Ochoa tapped on his chin with his left forefinger. *Maybe there was a better way than a risky meeting with the sheriff and buying back his own cocaine.*

I'd no more than gotten to my desk after my conversation with Wes when Betty Filmore stuck her head into my office.

"Commander Wilson on line two for you, Sheriff."

"Thanks, Betty," I said, punching line two and picking up the phone. "Morning, Commander."

"Mornin', Sheriff. Have you got a sec?"

"Yes, sir. Fire when ready."

Commander Wilson snorted. "Okay, Hardin. I guess you're up to speed on the approaching tropical storm?"

"Yes, sir," I replied. "Looks like it could blow up into a nasty hurricane."

"Exactly what my weather boys are telling me," Wilson said. "Which is why I'm calling you. I'm taking the *Bluefish* out to sea and up the coast to the Coast Guard Station at Port Aransas. And all of our small craft are going up the Intercoastal to join the cutter and sit out the blow."

I put my feet up on my desk and leaned back into my desk chair. "Damn. I hope the Mexican Navy doesn't decide to attack."

Wilson laughed. "Yeah, well, fair warning, Hardin. The coast is going to be wide open before, during, and for a while after the storm."

I put my feet on the floor and paid attention. "You think the cartels will use the storm to their advantage?"

"Could be, Hardin," Wilson replied. "They may try to move as much product as possible before the storm hits."

I took a deep breath and blew it out. "Jesus, what a country."

"Ours or theirs?" Wilson said.

"The whole damned shebang," I said. "All so a few dirt-bags can snort some white powder up their noses."

"Uh-huh. Problem is, Sheriff—it's a hell of a lot more than a few. And some of the dirt-bags, as you call them, are pretty high up the food chain."

I paused for a second. "I say again—what a country."

"Well, it is what it is, Hardin. But be advised, the local gunboat is weighing anchor in 48 hours, unless the storm track changes."

Chapter 16

Ochoa's plan was both bold and risky. He'd use Hurricane Adair as his "Fifth Column." He knew the storm would force the Coast Guard to move their cutter and utility boats to safe harbor.

Through his informants, he also knew the DEA office in Brownsville was now holding his 23 kilos of cocaine. He was counting on the DEA sending nearly all of their people up to Corpus Christi to wait out the storm.

Ochoa also knew one other thing: that much high-purity cocaine would be very tempting to the crew he sent to recover it. Ochoa flipped open his cell phone and called the communist.

"Alexsie, please come up from the beach and join me in my study."

Yazov frowned and looked at the topless Mexican beauty sharing his large beach towel. He reached over and slid his hand under the elastic of her bikini bottom. "Save this for later," he said in Spanish. "I have to go to work."

The woman smiled and arched her hips slightly. "Are you sure you must go," she said, looking up and down the deserted beach.

Yazov teased her for a moment with his fingers and then removed his hand. "Señor Ochoa is not a man I choose to keep waiting. But I shall return," Yazov said with a laugh. He was a big fan of the long-dead American general Douglas MacArthur.

Yazov stood and looked out across the Gulf of California. *Truman was a fool*, he thought, watching the gentle surf break on the sandy beach. *If he'd let MacArthur have his way, the Chinese would've been bombed back into the Stone Age.*

In ten minutes, Yazov was in his boss's study. Ochoa was seated in his favorite leather chair. He looked for a long moment at the big Russian. "Cognac, Alexsie?"

Yazov knew this was not a normal meeting. Something big was up, and the old man was priming the pump. "Yes, sir. Thank you," Yazov replied, bending his rule about alcohol in the presence of evil.

Ochoa poured a measure of Fussigny into two glasses and handed one to Yazov.

Yazov hefted the heavy crystal and noted the etched swastika. "Your father's?" he asked, moving the cognac under his nose, enjoying the montant aroma.

"Yes," Ochoa replied. "A gift from Hermann Göring."

Yazov took a sip of the rich, velvety liquor. "Outstanding, sir. Both the cognac and the crystal."

"Indeed," Ochoa said, pausing while he finished his cognac. "I called you in, Alexsie, to discuss the Matamoros operation."

Yazov tossed back the two fingers of Fussigny and walked over and carefully placed his empty glass on the bar. "Yes?"

Ochoa set his glass on a side table, tugged on the right leg of his neatly creased trousers and smoothly crossed his legs. "I want you to personally oversee the recovery of my lost cocaine shipment."

Yazov wrinkled his wide brow. "I thought your people were planning to meet with the American sheriff in Matamoros and work out a deal. And I was to grab the Roughton woman as insurance."

Ochoa almost smiled. "I have a better plan."

"A better plan?" Yazov said sharply, too sharply. He knew he'd made a mistake. Psychopathic degenerates like Ochoa were not to be questioned, not if one wanted to continue walking on the topside of the grass. But Ochoa had blindsided him.

Yazov backed off and tried to repair the damage. "But I have made preparations to abduct and hold the woman."

Ochoa stared at the insubordinate Russian until Yazov dropped his gaze. "If my plan is carried out *precisely*, Alexsie, I will have no need of the woman. Do with her as you will—after my cocaine is recovered."

*****

I'd called all my deputies and reserves into a large room in the courthouse annex. "Take a seat, gentlemen," I said, tapping on an old conference table with a gavel some judge had left behind.

"Okay, fellows, listen up," I said, turning my laptop around so they could see the latest storm track projections for Hurricane Adair. "If Adair stays on this track, looks like she'll come ashore just south of Boca Chica, in about fifty hours. And then right over us and up the Rio Grande Valley.

"Pressure's around 900 millibars with gusts to 200 miles per hour. If this holds up at landfall, we're looking at a Cat-5 hurricane."

A murmur ran through the room. "That's right, gentlemen. Prepare for the worst. I want mandatory evacuations of Padre Island starting at noon today. I want everybody off the island, and the causeway closed eight hours before landfall. Questions?"

Deputy Rodriquez raised his hand.

I pointed to him. "Alex?"

"Can we expect any help?"

"Not until after the storm passes. Then we'll likely see DPS troopers and, if necessary, the National Guard.

"Any other questions?"

One of the reserve deputies raised his hand.

"Yes, Mack?"

"What about the border crossings, Sheriff?"

"I want them closed eight hours ahead of landfall. And I mean locked down. Anything else?"

No one raised their hands. "Okay, gentlemen, get to it. And good luck."

*****

I went back to my office and started working the phone. My first call was to Rory.

"Hey, babe, just so you know, I'm ordcring a mandatory evac of the island starting at noon."

"It's going to be bad, isn't it?"

"Unless the storm weakens or changes course, yeah, it's going to be pretty damned bad. Can you stay at the ranch?"

"Yes. Dad's got all the hands getting things battened down."

"Okay, Rory, keep me posted as long as you can. I wish I could be with you, but I've got a lot on my plate."

"Don't worry about me. Dad and I have ridden out many a nasty storm at the ranch. The main house walls are two feet thick."

"Okay, get squared away and stay safe."

"You too, cowboy. It's liable to get real western before this is over."

I paused for a moment. "I've given orders to arrest looters and use all force necessary. This isn't going to turn into New Orleans."

I'd just hung up with Rory when Wes knocked on my door and stepped into my office.

"Hardin, I'm taking Lacey, Buck, and Dottie up to San Antonio on my plane. You want me to check with Rory? I can squeeze in a couple more people."

"Thanks, Wes, but I just got off the phone with her. She and Robert Lee are going to ride it out at the ranch."

Wes nodded. "They should be fine. The main house is built like the Alamo." He hesitated for a second. "If you want us to, Buck and I can rent a car and come on back."

"No, y'all stay in San Antonio till the storm moves through. Besides, all lanes are going to be reversed for evac. You'd have a hell of a time trying to get back down here."

Wes grimaced and nodded. "Roger that. Okay, then, I'm off. See you on the other side, Hardin. And watch your six."

Chapter 17

Yazov didn't like last-minute changes, but he had to hand it to the little Nazi bastard; the plan was brilliant.

As instructed, Yazov assembled a team and flew them to Monterrey in Ochoa's Army surplus Huey helicopter. Once the worst of Hurricane Adair passed Brownsville, Yazov and his para-military force would fly at tree-top level, cross the Rio Grande, and assault the Brownsville DEA office. The storm would force the Americans to reel in and tether the mini-blimps along the border. And without their "lookdown" radar, they'd never see him coming.

They say a rising tide floats all boats. Well, an approaching hurricane drives all rats to higher ground. Every drug-dealer wannabe and his stash were scurrying to get inland.

It was like shooting fish in a barrel. We picked them off at the causeway, coming off the island, and we nailed them coming across the bridges at the border. My officers arrested so many, we didn't have any more room in the jail. And I was starting to worry about the storm surge. If Adair made landfall as a Cat-5, we could get a 20-foot storm surge, which would flood the jail and drown most of the prisoners in their cells.

Deputy Tom Allen and I walked through the jail, looking at the assortment of people we'd picked up. Most were strung-out bottom-dwellers, the lowest rung of the food chain.

I shook my head and looked at my deputy. "Tom, get on the horn to all the deputies. Tell them to seize any contraband they find, but don't make any more arrests unless absolutely necessary."

Tom looked at me and nodded. "What about the prisoners we're holding?"

I looked around and listened to the din in the jail. "Get ahold of somebody at Border Patrol and see if we can borrow a couple of their buses. I'll call Sheriff Riviera up in Kingsville and see if he has cells available. Or maybe we can stash some prisoners at the Naval Air Station. And Tom . . ."

"Yes, Sheriff?"

"Kick loose anybody in here on a misdemeanor charge. Just transport the for-real bad guys. I'll work it out with Judge Wentworth . . . after the storm."

We got lucky and got two buses from the Border Patrol, and Sheriff Riviera had room in his jail. One problem solved. But looking out a window at the sky, I could see a bigger problem was fast approaching.

I drove down to the causeway that crossed Laguna Madre and linked South Padre Island with the mainland. Deputy Rodriquez was on station and had his sheriff's cruiser blocking the road.

"Everybody off the island, Alex?" I asked.

Alex looked at me and shrugged. "I made a run over there before we shut down the causeway. Looks totally abandoned. But, hell, Sheriff, there's always some jerk who thinks he can ride out the storm. So, no guarantees."

I looked across the bay, which was now covered with whitecaps. "Well, we did all we could, Alex. If a few crazies decided to stay and try to ride out the storm, so be it. We'll police up any bodies the sharks don't get, after the storm."

Then we caught a break. The storm was weakening as it approached the coast. The CNN weather jocks were now predicting Adair would make landfall as possibly a Cat-3. Still no walk in the park, but a damn sight better than a Cat-5. And the projected landfall had moved up the coast to Kenedy County. Other than the King Ranch, most of Kenedy County was sparsely populated. More good news, unless you were one of the sparse.

*****

Yazov was watching the developing weather situation on CNN International. He switched off the TV and walked out of the hanger.

He located the chopper pilot and handed him a new set of coordinates. “New lat-long.”

The pilot looked at the piece of paper. “These coordinates are not for the DEA helipad in Brownsville.”

“Change of plans from the old man himself,” Yazov replied. “We’re to pick up a passenger before we make the assault.”

The pilot hesitated and looked unsure.

“Look, Captain,” Yazov said, “I’m checked out in this bird. If you choose to not obey Ochoa’s orders, I will have no choice but to terminate your services and fly the mission myself.”

Yazov’s tone left no doubt in the pilot’s mind what *terminate* meant. “No problem, Señor Yazov. The new coordinates are but a small distance from our primary objective.”

Yazov smiled and winked at the pilot. “Very good. And I assure you, Captain, your cooperation will not go unreported to Señor Ochoa.”

Adair came ashore as a strong Cat-3. At the last minute, as predicted, she had wobbled slightly to the north, sparing the condos and hotels on the southern tip of South Padre Island from even worse damage.

Arroyo City, in northern Cameron County, and Port Mansfield, near the Kenedy County line, weren’t as fortunate. They were in the direct path of the storm, and they ceased to exist.

As the storm moved inland and began to lose a bit of steam, Yazov lifted off from Monterrey. The flight was rough, but ninety minutes later they touched down in front of the main house at the Roughton Ranch.

Robert Lee heard the chopper over the bands of heavy rain. He looked over at Rory and his ranch foreman, Ike Toms. "What in tarnation?" he said, looking out a window, trying to see through the rain squall. "Looks like a military chopper. Maybe National Guard?"

Yazov pounded on the massive wooden doors of the main ranch house. Ike walked over and opened one of the double doors just enough to see who was on the other side.

It was all the opening Yazov needed. He put his shoulder hard into the door, the edge of the heavy wood catching Toms in the forehead.

Yazov was inside before Robert Lee or Rory could react. "Stand fast and nobody will get hurt," Yazov said, glancing at the unconscious and bleeding man on the floor. "An unfortunate accident," Yazov said, covering Rory and Robert Lee with his model 1911, Colt .45 automatic.

"What in the hell is going on?" Robert Lee asked, moving to shield Rory.

"Stand fast, old man," Yazov snapped. "What's going on," Yazov motioned toward Rory with his pistol, "is the sheriff's girlfriend and I are going to get on that helicopter and fly down to Mexico."

"You're kidnapping my daughter?" Robert Lee said, the anger building in his voice.

"Very perceptive, Mr. Roughton. And I suggest if you want to see your daughter again, you do exactly as I say."

From Roughton Ranch, it took about fifteen minutes to fly to the DEA office in Brownsville. As the pilot descended, Yazov gagged Rory and handcuffed her hands through the metal seat back.

"Make a sound and you die," Yazov said, his face an inch from hers. "And so will Sheriff Steel. Understand? Nod if you understand."

Rory nodded and glared at her captor. The hatred in her eyes impressed Yazov. *This one may be a keeper,* he thought as he grabbed an AK-47 and moved to the door of the helicopter.

Before the skids were firmly down, Yazov and two Nicaraguan mercenaries were out of the chopper and running through the rain to the front door of the DEA building.

Yazov tried the door and turned to his men. "It's open," he said just loud enough to be heard above the wind and rain.

Yazov motioned for his men to enter the building. He followed close behind with his AK-47 up and off safe.

Bill Johnson had volunteered to stay behind with one other junior agent. One of the Nicaraguans pumped two rounds into Johnson's chest and stepped over the dead agent's body. The remaining DEA agent in the building was in the men's room. He came out wiping his hands on a paper towel. "Jesus, Bill, did you hear that thunder?"

The second mercenary stepped from behind a file cabinet and shot the young agent in the side of the head.

Yazov looked at the dead DEA agents as he stepped past their bodies. "No, my friend, I don't think he heard anything," Yazov whispered, motioning for his men to move ahead.

They found the evidence area, which was caged like a jail cell. Yazov handed his rifle to the nearest Nicaraguan and slipped off his backpack. He removed a small shaped charge filled with plastique explosive. "Take cover, gentlemen," Yazov said, arming the fuse.

The high-energy, focused blast of the shaped charge made short work of the heavy steel door. It took longer to find the cocaine than it had to shoot and blast their way in.

Yazov carefully placed the one-kilo green plastic bags of cocaine in his backpack. He smiled when the tally was a kilo short. *Either someone has sticky fingers, or the DEA is setting up a sting. No matter*, he thought, glancing at his two companions, *Ochoa's never going to know the difference*.

Yazov finished packing the cocaine into his backpack, pulled the drawstring tight and buckled the flap. He nodded to the mercenary holding his rifle and retrieved his AK-47. Yazov smiled, nodded again, and then calmly shot both Nicaraguans. One round each in the chest, followed by a *coup de grâce* round in the head.

Backpack slung over his shoulder and rifle in hand, Yazov made his way past the four bodies and back to the helicopter. He opened the door on the copilot's side, stowed his AK-47 and tossed the backpack on the floor in front of the copilot's seat.

"We had some trouble, comrade," Yazov said, drawing his .45 and pointing it at the pilot. "Please get out of the chopper."

The pilot looked in disbelief at Yazov, but he wasn't going to argue with a cocked .45. Instead he released his seatbelt, opened the door and started to step out. But before he could exit the chopper, Yazov shot him just below his left armpit. The force of the 230-grain hollow-point bullet knocked the pilot from the Huey.

Yazov walked quickly around the nose of the chopper. He stepped over the dead pilot and climbed into the right seat. He looked back at his bound and gagged passenger. All the color had drained from her face. But the anger was still heavy in her eyes.

This one does indeed have fire in her belly, Yazov thought as he twisted the collective, powering up the turboshaft engine. As the RPMs increased, he pulled back slowly on the cyclic. To offset the torque, he pushed lightly against the left pedal. When the bird felt light on her skids Yazov eased her forward and climbed to 500 feet. His heading was due south.

He'd made arrangements to refuel the Huey at a small airstrip south of Matamoros. From there he'd fly to Tampico. He'd contacted a fellow Russian working for a rival cartel, and worked out a deal to sell Ochoa's Huey. *What the hell*, Yazov thought, smiling to himself. *I'm stealing the little prick's cocaine; I may as well steal his chopper.*

From Tampico, he and his female companion, and Ochoa's dope, would board a fast boat to Cuba. The plan was perfect—he hoped.

Chapter 18

The first call I got after the storm was from Robert Lee Roughton. Robert Lee hated cell phones, but he was on one now and he was a bit more than highly agitated.

"Hardin, they've got Rory!" Robert Lee said so loudly I had to hold my phone away from my ear.

"Calm down, Robert," I said. "Who's got Rory?"

"How the hell should I know!" He was shouting now. "Some goddamned big Eastern European sonofabitch flying a Huey."

Something clicked in my memory bank. "Could he have been Russian?"

There was a short pause on the line. "That's it," Robert Lee replied. "I knew I knew that accent. Yes, I'd bet money on it. Do you know who it is?"

I ignored the sinking feeling in the pit of my stomach. "No, I don't, Robert. But we've gotten reports of Russian Mafia-types doing some work with the cartels. The Ochoa Cartel in particular."

"Jesus," Robert said, all the bluster now gone from his voice.

"Robert, get hold of yourself and tell me every damned thing you can remember."

Robert took a deep breath, composed himself, and told me everything about the abduction.

"Was there a ransom demand?" I asked when he finished.

"Yeah. The Russian gave me a typed sheet of paper with his demands."

"Read it to me."

"Hang on a sec, Hardin."

I grabbed a notepad and a mechanical pencil. "Fire away, when you're ready."

"Okay. The note says I'm to wire $2 million to an account in the Caymans. Upon receipt of the money, Rory will be flown to Mexico City and released. And it says I have ten days to make it happen, or he'll start sending me pieces of her."

My blood was starting boil but I concentrated on the details like it was any other kidnapping, which of course it was not. "Can you make the payment?"

"Yes."

"Okay, Robert. Make it happen," I said as professionally as I could. "The main thing is to get Rory back, unharmed. Then we'll run this commie bastard to the ground and feed his carcass to the hogs."

"Understood," Robert said, perking up a tad. "Do you want the ransom note?"

"Absolutely. And try not to handle it any more than you already have. Put it in a plastic bag and I'll send a deputy and a sketch artist to your ranch."

"Done. And don't worry, Hardin, I'll never forget the Russian's face or voice."

Yazov made it to the refueling stop outside of Matamoros without incident. It was a small, private airstrip. The kind that accepted only cash, kept no records, and asked no questions.

Yazov cut the power and turned to look at Rory. "If you promise to behave, I'll take off the cuffs and remove the gag."

Rory nodded and mumbled something.

Yazov snorted and climbed out of the Huey. He stopped for a minute and talked to the refueling crew, and then climbed into the rear of the Huey.

He removed Rory's gag and then uncuffed her hands. She rubbed her wrists to get the circulation going and glared at her abductor.

"Relax, Ms. Roughton. You behave yourself and you'll get to see a bit of Cuba and have one hell of yarn to tell your grandkids."

"Cuba?" Rory said.

"Yes," Yazov replied, motioning for Rory to step out of the chopper. "There's a toilet in the hanger, if you need it."

Rory nodded and turned toward the hanger.

Yazov grabbed her right arm. His grip was like a steel trap. "No funny stuff, young lady, or I'll send one of your nipples to your father as proof of life. Understand?"

"I understand," Rory replied.

"Very good," Yazov said, releasing his grip. "Now be quick about it. As soon as the chopper is refueled we're leaving."

Rory glanced at the Huey. "That bird doesn't have the range to make Cuba."

"I'm impressed, Ms. Roughton. You fly?"

"All the damn time, in chartered aircraft."

"I see. Well, the Huey has a range of about 315 miles. More than enough to get us to Tampico."

"Tampico and then a boat to Cuba?"

Yazov looked at her and smiled. "If you need to pee, you'd better hurry. When the refueling is complete, we take off."

A little over two hours later, Yazov landed the Huey on a private airstrip west of Tampico. As he powered down the engine, he turned and looked over his shoulder at his passenger. "End of the line, Ms. Roughton. We'll spend the night at a friend's compound and get you some clothes and anything else you might need."

"How about a 9mm Beretta?"

Yazov laughed. "I like your style. I think I'm going to enjoy your company."

Rory gave him the finger and the big Russian cracked up. She nodded toward the front of the chopper. "I think you have a visitor."

Yazov turned back to the front. "Ah, yes. My good friend Comrade Vasily. The new owner of this helicopter. Time to go," Yazov said, grabbing his backpack containing Ochoa's cocaine, but leaving his AK-47. He still had the Colt .45 on his hip.

The two Russians met in front of the cockpit and exchanged hugs and a bit of Russian. Yazov motioned for Rory to join them.

"Comrade Vasily, allow me to present my friend, Ms. Rory Roughton," Yazov said, switching to English. "After we rest up and get some supplies, she has agreed to spend a few days in Cuba with me."

Vasily looked at Yazov's backpack. "You seem to be travelling very light and very fast, comrade."

Yazov shrugged. "Yes, just some travel documents and a change of clothing. But we'll resolve that situation in Tampico. Do you have the money for the Huey?"

Vasily nodded. "Yes, the money is at my compound. Circulated $100 bills with non-sequential serial numbers, as you requested."

Yazov raised his right eyebrow. "Five hundred thousand dollars?"

Vasily nodded. "Again, as you requested."

Yazov smiled. "Then, my friend, you are the proud new owner of a very fine helicopter. The AK-47 stowed by the copilot's seat is my gift to you."

Vasily took them to his compound in the Zona Dorado, an upscale suburb of Tampico. A female member of Vasily's house staff showed Rory to her room. She was relieved to see she was getting her own room and bath. When the maid left, she tried the door, but it was locked from the outside.

Rory looked around. The room was nicely furnished and spotless. Fresh clothing had been laid out on the bed. The room's two windows were set high in the adobe walls and, in any event, were too small to climb through.

Rory stripped off her khaki slacks, blue denim shirt, and underwear, and took a hot shower. Afterward, she put on the jeans, blouse, and underwear that had been left for her. To her surprise, everything fit quite nicely. The only thing missing was a bra, so she put on the one she'd been wearing. She didn't like the idea of going braless in front of the big Russian. So far he'd been on his best behavior, at least around her. But there was no reason to put any ideas in his big bald head—either one of them.

Chapter 19

Lee Fairchild closed his cell phone and glanced over at Peter Weller, agent-in-charge of the Corpus Christi DEA office. "No answer. And that's the third time I've called."

Agent Weller nodded. "Weather's clearing fast. We've got a Blackhawk helicopter at CC International."

"Tell the pilot to get ready to take me and two agents to Brownsville. We'll be at the hanger in thirty minutes."

The flight was fast and rough.

"Circle the building," Fairchild ordered, looking down at the DEA office building. The pilot did a slow, low-level circle of the building. Fairchild scanned the building's exterior through his binoculars.

He turned to the two agents accompanying him and keyed his mic. "Front door's open and there's a bit of smoke drifting out."

The agent sitting next to Fairchild keyed his mic. "Damage from the hurricane?"

Fairchild shook his head. He had one of his feelings. "Maybe."

The pilot glanced back at the senior DEA agent. Fairchild nodded and gestured downward with his right index finger.

The three DEA agents were out of the chopper as the skids settled. Guns up and out.

"Sheriff, I've got a priority call for you from DEA Agent Lee Fairchild. Line one."

"Okay, thanks, Betty. I've got it."

"Lee, this is Hardin, what's up?"

"Plenty, Sheriff. Someone hit our office during the storm."

"*Hit*?"

"Yes. I've got two agents KIA and 22 kilos of Ochoa Cartel cocaine are missing."

I felt like somebody had punched me in the solar plexus. There was no doubt now who'd grabbed Rory.

"Hardin, you still there?"

"Yes, I'm here, Lee."

"Okay. This is federal jurisdiction, Hardin, but we'll be working closely with your office and the other law enforcement agencies."

I paused for a second. "There's more, Lee."

"*More*?"

"Yeah. Rory Roughton was kidnapped around the time your office was knocked over."

Lee blew out his breath. "Jeezus . . .! You think there's a connection?"

"Well, Robert Lee, Rory's dad, said the abductor was a big Eastern European type, probably Russian. And they came in a military-looking Huey.

"Ochoa is reported to be using Russian mercs. I doubt anyone else would have the balls to shoot their way into a DEA office. And even if they did, they sure as hell wouldn't have the balls to steal Ochoa's coke."

"Agreed," Fairchild replied, anger boiling over in his tone. "What did they ask for?"

"Two million. Wired to an account in the Caymans within ten days."

"Is Mr. Roughton going to comply?"

"Yes. And then I'm going to hunt down that Russian bastard and castrate him."

Fairchild's tone softened. "Listen, Hardin, I know you and I have had our differences in the past, but anything you need, you let me know. I've got two young agents, not much more than kids, murdered. I want that Russian's head on a tray."

"Done. Anything else, Lee?"

"Yes. There are two dead Latin males in our office: full camo, AK-47s, single tap in the chest and one to the head. But my guys never got off a shot."

"I see," I said, my brain going into overdrive. "My guess is the Russian grabbed Rory, flew to your building in the Huey, killed your guys, stole the dope and then executed his buddies. No witnesses except the chopper pilot."

Lee cut in. "Somebody in a flight suit is lying on our helipad, shot through and through, ribcage to ribcage," Lee said. "I'm guessing he is, was, the pilot."

I tapped on my chin with my left fist. "Make that no witnesses. And that also means the Russian can fly a Huey."

"You're forgetting one witness, Hardin."

I paused for a moment and realized I'd missed the obvious. "Yeah. No witnesses, save for Rory."

It took Robert Lee three days to get the two million together and wired to the numbered account in the Caymans. It took Wes only about an hour to fly the King Air and his passengers, Buck, Lacey, and Dotty, back to Brownsville—all eager to help.

Two days after Robert Lee wired the money to the Caymans, we'd had no word on Rory being released. Wes was working the "back channels" and had learned a couple of very interesting things.

Wes, Buck, and I met at my bayside bungalow shortly after seven in the evening. It was now Day Six since Rory had been kidnapped.

"Okay, fellows, here's what I've learned so far," Wes said, pausing to take a sip of his tequila. "It seems Ochoa's Russian merc, and probably the SOB who tried to shoot me down, made off with

FreddieO's favorite Huey. I'm guessing it's the same Huey that was used to grab Rory and hit the DEA office."

I lit a semi-good cigar one of my constituents had given me, took a deep pull, coughed, and looked at Wes. "You got a name on the Russian?"

"Yazov . . . Alexsie Yazov. Speaks English, German, Spanish, and of course, Russian. A big bald-headed SOB."

"That fits with Robert Lee's description," I said. "Damned good work, Wes."

"Thanks. It gets worse," Wes continued. "Turns out ol' Alexsie has deep ties in Cuba. Both with the local commies and the Cuban mob. His ties in the government reportedly reach the highest levels."

Buck leaned forward in his chair. "You think Yazov has taken Rory to Cuba?"

Wes shrugged. "Could be. Word is he dumped Ochoa's Huey in Tampico. Sold it to a rival cartel."

I shook my head. "Damn. This Russian is either the dumbest bastard on the planet, or the coolest customer I've ever come across."

Buck looked at the floor for a moment, then raised his head and asked a damned good question: "What the hell do we do if Yazov is holding Rory in Cuba?"

I shook my head and looked at Wes.

"I'm working on it," Wes replied, swirling the remaining tequila in his glass, and then downing it in one swallow. "I'm working on it."

*****

Yazov lowered his binoculars. He could see the coast of Cuba coming up—fast. The old trawler looked like a hundred others plying the waters off Cuba. But beneath the rough, weathered exterior, she was anything but an old rust bucket.

Her twin turbo diesel engines could ring up 30 knots if needed. Behind blacked-out portholes on the port, starboard, and stern were 20mm cannons. She was not only fast, but packed a hell of a wallop. The Cuban mafia used her to transport everything from drugs to counterfeit U.S. $100 bills.

Yazov's plan was to lie off the Cuban coast till dark and then quietly enter Havana Harbor. Once safely tied up, he'd take the coke in to Old Havana and make the sale. Afterward, he'd decide what to do with the girl.

Two days earlier, he'd used the ship's satellite phone and confirmed that Rory's father had wired the ransom money into his Cayman Island account. Yazov provided the Cayman bank with a Panamanian account number and instructed them to transfer the two million dollars. Once his business in Havana was completed, he'd move the funds again to Tortola in the British Virgin Islands. Yazov was anything but careless.

Late the next day, Wes called me on my cell phone.

"Hardin, it's Wes. Are you where you can talk?"

I was out surveying storm damage. "Yeah, I'm over on the island. Damn, what a mess."

"Yeah, I bet," Wes said. "Well, hopefully Barack can get federal aid down here a bit quicker than 'W' did to New Orleans."

"Amen, brother," I said, looking at the debris and destruction just a glancing blow from Adair had caused. "So what's on your mind, Wes?"

"Well, my sources tell me FreddieO is turning Mexico upside down looking for our Russian friend."

"And?"

"And, I think our commie buddy has departed Mexico. The money Ochoa is offering for information on Yazov would've turned something up."

"Cuba?"

"That's the consensus of opinion."

I took a deep breath and exhaled. "What I don't understand is why Yazov hasn't released Rory. Hell, he got his damned money."

Wes didn't say anything.

"You still there?" I asked.

"Uh-huh," Wes replied.

I could tell from his tone there was bad news coming. "Let's have it, Wes," I said. "All of it."

"Well, I also heard that Yazov likes the ladies. He may have decided to hold on to Rory . . . at least for a while."

"What does the commie bastard do when he gets tired of them?"

Wes hesitated.

"Wes," I said, knowing I didn't want to hear the answer.

"It's not good, Hardin."

"He kills them?"

"That's the word."

I took a deep breath and exhaled slowly. "When do we leave?"

"I figured that'd be your response. Soon, Hardin. I've got a seaplane lined up and I'm working on pinpointing Yazov's location."

"A seaplane? Jesus, Wes, can you fly a seaplane?"

"Hell, Hardin, I fly a King Air."

"Yeah, but you don't take off and land on water."

Wes chuckled. "No worries, Stainless, I read Jimmy Buffett's book."

"Buffet has an instructional book out on flying seaplanes?"

"More or less," Wes replied. "Look, Hardin, it's the only way. We'll come in low, below radar, I'll set her down in a deserted cove and you and Buck can raft in and get Rory."

"And shoot the Russian," I added.

"I think it best," Wes replied so offhandedly I almost laughed.

"When do we shove off?"

"Just as soon as my contacts get a fix on Yazov's location. The seaplane is an old Grumman Albatross and she'll be waiting for us in George Town, Grand Cayman."

"How the hell are we going to pay for this operation?" I asked. "I can't exactly put 'seaplane rental for invasion of Cuba' on my expense report."

Wes chuckled. "You still have the kilo of cocaine you checked out from the DEA office?"

I felt a familiar hollow feeling in the pit of my stomach. "Yeah."

"Could it be that all chain-of-custody records for that little transaction were lost during the hurricane and break-in?"

"I'll have to check with Agent Fairchild," I replied. "And he's a by-the-book SOB. But he did say he'd do anything to help get the guy who killed his two agents."

"Okay, there you go. You work it out with Fairchild and I'll take care of everything else," Wes paused a half second. "Just one more small detail, Stainless. This little operation is totally unsanctioned. The Cubans catch any of us, they'll execute us. If the Marines at Gitmo pick us up on radar—end of mission."

I took a breath and blew it out. "Times like this, I wish Meyer Lansky was still in charge down there," I said, only half kidding.

Wes chuckled. "Yeah, what the hell was Fidel thinking?"

Chapter 20

Shortly after midnight, the captain of the *Hades Sabre* entered the narrow channel that lead to Havana Harbor.

Yazov went below to Rory's cabin. He knocked and then opened the cabin door. Rory was sitting on her bunk, her knees drawn up against her chest.

Yazov looked at her for a long moment. "You continue to cooperate and we'll both get out of this alive. Understand?"

Rory nodded. "Yes, I understand. Are you in danger, too?"

Yazov snorted. "One is always in danger in this business."

"Then take the ransom and disappear," Rory said.

"Want to go with me?" Yazov asked, smiling.

Rory took a breath and exhaled. "Look, Alexsie, you've treated me well and I appreciate it. But I'm not running off with a Russian mobster. Turn me loose and I'll call off Sheriff Steel."

Yazov laughed. "Your boyfriend, the Sheriff of Cameron County, is coming after *me*?"

"You can count on it. And he'll be bringing some interesting friends."

"Indeed? A posse?" Yazov said, raising his bushy black eyebrows. "Well, it will be interesting to see how they intend to apprehend me here in Cuba."

I called Lee Fairchild and arranged to have lunch at Lupe's. He was seated at a table and waiting for me when I got there.

"Lee, thanks for coming," I said, pulling up a chair.

The waitress came over to take our order. "Sheriff, Agent Fairchild, what'll it be today?"

We both ordered the daily lunch special and sweet tea. I waited until she headed to the kitchen with our orders. "I know where Rory and the Russian are," I said. "And we're going after them."

"*We*?"

"Yeah. Me, Wes, and Buck," I replied. "You're welcome to tag along, Lee."

Lee put both elbows on the table, clasped his hands together and rested his chin on his thumbs. "Boy, that I could," he said, looking over the tops of his glasses. "But I'd be a hindrance to the operation. Hell, Hardin, a federal agent on some kind of illegal operation . . ."

I looked at Lee, not sure whether to laugh or not. "You're kidding me . . . Right? Lee, our government is up to their ears in illegal operations. Hell, they've probable bugged every establishment in Brownsville."

Lee ignored my remark. He pulled off his glasses and cleaned them with his napkin. "Where are they, Hardin?"

I looked around the café; nobody appeared to be paying any attention to us. I leaned forward. "Cuba."

Lee put his glasses back on and stared at me. "You want to start a war?"

"If I have to. Whatever it takes, Lee, I'm getting Rory back and I'm going to terminate Comrade Yazov—with extreme prejudice."

"Yazov? Alexsie Yazov?" Lee asked.

Why was I not surprised? "You know him?"

"We know him, Hardin. He works for Ochoa." Lee paused for a long moment. "How good is your intel?"

I exhaled and looked at Lee. "It's as good as it gets . . . considering the source."

"Wes's contacts?"

I took a sip of my tea and nodded. "Bingo."

Lee rubbed his palms. The sound was like old sandpaper scraping together. "I was never here, we never had this conversation," Lee said, and paused. "Other than going along, which would put Rory in more danger . . . what can I do to help?"

"Deep-six the chain of custody on the kilo of Ochoa's cocaine."

Lee nodded. "Short of funds?"

I nodded. "Yes."

Lee looked slowly around the café. "Done. Just one thing, Hardin . . ."

"Yes?"

"Put two in that Russian bastard for me; one for each of my agents."

Yazov returned to the *Hades Sabre* just before noon. He paid off the captain and went below to collect Rory.

Her cabin door was open and she was sitting on her bunk with her belongings packed.

"I see you're ready to get off this scow?" Yazov said, glancing at the suitcases he'd bought for her in Tampico.

Rory looked up at Yazov. "Yes, I'm ready to get back on land . . . even Cuban land."

Yazov laughed and grabbed her bags. "Then by all means, we should go."

Rory sighed. "Where to now, comrade?"

Yazov smiled. "I have a compound just outside of Cienfuegos, about 240 kilometers southeast from here. My home overlooks Playa Rancho Luna, one of the finest beaches in all of Cuba."

Rory nodded. "I'm impressed. But why take me? You undoubtedly have the ransom money by now, and I assume you've sold the cocaine. Put me on a plane to Mexico City, and I'll call off Steel and his band of brothers."

Yazov tilted his head toward the cabin door. "All in good time, Rory. I will explain everything on the way. Don't worry, no harm will come to you."

*****

In a faded, peeling, pink-and-white stucco building in the old section of Havana, two narco-traffickers were overseeing the cutting of Yazov's cocaine. To discourage theft, the all-female crew was naked except for G-strings.

The older of the two men half-turned, never quite taking his eyes off the women or the coke. "Did you have that Russian pig followed?"

"Sí, exactly as you requested. Yazov went straight to Banco Nacional. It appeared from all the handshaking and patting on the back that he made a rather large deposit."

"One point five million?"

"Not yet confirmed."

"After the bank, where?"

"To the docks where he boarded the *Hades Sabre*."

The older man snorted. "So that's how he got the coke into Cuba."

"Yes. The same boat we've used many times in our runs to Florida."

The older man tapped his walking stick sharply against the tile floor and pointed to a particularly large-breasted woman. "Watch what you're doing, or I'll replace you."

The young woman nodded and redoubled her efforts.

"After the boat, what?" the older man asked.

"Yazov and a young lady from the boat hired a rental car and drove southeast on Highway One."

"Are we tailing him?"

"Sí, señor. All the way to his destination."

The older man nodded and continued to watch the women process the coke. “I want this dope on the street in Miami in 36 hours.”

“Sí, señor. And the Russian?”

“I will deal with Comrade Yazov. And I will arrange a visit with our good friends at Banco Nacional.”

Chapter 21

I gave the kilo of cocaine to Wes, and he'd *placed* it with one of his dealer buddies—cash problem solved.

In less than ten days, I'd gone from being a sworn law enforcement officer to a co-conspirator in a drug deal. Worse yet, I was about to participate in an invasion of Cuba and the murder of a Russian national. Ian Fleming had nothing on me.

It took a few days for Wes to get a line on Yazov's location. He finally called and said to meet him at Red's BBQ. And to bring Buck.

After we ordered, Wes pulled a map of Cuba from his back pocket. "Well, Yazov's in Cuba alright." Wes said, spreading the old Michelin road map across our table.

We anchored the map with salt and pepper shakers and hot sauce bottles.

Wes took a pen from his shirt pocket and pointed to a spot along the southwest coast of Cuba.

"Cienfuegos, gentlemen," Wes said, tapping on the map with the tip of his pen. "That's where dickhead is holed up. Turns out he has a pretty fancy compound just above the beach, here at Playa Rancho Luna."

I looked hard at Wes. "Is Rory with him?"

Wes nodded. "According to my source there's a woman with Yazov who matches Rory's description."

I nodded. "When do we go?"

Wes looked at me and Buck. "We fly to Grand Cayman tomorrow and tag up with the Grumman."

Buck had been studying the map while Wes and I had been talking. "What about this little inlet here?" Buck asked, leaning closer to read the name. "Playa Arimao?"

"Good eye, Buck," Wes said, moving his pen to the U-shaped inlet. "It's perfect. Just a short hike to Yazov's villa and protected by a low range of hills."

I looked at the map and tapped on a small airplane symbol with my fingernail. "There's an airport at Cienfuegos. Will they have radar?"

Wes nodded. "Most likely, but we'll be shielded by the hills. And I'll bring the Grumman in right at wave-top."

"Daylight insertion?" I asked.

"Got to be, fellows," Wes replied. "I'm going to get checked out in the Grumman when we get to the Caymans. Touch-and-goes, etcetera, but I won't have enough stick time to attempt a water landing at night."

Buck and I glanced across the table at each other and then back at the map.

I lowered my voice. "Weapons?"

"Ours or theirs?" Wes said with a chuckle.

"Let's start with ours," I said.

Wes smiled at me and Buck. "Don't worry, fellows, I've arranged to have the standard drug-dealer's arms package stowed on the Albatross."

I felt myself sink deeper into the abyss. "What about Cuban military?" I asked.

Wes used his pen and pointed to the airport I'd just mentioned. "Jaime Gonzáles Airport. Castro used to keep attack helicopters stationed there, but it's currently reported as inactive."

"*Reported*?" Buck said.

Wes nodded. "According to my source."

"Okay, Wes," I interrupted, "how do we get to the beach, grab Rory, and get back to the Albatross?" I cringed and paused for a half second. "If it's alright with y'all, I believe I'll call it a Grumman."

"You superstitious, Stainless?" Wes asked, winking at Buck.

I stammered for a second. "No, not really. It's just that an Albatross is not exactly a good-luck symbol."

Wes nodded. "Okay, Grumman it is."

"So?" I said, looking at Wes.

"So, we'll have an inflatable rubber raft in the Alb . . . I mean, Grumman," Wes said. "I'll stay with the plane and keep the engines turning over. You and the Buckmeister raft to the beach and climb the hill to this point." Wes tapped on the map with his pen. "Then you'll enter Yazov's compound, grab Rory, shoot the fuckin' commie bastard, and haul ass back to the plane."

Buck snorted. "Hell, is that all? I thought this might be tough."

"Tough enough," I said, glancing at Buck and then back at Wes. "Anything else?"

"Just this. Anything my source knows, so does our friend Ochoa."

Buck looked up from the map. "You think he might try to grab Yazov while he's in Cuba?"

Wes chuckled. "Hell, no. He's not that crazy."

It took Yazov and Rory about three hours to negotiate the 240 kilometers to Cienfuegos.

Yazov stopped at a traffic light and checked his rearview mirror. Old habits die hard. He glanced at Rory. "My place in just south of town, but we should stop here and get something to eat. And buy some supplies."

Rory sat up in her seat and ran a hand through her dark hair. "I could eat . . . before you drop me at the airport."

Yazov grinned. "You're hurting my feelings, Rory. I'm starting to feel you don't care for my company."

Rory half-turned in her seat and looked at the big Russian. "Actually, for a commie . . . you're not too bad," Rory said and then laughed. "Must be some kind of captor-hostage mind warp."

Yazov knew he was falling for this South Texas firebrand. He'd never known anyone like her. He could still kill her, if it came to that, but he hoped it wouldn't. In fact, he wasn't at all sure how this situation was going play out.

"I know a good seafood place along the bay. It's called Finca del Mar. Beautiful view of the bay, damned good food, and a well-stocked bar. Sound okay?"

"I'm with you," Rory replied, a hint of sarcasm in her voice.

About ten minutes later, Yazov pulled into the restaurant's parking area.

Rory looked around as Yazov parked the car. "Wow. You weren't kidding about the view."

Yazov smiled. "Bahia de Jagua. Named after Spanish King Ferdinand the Seventh."

Rory looked a Yazov and nodded. "Salt water?"

"Yes," Yazov replied, gesturing with an open hand. "The bay is shaped like a fat plum with a narrow stem opening to the sea."

"Quite a natural port," Rory said.

Yazov nodded. "Yes. At one time, we considered stationing nuclear subs here. But Castro wanted too much in return." He laughed. "And your government would've gone ballistic—no pun intended. Shall we dine?"

I informed my deputies and the requisite city officials that I was going to be out of town for a couple of days, checking out a lead on Rory Roughton's kidnapping.

The next morning, Wes, Buck, and I caught a United commuter jet out of Brownsville and flew to

Houston. We had a quick bite at the airport and caught the one o'clock United flight to Grand Cayman. In three hours we were clearing customs at Owen Roberts International Airport.

I'd spent a fair bit of time in Grand Cayman when I was with the DEA, but I wasn't too sure if that would be an asset or a liability.

"Agent Hardin Steel, as I live and breathe."

I looked up at the approaching immigration officer; right about now, it didn't feel like an asset.

I watched Deputy Chief Amos Kincaid as he approached. "Immigration," I whispered to Wes and Buck.

When he was in range, Kincaid extended his right hand. "Hardin! Bloody good to see you again. Are you still with DEA?"

Jeezus! Could he possibly draw any more attention to us? I shook his hand. "No. I clocked my twenty and retired, Amos."

"Retired? You're too young to retire, Hardin."

I nodded and smiled. "Retired from the feds. I'm now the Sheriff of Cameron County, Texas."

Amos though for a moment. "South Texas, isn't it?"

"You know your geography, Amos," I said, motioning to Wes and Buck. These are two of my runnin' buddies from Brownsville."

"Running? Good God, you still jog?" Amos said, looking at the three of us.

I laughed. "Only when someone with a gun is chasing me. No, it means we're buddies, friends."

"I see," Amos said, still sizing us up. "So what brings you and your *running* buddies to the Caymans?"

"Just a bit of R&R, Amos," I said, glancing at Wes and Buck, who both nodded.

"Good show," Amos said. "This is certainly the spot for a bit of R and R, or as I like to say, I and I."

"I and I?" I asked.

"Yes," Amos replied, lowering his voice, finally. "Intoxication and intercourse."

We all laughed. "Well, Amos, very good to see you again."

Amos shook my hand again. "The pleasure's all mine. By the way, you're not carrying, are you?"

I laughed. "Hell, no. I'm not here on business, Amos."

Amos nodded. "Forgive me for asking, but we had a couple off-duty FBI guys down here not too long ago, and they forgot to register their weapons. My boss got his knickers in a hell of a twist."

"No worries, Amos, we're unarmed and generally harmless."

"Good show. Please enjoy your stay. By the way, where are you staying?"

"The Hyatt," I said, glancing at Wes and Buck.

Amos nodded. "You know it's now the Grand Cayman Beach Suites."

I nodded. "Yes, I know, but I like the old name better."

Amos smiled. "As do I. I remember when Hackman and Cruise were down here filming *The Firm*. They shot some scenes there."

"I remember," I said. "Damned good movie."

"Yes, and it was a damned fine hotel until Hurricane Ivan hit in 2004."

"Ivan?" I said.

Kincaid nodded. "Yes. As if it's not bad enough we've got the commie bastards off to our east, we had to get hit with a commie-named storm."

I looked at Wes and Buck and shook my head. "A bloody shame, Amos."

"So right," Amos said, glancing at his watch. "Well, I must be off. Good to see you again, Hardin." Amos glanced at Wes and Buck. "And good to meet you gentlemen. If there's anything I can do for you while you're on the island," Amos fished in his uniform shirt pocket and produced a card, "just ring me up."

"Will do, Amos," I said, taking his card. "And good to see you again."

The three of us watched Deputy Chief Amos Kincaid stride purposely into the airport crowd.

"Damn, Hardin," Wes said, "I didn't know you were an international celeb."

I shrugged. "What did Bogie say: 'In all the gin joints in the world'?"

"Something like that," Wes said, winking at Buck. "Come on, let's shag ass for the hotel before a TV crew shows up to interview Stainless."

As we headed for the airport exit, I turned and looked at Wes. "What about the Grumman?"

Wes pushed open the exit door. "We're to meet the plane's owner in the hotel bar at five."

*****

We took a cab to Seven Mile Beach and checked into the former Hyatt. Wes had rented us a three-bedroom suite. I'd mentioned the cost, but he'd shrugged it off. I guess drug smugglers are used to traveling first class.

We cleaned up a tad and headed down to the bar around five.

"There he is," Wes said, motioning to a very fit and tan-looking guy standing at the bar. "Come on."

"Tommy," Wes called out.

The man turned and looked in our direction. "Hey, Wes, fellas, glad you all made it okay."

"Tommy, I'd like you to meet Hardin Steel and Buck Bateman."

"A real pleasure, fellas. Wes has told me all about you."

Tommy's accent was hard to place; maybe Pacific Northwest? He was about my height and solid. And very tan for a blond-haired, blue-eyed individual. His most distinguishing feature, however, was his ears. He'd evidently wrestled . . . a lot.

"Buck, Hardin, this is Jack Thompson," Wes said. "But as you probably gathered, he goes by Tommy."

Buck and I both shook hands with the Grumman pilot.

"Let's grab a booth and get some drinks." I gestured to an open booth near the pool, but not too near.

We sat down and ordered a round of cocktails from a very good-looking cocktail waitress. While we waited for our drinks, we watched a half-dozen beauties in very scanty bikinis frolicking in the pool.

"Nice place," I said, grinning at the others.

Tommy nodded. "You should have been here before the hurricane, when it was the Hyatt."

I nodded. "I was . . . many times."

The waitress arrived with our drinks. Tommy hoisted his and said, "To the good old days."

Wes laughed. "Yeah, may they never come this way again."

We all laughed and clinked glasses.

Wes set his glass on the table and looked at Tommy. "Everything in order and ready to go?"

Tommy took a long sip of his drink and nodded. "Yep, the plane's fueled, armed, and ready to go. I'll check you out tomorrow morning."

Wes nodded. "Where is she moored?"

Tommy watched a particularly voluptuous young lady dive into the pool. "She's tied to a buoy in the North Sound. The Barcadere Marina."

I looked at Tommy. "What kind of word is *Barcadere*?"

Tommy smiled. "It's a bit of a bastardization of the French word *débarcadère*, which loosely translated means 'landing place'."

I nodded. "I like it. Fits right in with the flavor of this operation."

Wes looked at Buck and me and then at Tommy. "Tommy, why don't you tell the boys a little bit about yourself and how you came to be the proud owner of the Grumman Albatross?"

Tommy set his drink down and leaned in to the table. "I'd just graduated from UT, as in University of Texas, law school, but I was having trouble latching on with a big firm," Tommy laughed. "For some reason my cauliflower ears just didn't fit their button-downed lawyer image."

"Wrestler?" Buck asked.

"Yeah, high school and four years at UT," Tommy replied. "I just couldn't get used to the head-gear . . . and now I'm paying the price. Anyway, I needed some cash and I'd had a pilot's license since I was sixteen."

"And you ran into Sky King, here," I interrupted, glancing at Wes, "and decided go into the 'import-export' business?"

Tommy smiled and nodded. "Yep, that's about it. And the rest, as they say, is history."

I looked at Tommy. "Is the Grumman clean?"

"As a nun's dildo."

We all cracked up. "Good to hear," I said, still grinning.

We spent the rest of the evening getting better acquainted and prepping ourselves for Wes's check-flight.

The next morning at eight sharp, we met Tommy on the main dock at the Barcadere.

"Mornin', fellas," Tommy said. "Looks like we've got a perfect morning, weather-wise. Come on, I've got a rented Zodiac tied up just down the dock."

We walked a short distance down the dock to the Zodiac and all piled in. The boat driver was a local named Oscar. Tommy had hired him to run us out to the Grumman and pick us up when we returned.

With his passengers safely aboard, Oscar fired up the 40-horsepower engine and we headed out to the Grumman.

Once clear of the dock, Oscar pushed the throttle open and brought the inflatable boat quickly up on plane. A few minutes later, we were approaching the Grumman. Oscar eased off the gas, and the 15-foot inflatable dropped smoothly off plane and slowed.

I wiped some spray from my face and leaned toward Tommy. "What'll this souped-up raft do?"

"Flat out with this engine," Tommy replied, "about 32 miles per hour."

I nodded. "Is this the boat we're taking with us?"

Tommy shook his head. "No. The Grumman could carry the Zodiac, but the problem is getting her in and out of the plane. It just has one loading hatch on the port side. It's fairly small and set pretty high above the water line.

"No, for this little operation, I've loaded two four-man inflatable rafts. One to use for the rescue and one as a backup. Wes will bring you boys in close, and then you'll toss out one of the rafts and row like hell for shore."

I glanced at Buck, who was listening intently, and rolled my eyes.

Oscar eased the Zodiac up along the port side of the Grumman, near the tail. Tommy stood up and grabbed a lever just to the left of the hatch and pulled it down. A retractable step popped out below the hatch, and he tied off the Zodiac and opened the hatch.

Tommy held us steady while Wes, Buck, and I climbed into the Albatross. Once we were clear of the hatch, Tommy followed.

Oscar slipped the line and gently pushed the Zodiac away from the aircraft.

Tommy threw Oscar a salute. "I'll circle the marina and waggle the wings a couple of times before we make our final landing."

"No problem, sir," Oscar said. "I'll be waiting. Safe flight."

Tommy nodded, closed the hatch and made his way forward. "Well, here she is, boys. Whadda you think?"

I looked around the interior of the plane. "Damn, she's a lot bigger than I thought she'd be."

Tommy smiled like a proud papa. "Yep, biggest damn plane in the Grumman line. Right at 60 feet long and 80 feet across the wings."

Wes was up front, looking over the flight controls.

"You take the right seat, Wes," Tommy said. "Hardin, you and Buck take the two seats behind the pilot and copilot seats." He turned and winked at Buck and me. "You'll get a good show from there."

Tommy spent about fifteen minutes going over the instrumentation with Wes. I paid attention, just in case.

"Starting one," Tommy said, firing up the starboard engine.

The big Wright R-1820, 9-cylinder, 1450-horsepower engine coughed and blew some white smoke out the exhaust stacks, then caught and began turning smoothly. Tommy repeated the cycle on the port engine.

"Okay, Wes, I'll do one takeoff and landing so you can get the feel of it," Tommy said, reaching up to advance the throttles. "Piece of cake . . . sort of."

The North Sound was smooth, as was Tommy's takeoff.

Tommy keyed his mic. "I'll do a slow go-round and set her back down. Then she's all yours."

Wes nodded and looked back at me and Buck. "No worries, fellows, it's just like flying a pregnant King Air . . . with pontoons."

Tommy landed with barely a splash. He brought the big Grumman into the wind and idled down. "Okay, Sky King, your turn."

Wes took the yoke, and Buck and I tightened our seat belts to the max.

"Okay, Wes," Tommy said, pointing out the cockpit window. "Put the nose about 10 degrees starboard of your line."

Wes gave him a quick glance. "Don't worry, Wes, the torque will bring her nose on line. Twenty-five hundred RPMs on the engines. Flaps down 15 degrees."

Wes did a quick check, nodded and pushed the throttles forward.

"Rotate at 80 knots," Tommy said, looking straight ahead. "She's going feel a bit sluggish till were up."

Talk about loud. Even with the headset on, it was the loudest, and sexiest, aircraft I'd ever been on.

At 80 knots, Wes pulled back gently on the yoke and the aged Albatross broke free of the water's grip.

"Very nicely done, old man," Tommy said. "Now make a nice loop and bring her around for a touch-and-go."

The first landing was a bit rough, but the next four were perfect.

Tommy punched Wes in his left shoulder. "Nice flying, especially for a King Air driver. I'll write you up a type rating back at the bar."

Fifteen minutes later we were tying the Grumman to the buoy and, true to his word, climbing into Oscar's Zodiac.

Back at the hotel bar, Tommy bought the first round of drinks, Cuba Libres, which seemed fitting.

Tommy lifted his drink and inclined it toward Wes, Buck, and me. "I have, I believe, learned two things today: first, old Wes here is a natural-born seaplane flyer, and secondly, that I'm going with you on your little *mission.*"

I half-choked on my rum and coke. "What?"

Tommy nodded. "Yep, my mind is made up. I'll fly left-seat, and Wes can copilot. No reflection on your flying, Wes. You were brilliant for your first time in a seaplane. But it was under perfect conditions: calm seas, and nobody was shooting at you. And remember, boys, what if Wes takes a bullet? Who flies you home then?

“And besides, fellas, not to put too fine a point on it, it’s my plane.”

I looked at Wes and Buck. Both nodded. “Okay, Tommy, you’re in,” I said, holding up my glass. “May we be invisible to radar, merciless to our enemies, and long gone before Fidel finds out we were there.”

Chapter 22

Yazov had been preoccupied with business matters for the past few days—mainly banking transactions—and had had little contact with Rory, other than at meals. She seemed to have accepted her temporary fate and settled into life within the gated villa. But Yazov's instincts told him he must win her over, turn her loose, or kill her. Right now he was hoping for the first option.

He closed his computer and walked out of his office into the main living area. Rory had the windows and curtains open, and a fresh sea breeze was wafting through the house.

"Care for a swim before dinner?" Yazov asked.

"Ocean or pool?" Rory asked.

Yazov smiled. "I think, for now, we'd better stick to the pool. I don't want you to swim away."

"If you put me on a plane, I could just fly away."

Yazov rubbed the stubble on his chin. "Still think the good sheriff is coming to rescue you?"

"Not a doubt in my mind. Unless you let me go."

Yazov sat down in his favorite chair and stared out at the beach. "What if I made you a partner?"

"A partner? What kind of a partner?"

"Fifty-fifty in all my business ventures . . . and in my life."

"Alexsie," Rory paused and looked at the Russian. "I'm not in love with you."

"Get to know me. Give me a chance. You might be surprised."

Rory stood and walked to one of the open windows and looked down at the pool and the beach beyond. "I was surprised when you killed those men. And I was surprised when you kidnapped me."

Yazov took a deep breath and let it out slowly. "Those things I did, I had to do or face death myself. Have I not treated you with respect? Have I laid a hand on you?"

"I'll admit it, Alexsie, you *have* surprised me. And I'll admit, I've grown fond of you."

"Then why not take a chance? Life is very short, Rory. And opportunities are few and far between."

Rory paused for a moment. "Where would we live? Here in Cuba?"

Yazov rose and walked over to Rory. "Why not? Is it not beautiful? Do we not have everything we need, including friends at the highest levels of government? With the right partner, it could truly be paradise."

Yazov reached for her and took her in his arms. He kissed her deeply on the mouth and reached behind her and undid the knot holding her halter top.

Rory gasped softly as the cloth fell away, exposing her firm breasts and erect nipples.

Yazov led her to the sofa and slowly removed the rest of her clothing, and then his. He gently pushed her back on the couch and spread her firm, tan legs. He entered her just as a glint of silver reflected off a low-flying aircraft headed toward the coast. A reflection neither he nor Rory saw.

Tommy had flown the last 200 miles skimming the waves. The natural bay at Playa Arimao was about a mile long by a half mile wide. A small range of hills protected it from radar at the Cienfuegos airport.

Gitmo, at the southern end of the island, may have detected the Grumman, but hopefully they'd think it was a plane inbound for the local airport. Although the low flight level was sure to attract a bit of attention.

Tommy eased back on the power, dropped the flaps and yelled over his shoulder for everybody to get ready. A couple of minutes later, he gently flared the Grumman and set her down in the bay.

He brought the big seaplane as close to the shoreline as he dared. "Pop the hatch and get ready!" Tommy yelled, cutting the engines back even more. "I'll keep the bird offshore, just out of rifle range, until you get back. But no more than 90 minutes, fellows. We're bound to attract attention floating around out here. And I don't want Fidel scrambling his MiGs."

Tommy idled the engines, and I threw one of the inflatable life rafts out the hatch, pulling the cord as it cleared the fuselage. Sort of like Tom Hanks in *Castaway*, except our plane wasn't sinking—yet. Buck held the raft close with a rope.

I grabbed two sets of oars and climbed out of the Grumman and into the raft. Wes followed me, carrying a duffle bag containing our weapons. Buck came last, managing to close the hatch and not fall out of the raft.

Buck took one of the oars and pushed us away from the seaplane. "Goddamn. I'd hate to try that little maneuver in rough seas."

I nodded and started paddling. "Amen, brother."

With two of us paddling we covered the 100 yards in nothing flat. We hit the beach and pulled the raft into a small cleft in the hillside.

Wes unzipped the waterproof duffel and removed three M-16s. He handed a rifle and a 30-round magazine to both Buck and me. A second 30-round magazine was taped "piggy-back" to the first magazine. Sixty rounds apiece. We'd live or die with 180 rounds of .223 caliber ammunition.

Wes fished around in the duffle and pulled out a waterproof pouch. "Okay, fellas, here's a rough map I got from one of my contacts in the Ochoa Cartel."

Wes spread the map on the gravelly beach. "Listen up. We're here," Wes said, pointing to a spot on the map, "and here is where the big Ruskie's villa is supposed to be."

"*Supposed to be*?" I said, looking up at Wes.

"Don't worry, Stainless," Wes replied. "According to my guy, there's only one large house on the bluff above Playa Rancho Luna. We top this hill," Wes said, pointing to the hill immediately to our front, "and work our way across this little peninsula, here." Wes pointed to a spot on the map. "Then we take the house, kill the Russian, and rescue the maiden in distress. Piece of cake."

I pulled the bolt back on my M-16 and released it, chambering a live round. "Yeah, nothing to it. Let's move out."

It took about twenty minutes to work our way into position. Buck had a close encounter with some kind of snake that cost us a few minutes, but other than the reptile we'd run into no resistance.

I glanced at Wes. "Wow, your guy wasn't kidding about a 'large house'," I whispered.

Wes nodded. "Why do you think everybody wants to get in the drug business?"

Buck smiled and winked at Wes. "Big houses in Cuba?"

Wes flipped Buck the finger. "You're the cop, Stainless. How do you want to do this?"

"Spread out." I said, looking at the house, which was really a compound. "I'll go in the front, you two take the sides or the rear. And watch your background if you have to shoot. We don't want to hit Rory."

I looked at my watch. It read 9:30 a.m., local time. "Okay, I've got 9:30. Set your watches. We go in at 9:40."

We spread out and started to move in on the compound. I lost sight of Buck and Wes as I made my way to the front. Fortunately, Yazov liked his view of the bay. His security fence was only five feet high and the wrought iron gate was unlocked.

Yazov must feel right at home, I thought as I lifted the gate latch with the barrel of my M-16.

I used some boulders and cactus for cover and worked my way to the front door. The large windows on either side of the massive wooden door were open, and the cloth curtains were moving easily in the light breeze.

I risked a quick glance in one of the open windows. There was a pile of clothes on the floor in front of a sofa. On the sofa, a naked man and woman were sleeping. The woman was Rory, and from Robert Lee's description the man had to be Yazov.

I should have just backed off, but there was no way to recall Buck and Wes. I whispered, "Fuck," and stepped quietly through the open window.

I took a quick look around but couldn't see or hear anybody, save for my naked girlfriend and her commie lover snoring softly on the sofa.

"Wakey, wakey, kids. Daddy's home," I said, prodding the big Russian in the ass with the barrel of my M-16.

Yazov was instantly awake. It took Rory a moment or two to shake the cobwebs.

"Am I dreaming?" she said sleepily, just as Wes and Buck came in through open windows on opposite sides of the living area.

"If you are, it's a damn nightmare," I said, glancing at my two smirking companions.

"Both of you, get dressed," I said, nodding toward the pile of clothes on the tile floor.

Rory looked at me. "Hardin! Is that really you?"

"In the flesh, babe, if you'll pardon the pun. Now get some damn clothes on."

I motioned for Wes and Buck to turn around for a half-second and give Rory a chance to get dressed. They, of course, were having none of it.

Wes starting chuckling. "Now what, bwana?"

I shook my head. "Fuck if I know."

I've got to admit Yazov was a gentleman. He did his best to shield Rory from view while they both got dressed.

"Okay, you two," I said, motioning to my *ex*-girlfriend and the Russian, "just sit there on the couch while I figure this out."

"Shoot the damn Ruskie and let's haul ass," Wes said, glancing at his watch. "We don't have a lot of time, Hardin."

"No!" Rory shrieked. "You can't shoot him, Hardin. He never laid a hand on me."

Wes and Buck both laughed.

"Yeah, I can see that," I said, frowning at my two buddies.

Rory blushed. "Not until just now . . . and it was consensual."

A quick thought flashed through my mind. The promise I'd made to Lee Fairchild—to put two rounds in Yazov. I raised my rifle.

"No, Hardin. Don't do it. Please," Rory said, tears now streaming down her cheeks.

Wes took a step toward me. "It's your call, Stainless."

I nodded and slowly lowered my weapon. As I did, Yazov glanced toward the front of the compound. There was a different look in his eyes.

"What?" I said, bringing my rifle back to bear.

"I think we have company," Yazov replied, tilting his head toward the front of the house. "And I am not expecting any company."

"Bad guys?"

Yazov nodded. "Perhaps. If you would permit me a quick look?"

I motioned with my head toward the door. "One false move and I'll drill you. Understand?"

"Understood," Yazov said, moving toward an open window beside the front door. He glanced out the window for a second and then turned to me and held up six fingers.

I kept my rifle on Yazov and moved closer, taking a quick peek over his massive shoulder. Six armed men were climbing out of two beat-up Toyota pickups. They were all carrying AK-47s.

"I believe we've got us a little problem," I said, just loud enough for Buck and Wes to hear.

Buck glanced at Wes. "Let's take Rory and get the hell out of here."

I took another quick peek. The men were deploying around the house. In a few seconds, we'd be surrounded.

I shook my head. "Too late."

Yazov half-turned and looked at me. “Let me get a weapon. I know who sent these men. They will leave no one alive, not even the girl.”

I looked hard at the Russian.

“I give you my word, Sheriff Steel.”

I grimaced when he said my name, but I wasn’t surprised. Hell, he obviously knew all about me . . . and Rory.

I glanced at Wes and Buck. Both of them shrugged.

“What the hell,” Wes said. “We’re going to need him to get out of this mess.”

One of the men in front opened fire. The rounds tore through the front door, punching neat round holes in the hard wood.

“Jesus! Not too damned subtle, are they?” Buck yelled, grabbing Rory and ducking behind the sofa.

I looked at Yazov. “Get a weapon.”

Yazov sprinted for a closet with double doors off to the side of the living area. He ripped open the doors, exposing a small armory. He grabbed an AK and a handful of magazines.

We were now being fired on from three sides. I looked over at Wes and Buck and motioned toward the rear of the house. “See if you can flank ’em. We’ll cover you.” Yazov and I cut loose on full auto. “Go now!”

Wes and Buck stayed low and sprinted to the rear of the house. The shooters in front temporarily ceased firing, caught off-guard by the volume of return fire.

Yazov looked at me and grinned. “They thought I’d be alone.”

I couldn't help but smile back. The big bastard did have a certain panache about him.

I nodded. "Yeah, well, they'll get fully educated in a couple of minutes when Buck and Wes flank 'em."

I worked my way over to a huge ceramic flowerpot filled with dirt. I had a clear field of fire out one of the open windows. I could see just the back of one of the shooter's heads. I used the flower pot for a rest and removed the back of the bad guy's skull. One down, five to go.

I looked over at Yazov and motioned with my head for him to get closer to the windows. He didn't need much coaxing. For a big guy, he slithered with the best of them. He worked his way across the floor to a position behind a brick planter.

One of the attackers made a move for the front door and Yazov cut him nearly in half. He looked over at me and held up two fingers. Seconds later, I heard both Wes and Buck cut loose. There was no return fire from the sides of the house. I held up four fingers. Yazov nodded and winked at me.

The last men standing on the opposing team finally figured out they'd walked into a hornet's nest. They made a run for the nearest pickup, and Yazov and I cut them both down. And that made six.

"Buck, Wes!" I yelled at the top of my lungs.

"Yep, I'm here," Wes said, stepping through an open window.

"Ditto," Buck said, coming in from the opposite side.

I pointed my weapon at Yazov. "Please drop your weapon."

Yazov nodded and laid his AK on the tile floor and stood up. "Now what?"

I walked over and picked up the rifle. Smoke was still rolling out of the barrel. I looked at Wes and Buck. "What do you think, fellas?"

Wes looked at Buck and then at me. He gave me a thumbs-up, like an old Roman emperor in the Colosseum. I nodded and looked over at Buck, who did likewise.

"Okay, it's unanimous. The Russian lives," I said. "Now, let's get the hell out of here before the cavalry shows up."

"What about Rory?" Wes asked, motioning toward Rory, who'd just come out from behind the sofa.

I took a deep breath and exhaled. "What'll it be, babe. The Russian, or back to the good ol' U.S. of A. with us?"

Rory looked at me. "What about Alexsie?"

I cringed. "*Alexsie*?"

I don't know why I was surprised she knew Yazov's first name. Hell, she'd just had sex with him.

"Well, I don't know," I said, turning and looking at the big Russian. "How about it, *Alexsie*? Want to go back to the States with us and face charges?"

Yazov smiled and raised his eyebrows. "I think not." He paused for a moment and looked over at Rory. "But I'll make you a deal. You take me as far as a neutral port . . . and I'll help you get that sawed-off Nazi bastard."

I looked at Yazov. “Ochoa?”

Yazov nodded. “Yes. He sent those men. And after they’d killed me, they would have raped and killed Rory, and sent the photos to the little pervert.”

While I was thinking about Yazov’s proposal, Wes looked over at me and tapped on his watch. “Time to go, people.”

I looked at Buck, who glanced at his watch and nodded.

I grimaced and shook my head. “Okay, comrade, you’ve got a deal,” I said, knowing I should probably just shoot Yazov and be done with it.

I handed Yazov back his AK. “Here, pal, you may still need this.”

Yazov took the rifle, ejected the magazine and shoved in a fresh one. “Thank you. And your friend is right, we should be going. Someone is bound to have heard the shooting.”

The return trip was downhill and fast, especially since Buck didn’t run into any snakes. When we hit the beach, I waved my arms to get Tommy’s attention. I needn’t have bothered. He was watching the beach with binoculars.

We launched the raft, and we managed to cram five bodies into the four-man inflatable. As we paddled into the bay, Tommy brought the plane’s engines up from idle. In seconds, the Grumman was pushing a bow wave and closing the distance between us.

In five minutes we were all on board the seaplane. The inflated raft was too bulky to get through the hatch, so I used my pocket knife to puncture it in several places. As I secured the hatch, the raft was already sinking low in the water.

Tommy turned from the left cockpit seat and looked aft. "All set?" He paused half a beat. "Who the hell is that?" he asked, gesturing toward Yazov.

I clasped Yazov's shoulder. "I'll take the AK now, comrade."

Yazov nodded and handed me the rifle.

"This is Comrade Alexsie Yazov," I replied stowing my M-16 and Yazov's AK-47. "He'll be coming with us. And I suggest we shake a leg. We had a small firefight at Alexsie's compound, and we could be having company very shortly."

Tommy nodded and reached up for the throttles. "Wes, get in the copilot's seat. Everybody else, find a seat and buckle up."

I got in the seat behind Tommy and motioned for Alexsie to sit behind Wes. "Rory, there's a seat just ahead of the bunks, behind Alexsie. Take that one and buckle up tight."

Tommy checked the flaps and then increased power.

Yazov leaned over toward me. "Grumman Albatross, is it not?"

I nodded.

Yazov smiled. "Very inventive. Short of a submarine, a seaplane is the best way to get close to mainland Cuba."

I looked at Yazov. “Yeah, well, I just hope it gets us far from the mainland of Cuba.”

Yazov chuckled. “I share that sentiment.”

The roar from the engines was impressive. When the plane hit 80 knots, Tommy called out, “Rotate,” and pulled back on the yoke. Wes mimicked Tommy’s motion, keeping his hands lightly on the yoke—just in case.

The buffeting of the hull by the waves ceased and we were airborne.

Tommy leaned toward Wes. “I’m going to keep her right on the deck. I heard a little chatter out of Gitmo. Seems they had us on radar and then we disappeared. When we pop up again, they’re liable to be real curious.”

I leaned forward between Tommy and Wes. “Have we got the range to make Brownsville?”

Tommy looked over at Wes. “Check the charts. They’re in the black case behind your seat.”

Wes retrieved the maps, plotted headings and scaled off distances. When he had a number he leaned toward me and Tommy. “I make it 975 nautical miles from George Town to Brownsville. And add to that the roughly 500 nautical miles to Cuba and back . . . that’s around 1975 nautical miles total. Assuming we go back to Grand Cayman. If we cut the dogleg,” Wes said, using his pencil to mark a direct route from our current position to Brownsville, “it’ll be a hair shorter.”

Wes and I looked at Tommy and waited.

Tommy nodded. “Yeah, we can do it, with about 500 NMs to spare.”

I wrinkled my brow and looked at Tommy. "Jesus, just what *is* the range of this bird?"

Tommy turned his head just enough to see my face. "All out, down to vapors, just over 2400 nautical miles." Tommy laughed. "That's why there's a head in the back. The Albatross can stay in the air a long, long time."

"You have any problems taking us to Brownsville, rather than back to the Caymans?" I asked.

Tommy shook his head. "Not really, but it'll cost you boys a bit more."

I looked at Wes and raised my eyebrows.

"Not a problem, fellas," Wes said, smiling. "We're flying on Ochoa's dime."

Tommy glanced at Wes, but didn't say anything.

I looked at Yazov and grinned.

Yazov snorted. "The missing kilo?"

"You noticed?"

"Of course," Yazov replied. "And I am impressed." Then he laughed. "I think this little band of pirates might just have a chance."

"Of knocking off Ochoa?" I asked.

Yazov looked at me and cocked one bushy eyebrow. "Yes."

Chapter 23

Tommy called Owen Roberts' flight control and filed an amended flight plan. Wes gave him a new heading of 290 degrees, and Tommy brought the Grumman's nose around to the northwest.

Tommy leaned around to his right. "Get comfy folks, it's going to be a long flight."

Nine hours later, I could see the hotel towers on South Padre Island. I tapped Tommy on the shoulder. "Can you drop us off at my bayside house before you land in Brownsville? I need to keep Comrade Yazov under wraps."

Tommy looked at me and then at Yazov. "Okay. If air traffic control asks why I dropped off radar, I'll tell them I made a low-level run up the bay."

I chuckled. "Don't worry. If they get tough with you, I'm the county sheriff. Take a right at the causeway. The channel is the darker band of water near the center of the bay."

Tommy nodded. “I see it. Where do you want me to land?”

“My place is a couple of miles up the bay,” I said, pointing out the cockpit window. “Just west of Port Isabel.”

“Is there any place I can tie up?” Tommy asked.

“Yeah, I have a long, low dock. The water’s four or five feet deep at the far end. Just watch for boats when you set her down.”

“Roger that,” Tommy said, reducing power and lowering the flaps.

“I’ll slip into a uniform at my place and pick you up at the airport,” I said.

Rory, who’d been asleep most of the trip, leaned forward. “Hardin, has anybody notified my father?”

I half-turned and looked at her. “Not yet. I need to get our Russian guest sequestered at my place, and then I’ll call Robert Lee.”

Rory nodded. “Thanks, Hardin.”

The mention of Robert Lee reminded me of the $2 million ransom. I reached over and put my hand on Yazov’s knee. “That reminds me, old stick, there’s a small matter of a $2 million ransom.”

Yazov grimaced. “I wondered when you would get around to the money.”

“Where is it?” I asked.

“First Caribbean National Bank, in the BVI,” Yazov replied.

I let go of Yazov’s knee and glanced at Rory. “When you speak to your father, get an account number. Mr. Yazov here is anxious to return the ransom money to its proper owner.”

Yazov rolled his eyes and shook his big bald head.

"Isn't that right, Alexsie?" I said.

Yazov turned and looked at Rory. "The sheriff is quite correct. However, it is but a small price to pay for getting to know you."

I grunted. "Put a cork in it, Yazov. I'm liable to get sick."

Yazov tilted his head toward me. "Not much of a romantic, is he, Rory?"

For the first time since her rescue, Rory smiled. "He has his moments."

Buck, who'd been asleep in one of the two bunks fixed to the port-side interior of the Grumman, woke up when Tommy set the big Grumman down dead center in the middle of the Intercoastal Waterway.

Wes directed him to my dock where we offloaded passengers and gear, including our weapons. In less than ten minutes, Tommy was roaring up the bay, en route to South Padre International Airport.

"Okay, everybody, let's get this gear and the weapons off the dock and into my house," I said, grabbing my bags. "Alexsie, grab the duffle bag."

Buck and Wes grabbed their gear and we headed, more or less in single file, down the dock to my humble abode.

Yazov looked at my beach shack and chuckled. "You know, Sheriff, I would be willing to split the two million with you."

I smiled and nodded. "Thanks, comrade, but I think I've broken enough laws for one week."

Chapter 24

I changed my mind and sent Buck out to the airport to pick up Tommy. Wes volunteered to take Yazov into town to get him some clothes and shaving gear. When Rory and I were alone, I called her dad.

"Robert Lee, Sheriff Steel. I have someone here who'd like to speak with you." I handed the phone to Rory and went out on the dock to have a cigar.

In about ten minutes, a teary-eyed Rory came out of the house and joined me on the dock.

"Cigar?" I said to break the tension.

Rory smiled. "No, not right now." She paused and watched a stingray glide by just off the sandy bottom. "I just wanted to say thank you, and that I'm sorry. I really don't know what came over me in Cuba."

"Don't worry about it, Rory," I said, putting my left arm around her shoulders. "It's very common for kidnapping victims to bond with their captors."

Rory nodded and chuckled. "I'm afraid I did a bit more than bond."

"Like I said, Rory, it happens. Don't worry about it. I still feel the same way about you I always have. I guess the question is . . . how do you feel about me?"

Rory looked into my eyes, and then kissed me deeply on the mouth. "Like that."

"That'll do," I said. "Come on, I'll run you out to your ranch. I'm sure Robert Lee can't wait to see you."

When I got back from Roughton Ranch, Buck and Tommy were out on the dock with margaritas in hand.

"How'd it go with Immigration and Customs?" I asked.

"Not too bad," Tommy said, chuckling. "But they did give the plane a hell of a going over."

I nodded. "Clean?"

Tommy smiled and started to answer, but I cut him off. "I know. Clean as a nun's you-know-what."

Tommy and Buck both laughed.

"Yep, that clean," Tommy said. "Hell, seaplanes always get a lot of attention from Customs. Something about being able to land in water drives customs guys nuts. A lot of places require I land only at airports."

"How about Mexico?" I asked. "Think you could land in the Gulf of California. Say, just up the coast from Mazatlán?"

Tommy looked at Buck and then back at me. "Probably . . . if I didn't have to sit too long."

*****

An hour later, Wes and Yazov showed up. Each was carrying a good-sized new suitcase.

Wes saw me eyeballing the luggage. “Don’t worry, Stainless, they’re both Yazov’s, and he used his platinum AMEX card. Which is a damned good thing, because he spent a ton of money.”

Yazov shrugged. “Fortunately, my wallet was in my slacks . . . before I was so rudely interrupted.”

I let it slide. “Your AMEX card . . .?” I paused because I knew what was coming.

“Certainly. I never leave home without it,” Yazov said, giving me a wink.

“Uh-huh. So what did you buy?” I asked.

“Just some slacks, shoes, shirts, and a sport coat, or two,” Yazov replied. “Just the basics.”

Wes rolled his eyeballs. “Yeah, all from Nordstrom at the mall.”

I looked at Yazov. “So I guess you have access to funds other than the ransom money?”

Yazov looked at me and snorted. “Of course. Plus I recently completed a small aviation deal, the proceeds of which I deposited in my bank in Cuba.”

I nodded. “I’m glad to hear that, Alexsie, because I just dropped Rory off at her dad’s ranch.” I hesitated a half-second while I pulled a piece of paper out of my shirt pocket. “And here’s the account number he’d like you to transfer the $2 million to.”

Yazov grimaced like he’d bitten into a lemon.

“Uh-huh, and I’d like you to do it now,” I said, pointing to my laptop. “I have a Google window open. Just type in your banking information and make the transfer.”

Yazov looked at me as he walked over to my desk and gave me a wry smile. “No chance of a deal?”

“Nyet, nada, no. Understood?”

“Yes,” Yazov said, looking around the interior of my house, “but I think you’re making a big mistake.”

I nodded. “I’ve made ’em before. Now make the transfer.”

It took Yazov about five minutes. “You want to see the confirmation?”

“Print a copy,” I said, pouring myself a margarita.

Yazov nodded, and I could hear the printer chattering away.

I looked at Yazov. He looked like he could use a drink. “Cocktail, comrade?”

“A big one, I think,” Yazov said, striding over and handing me the printed confirmation.

I handed him a large margarita and looked at the confirmation.

“It’s a lot of zeros, is it not?” Yazov said, taking a long drink.

I folded the confirmation and stuck it in my shirt pocket. “Come out on the dock with the rest of the co-conspirators.”

Yazov smiled. “Indeed.”

I grabbed a handful of cigars and we joined the others.

“Cigar, anyone?” I asked.

They all replied in the affirmative and soon a cloud of smoke wafted landward.

I watched a pelican fold his wings and dive-bomb some hapless fish. “Okay, Alexsie, how do we take down Ochoa?”

Yazov took a deep drag on his cigar and thought about it for a few moments. "Like you were planning to do. We use the cocaine as bait."

"You still have the cocaine?" I asked.

"No, of course not," Yazov replied, smirking like he was talking to an idiot. "But Ochoa doesn't know that. All he knows is I took the cocaine from the DEA evidence lockup in Brownsville."

"What about the men in Cienfuegos?" I asked. "I thought you said they were Ochoa's men?"

Yazov took a drink of his margarita and looked out across Laguna Madre. "Does it matter who sent those men? If you and your friends had not been there, the situation would have ended as I described."

"So you're telling me Ochoa doesn't know you sold his dope to some Cuban drug dealers?"

Yazov blew a perfect smoke ring. "If you bought cocaine stolen from Ochoa, would you announce it?"

I shook my head.

"Exactly," Yazov said. "Evidently the buyers were afraid I might implicate them, which is why they sent the thugs to kill me."

"So you lied to me?" I said, anger starting to flush my cheeks.

"Don't be so naïve," Yazov said, his tone sharp as a stingray's barb. "What would you have done in my position?"

I thought about Rory, took a deep breath and exhaled slowly. "Probably the same thing."

Yazov nodded. "Alright then, can we put this behind us and concentrate on getting Ochoa? Because believe me, gentlemen, it will be no easy task. Many have tried and none have succeeded—or survived. And the unfortunate ones who were taken alive . . . prayed for a quick death."

We worked on our plan the rest of the afternoon.

"Okay, fellows," I said, leaning back in my chair, "we're all agreed?"

I looked at each man in turn. Wes and Buck nodded, Tommy gave me a thumbs-up, and Alexsie mumbled something I assumed to be in the affirmative.

Our plan was fairly straightforward. Alexsie would contact Ochoa and set up a meeting in Mazatlán. But instead of returning the cocaine, we'd grab Ochoa, load him on the Grumman, and fly him to Brownsville where we'd turn him over to the DEA.

Aside from the obvious problems associated with kidnapping the head of the most dangerous cartel in Mexico, there were two wild cards: Lee Fairchild and Alexsie Yazov. If I brought Lee up to speed on our little plan, he'd likely grab Yazov. But if I didn't confide in Lee, and we got in trouble, we'd have no backup.

Turning Yazov over to the feds to face murder charges wasn't going to go down too well with the big Russian. But, all things considered, I decided to bring Fairchild into the loop. If push came to shove, I'd take DEA backup over the commie.

*****

The next morning I climbed into a uniform and went to my office. My first call was to Robert Lee to confirm he'd received the two million. He had.

By eleven, I was pretty well caught up. I closed my office door, fired up a cigar and dialed Lee Fairchild.

"Lee, Hardin. You got a minute?"

"Absolutely, Hardin. How'd it go?"

I knocked the ashes from the end of my cigar into an ashtray. "Rory's back, safe and sound. Robert Lee got the ransom money returned this morning, and I've got a plan to get Ochoa."

There was a brief pause on the line. "So I take it you've got Yazov in custody?"

"I do, Lee. And I'm going to need him in order to get to Ochoa."

"Goddamn it, Hardin, that son of a bitch killed two of my agents."

"Actually, Lee, two Nicaraguan mercenaries killed your agents. And just so you know, Yazov punched both their tickets."

"In the eyes of the law, Hardin . . ."

"Yeah, I know," I interrupted. "But I need Yazov to nail Ochoa."

"You're asking *one* hell of a lot, Hardin."

I decided to take a long shot. "Would you like to go along?"

"When you grab Ochoa?"

"Exactly. You could keep an eye on Yazov and take credit for the takedown of Ochoa."

"Hardin, you must know Yazov is never going to agree to return to the States."

"If the government grants him immunity, he'll agreed to come back and testify against Ochoa," I said, hoping Yazov wouldn't make a liar out of me.

"Hardin, Yazov participated in the murder of two federal officers. And I don't give a shit if he pulled the trigger or not."

I was starting to get frustrated with Lee's reticence. "Goddammit, Lee, we've granted immunity to a hell of a lot worse, and for a hell of a lot less in return."

Lee paused for a long moment. "What if I say no?"

"Then I'll turn Yazov over to you and Ochoa will continue to murder and push dope."

"Where is Yazov now?"

"I have him stashed in Matamoros," I lied.

"I see," Lee said. "You know if Ochoa finds out Yazov is anywhere in Mexico, he'll be dead in 24 hours."

"Ochoa thinks Yazov still has his cocaine. And I imagine Ochoa has other plans for our Russian pal."

"Does Yazov have the cocaine?"

"No. He unloaded the dope in Havana."

"Are you positive?"

"Yeah, pretty positive, Lee. Evidently, there was some post-sale buyer's remorse. The Cubans sent a half dozen of their boys to bag and tag our Russian friend."

"Afraid Ochoa might find Yazov and ask him *hard* where his cocaine was?"

"That's the consensus of opinion."

"I'm dying to ask how you know all this."

"We happened to be rescuing Rory when the boys from Havana showed up."

"I take it since you're here, that the bad guys have gone under?"

"Yep, with help from Yazov."

Lee exhaled. "Jesus, Hardin, that'll make some headline: 'Texas Sheriff Teams Up with Russian Drug Dealer to Murder Cuban Nationals'."

I couldn't help but chuckle. "Yeah, well, it worked out okay."

Lee paused. "Let me get back to you, Hardin."

While Fairchild was making up his mind, we proceeded with our plan. Yazov contacted Ochoa—a phone call I would have loved to have been on—and set up a meeting in Mazatlán.

Tommy got the Grumman prepped and fueled and filed a flight plan from Brownsville to Mazatlán for two days hence.

We'd pull the same stunt we had earlier. Tommy would take off from South Padre International and then drop down and land in the Intercoastal. He'd taxi to my place and pick us up, along with our weapons and supplies.

The next morning Fairchild called me at my office. "Okay, Hardin, the Justice Department will grant Yazov immunity if you bring Ochoa back to the States to stand trial, and if Yazov testifies."

“Thanks, Lee,” I said. “I know it’s a tough pill to swallow.”

“Uh-huh. Two other conditions, Hardin.”

“I’m listening.”

“Once the trial is over, Yazov and his immunity will be deported back to Russia.”

“I doubt he’ll have a problem with that,” I said. “What’s the other condition?”

“I’m going along.”

Chapter 25

The next 24 hours were a blur. I delegated everything I could to my deputies, and postponed everything else. I knew a couple of judges were going to be pissed, but they'd get over it when I delivered Ochoa. And if I didn't, I'd likely be dead. So, what the hell.

At dawn the next morning, Tommy finished his preflight check and climbed into the cockpit of the Grumman. He called the tower and was cleared for takeoff.

I was just finishing breakfast with my three co-conspirators and the communist when I heard the roar of the Grumman's big radial engines. We all walked out on the dock and watched Tommy set the Albatross down in the bay.

"Showtime, fellas," I said, glancing at Lee. "You sure about this, Lee? You don't have to go along. We'll bring Ochoa back, or we'll die trying."

Lee shot a look at Yazov. "No, I'm in. I won't be leaving Mr. Yazov's side until Ochoa is behind bars."

I nodded and tossed the remains of my coffee into the bay. "Uh-huh. Well, this should be interesting. Grab your gear."

Tommy eased the Grumman up against the end of my dock. Thank God it was high tide, because the plane was heavy with fuel and riding deep in the water. I tied off the plane with a single line and popped the hatch. In five minutes, we had all the gear and everybody but me on board.

I took a long look at my humble abode, hoping it wouldn't be the last time I saw it, and let go the line. I managed to get aboard and closed the hatch behind me.

Tommy looked back down the cabin. I nodded and gave him a "wind 'em up" sign.

As we crossed the strandline and headed out into the Gulf, a Coast Guard chopper passed just beneath us. I could see Tommy key his radio and speak into his mike. After a minute or so, he turned and gave me a thumbs-up.

Wes looked over at Tommy from his copilot's seat. "Two-fifty-three degrees. About five hours flying time."

Tommy nodded and brought the plane around to the new heading.

*****

At his compound outside Mazatlán, Frederick Ochoa had assembled ten of his most loyal men. He addressed them in their native Spanish.

"It is imperative that Yazov be taken alive. The pilot and any passengers are of little consequence; use your own discretion. But recover my cocaine. Do these things, and I will pay you all a handsome bonus."

Ochoa looked at each man individually. Though hardened killers, none could hold his gaze for more than a moment. Satisfied, Ochoa dismissed his assassins with a causal wave of his hand.

Yazov had told Ochoa he would be bringing the dope in by private plane. He purposely neglected to mention it was a seaplane.

Based on this information, Ochoa was planning to meet Yazov at General Rafael Buelna International Airport, on the outskirts of Mazatlán. He'd made arrangements with the authorities to look the other way when his men grabbed the Russian, and the cocaine.

About three hours into the flight, Wes spelled Tommy and flew the last leg. When we were about fifteen minutes out, Tommy reached over and tapped Wes on his left shoulder. "I've got it."

Wes nodded. "It's your airplane."

Tommy took the yoke, eased back on the throttles and gently pushed the nose over. He turned and yelled above the noise of the engines. "Ten minutes, boys. Get ready."

As we'd done during our brief invasion of Cuba, we'd brought along two inflatable rafts. Tommy would bring us in close to shore, and we'd deploy in the rafts. Once ashore, Yazov would lead the assault on Ochoa's compound.

Tommy touched down and taxied as close to shore as possible. The beach appeared deserted and the surf was low. So far, so good.

Unbeknownst to us, one of Ochoa's sentries was glassing the beach, idly scanning for topless women. When the Grumman touched down, he hurriedly keyed his radio and notified the compound.

One of the senior security guards knocked on the door to Ochoa's study.

"Yes?" Ochoa said, swinging his feet off the sofa, a bit irritated at the interruption of his siesta. "What is it?"

The security officer opened the study door and stepped inside. "I am sorry to disturb you, Patrón, but a large twin-engine seaplane has just landed near the beach."

Ochoa was immediately alert. "A seaplane?"

"Yes, sir. From the sentry's description it sounds like an old Grumman."

Ochoa nodded and thought for a moment. "Recall the men from the airport. And prepare your men to repel an attack. I think Comrade Yazov has arrived."

We'd managed to get the rafts out the rear hatch, inflate them, and get aboard without anyone taking a swim. Wes and Lee took the lead in the first raft. Yazov, Buck, and I followed, close astern.

We were all armed with M-16s, including Yazov. Even though Lee had strongly objected to giving the Russian a weapon.

Ochoa had read and re-read *Infanterie Greift An*, written by his hero, Field Marshal Erwin Rommel. Like Rommel, Ochoa knew the best way to stop a seaborne invasion was while the troops were floundering in the water, trying not to drown.

He ordered his men to open fire while we were busy trying not to capsize in the surf. The first rounds came out of the heavy foliage at the far side of the beach and tore into the rubber rafts. The Field Marshal would have been proud.

A round hit Lee Fairchild in the mouth, blowing off the back of his head. Wes was nicked in the shoulder and was bleeding through his shirt.

Yazov and I returned fire while Buck wrestled with the oars. Our raft was deflating and taking on water as rounds flew by us like a stream of angry hornets.

I heard the Grumman's engines winding up and turned to see Tommy moving the Grumman out of rifle range.

Suddenly, the firing from the shore ceased and we heard a rather high-pitched man's voice yell for us to surrender, and throw our weapons into the sea.

I glanced at Yazov.

He looked at me and grimaced. "Ochoa."

I turned to Buck.

"We're sitting ducks, Hardin."

I nodded and looked at the other raft. Lee, or what was left of him, was draped over the stern of their sinking raft. The water washing over him turning crimson. Wes was holding a bloody bandana against his shoulder wound. He looked at me and shrugged.

I lifted my M-16 over my head and then tossed it into the saltwater. Buck and Wes followed suit.

Yazov was hunkered down in the front of our raft, still clutching his M-16.

"Yazov! Throw the damn rifle overboard," I yelled. "We haven't got a chance."

He looked at me, shook his head and yelled, "Fuck!" And tossed his weapon into the drink.

Ochoa's men advanced from the thick foliage and waded into the surf to take us prisoner. All except for Lee, whom they unceremoniously rolled into the surf.

One of Ochoa's men saw me watching Lee's body being pulled out to deeper water by the undertow. He nodded and spoke to me in broken English. "Do not worry, my friend, the sharks are used to feeding here."

Safely out of range, Tommy brought the nose of the Grumman around and watched the ambush play out through his binoculars. He knew we had only one chance, and a slim one at that. He brought the Grumman into the wind and powered up.

Even over the surf we could hear the Grumman's radial engines as Tommy took off.

The man in charge of feeding the sharks poked me in the kidneys with the muzzle of his AK-47 and sneered. "Seems your pilot is abandoning you."

I shook my head. "I doubt it, fuck-wit," I replied, watching the Grumman climb out and make a turn to the northeast.

The man jammed the muzzle of his rifle hard into my back. "What did you say, gringo?"

I didn't reply and instead looked over at Wes, tilting my head toward the departing Grumman.

Wes nodded. "He'll be back."

Another of Ochoa's men hit Wes in the back with the butt of his rifle. "*Silencio*, gringo!"

As we neared the base of the heavily vegetated hillside, the leader of our captors yelled, "*Alto*."

We stopped and watched as a short, slender, well-dressed man wearing driving gloves stepped out of the jungle. I risked a glance at Yazov, who nodded imperceptibly.

Ochoa eyed us like he was picking out a piece of meat for supper. "Well, Alexsie, I see you've returned, and I believe I recognize one of your compatriots."

Ochoa looked at me. "Sheriff Hardin Steel, is it not?"

I nodded. "In the flesh."

Ochoa almost grinned—almost. "Bring them up to the compound, and be very careful with my Russian friend. I wouldn't want anything to happen to him until he and I have a chance to have a *serious* conversation."

I glanced at Yazov. He blanched at Ochoa's comment. I figured he knew what a *serious* conversation with Ochoa would entail.

Ochoa's compound was more fortress than villa. The stone walls surrounding the compound were ten feet high, with guard towers at each corner. Without an invitation, it would be a very tough party to crash.

Our wrists had been bound behind us with plastic ties and we were led into Ochoa's study. Three of Ochoa's men stood guard. They didn't appear to be from the beach crew. I assumed they were a bit higher up the food chain.

"Gentlemen," Ochoa said, gesturing to several chairs and a sofa, "please have a seat."

We were all still a bit wet and sandy from our little romp in the surf, but if Ochoa minded, or noticed, he didn't mention it.

"Sheriff, my compliments," Ochoa said, pouring himself a brandy and taking a seat in a leather chair that seemed, somehow, a bit out of proportion.

"So, gentlemen, are you here to assassinate me, or take me back to stand trial?"

He was looking at me so I jumped in. "Our plan was to take you back to Brownsville and turn you over to the DEA."

Ochoa nodded and gestured toward Alexsie with his glass. "I see. And I suppose my dear friend Alexsie has agreed to testify against me in return for certain considerations?"

I shrugged.

Ochoa took a sip of his brandy. "Well, perhaps I can save your government the cost of a trial." Ochoa tilted his head toward the guards. "Please take Mr. Yazov to more *suitable* quarters."

The biggest of the three men guarding us grabbed Yazov by his bound wrists and jerked him roughly to his feet. I figured it was probably the last time any of us would see the Russian.

Ochoa turned to Wes. "Ah, the pilot who refuses to fly for me and who managed to evade a Strela surface-to-air missile. Are you wounded?"

"It was two Strelas," Wes said, looking at Ochoa. "And it's just a scratch. I'll be okay."

Ochoa snorted. "Time will tell, Mr. Stoddard. And who is the other, rather large gentlemen?" Ochoa asked, gesturing at Buck.

"Buck Bateman is my name, Mr. Ochoa. I'm a private detective from Brownsville."

Ochoa took another sip of his brandy and looked at the three of us for a long moment. "I see. A very interesting group of provocateurs, I must say."

Ochoa swirled his brandy around in the heavy crystal glass. "Gentlemen, I am not the monster you assume I am. And to prove it, I will give you all a chance to live."

I looked at Ochoa. "Does that include Yazov?"

Ochoa shook his head. "Do not concern yourselves with Mr. Yazov."

I looked at my two friends and grimaced.

Ochoa continued. "As I was saying, you three have one chance to live."

"What chance?" I asked.

"An exchange," Ochoa said, now looking directly at me. "Your lives in exchange for two others."

"I'm listening," I said.

Ochoa nodded. "I want the two men in Havana who bought my cocaine from Yazov."

Ochoa took two photos from a manila envelope and nodded to one of his men. The guard stepped forward, retrieved the photos and placed them on a table in front of me. The men's names and other information were at the bottom of each photo.

"You deliver those two men to me, alive, and your two friends are free to leave."

I coughed and cleared my throat. "Sir, we were lucky to get into Cuba and grab Yazov. We'll never pull it off a second time."

"Agreed, Sheriff," Ochoa said. "But I happen to know the two gentlemen in question are planning a trip to the Caymans. Seems they're not too keen on Fidel's banking system. You will grab them on Grand Cayman and fly them here. Is that understood?"

I looked at Buck and Wes. "The three of us?"

For the first time the hint of a grin appeared on Ochoa's face. "No. Mr. Bateman and Mr. Stoddard will remain here as my guests until you return. Any help you require you must secure on you own."

"I see," I said, taking a deep breath and looking at my two friends. "Will you see to Wes's wound?"

"But of course," Ochoa said, frowning at me. "We are not barbarians."

I suspected Yazov would shortly disagree.

"Can you contact the Grumman?" I asked.

Ochoa nodded. “Yes. We have your pilot on the radio, standing by for your instructions.”

Chapter 26

I waited in a small wooden rowboat with one of Ochoa's men. I manned the oars, keeping the boat just beyond the surf. Ochoa's man sat in the stern and covered me with his AK-47.

I heard the roar of the Grumman's engines as Tommy broke out of the overcast. He spotted us and did a flyover, waggling his wings, before turning into the wind for a landing.

I looked at Ochoa's man. He nodded and motioned with his rifle for me to start rowing. He didn't have to motion twice. I leaned into the oars and moved away from the beach.

Tommy was a long way offshore, so I stood and waved for him to bring the plane closer. A few minutes later, he pulled the Grumman alongside the rowboat.

Tommy idled the engines and came aft to open the hatch. "Are you okay, Hardin? Can you get in okay?"

I nodded and climbed through the hatch. Ochoa's man used one of the oars to push the rowboat clear of the plane. "Yeah, I'm fine, but Ochoa's holding Buck and Wes."

"What about our Ruskie buddy?"

"He's not part of the deal," I replied.

"What deal?"

"Fire this bird up and I'll explain everything on the way."

"Brownsville?" Tommy asked as we worked our way forward to the cockpit.

"For starters," I said, climbing into the copilot's seat.

Tommy slid into the left seat and buckled his seatbelt. "Are Buck and Wes okay?"

I looked over at Tommy, watching him run through his takeoff checklist. "Wes got winged in the shoulder. A flesh wound. Ochoa's promised to get him medical attention. Buck's fine. Fairchild took a round in the face. He's gone."

Tommy nodded as he brought the Grumman into the wind. "How do we get Wes and Buck back?"

I spent the next thirty minutes briefing Tommy. Then I leaned back in the copilot's seat and dozed off. I awoke with a start when Tommy dropped the landing gear.

"Sorry, Hardin," Tommy said when he saw me jump. "I can't risk another water touch-and-go. ATC in Brownsville will start asking some tough questions if we drop off radar . . . again."

I nodded and looked out the cockpit at the approaching airstrip.

"I'll file a flight plan for day after tomorrow," Tommy said, lowering the flaps and reducing power. "Brownsville to Grand Cayman."

I thought about Wes and Buck and wished we could go today, but the Cubans were still in Cuba. I tried not to think about Yazov.

Yazov was naked and manacled to a steel chair in a soundproof subterranean room beneath Ochoa's compound.

Ochoa had let one of his more sadistic psychopaths *soften up* the big Russian. Now it was time to get serious.

Ochoa motioned for the tall, broad-shouldered, Amazonesque dominatrix to throw a pail of water on Yazov. "Wake him up, Ursula."

The cold water hit Yazov in his cut and bruised face. He blinked several times to clear his vision. When he was able to focus, he wished he hadn't.

"Ah, good, you're back with us, Alexsie," Ochoa said and actually smiled. "You know my associate, Ursula?"

Yazov nodded.

"Good, good," Ochoa said. "I'm going to ask you a question and your answer will determine what I let Ursula do to you. Do you understand?"

Yazov nodded again.

"What? I can't hear you, Alexsie," Ochoa said, cutting his eyes to the Amazon.

Ursula reached down and squeezed Yazov's testicles until tears ran down his cheeks.

"Yes! I understand," Yazov replied, gasping as Ursula released pressure.

Ochoa nodded. "Very good, Alexsie. Now, I have only one question." Ochoa paused and looked at Alexsie. "Why?"

Yazov looked up through his bloodshot eyes. "*Why*?"

"Yes, Alexsie. Why would you steal from me?"

Yazov smiled and spit out a piece of broken tooth. "It seemed like a good idea at the time."

Ochoa nodded. "And how does it seem now?"

Yazov whispered something in Russian.

"What was that, Alexsie?" Ochoa asked. "I didn't quite get it."

Yazov grunted and shook his bald and now-bloodied head. "I underestimated our friend the Sheriff," Yazov replied, and then managed a smile. "But he did save my life in Cuba."

Ochoa pursed his lips. "I see. And he in turn has underestimated me. Well, my friend, unfortunately I can't have people thinking they can steal from me and get away with it." Ochoa glanced at the tall blonde. "I'm afraid Ursula is going to have to hurt you quite badly."

Ochoa moved off to the side and sat in a chair. He was going to enjoy watching Ursula work on the Russian.

Tommy and I landed in Brownsville and cleared Immigration without much of a problem. As I said before, being the county sheriff did have a few perks.

I left Tommy at the airport to take care of pilot stuff, and I took a cab to my place. I needed to clean up, get into a uniform, and check in with my office.

Betty Filmore, my dispatcher, looked up as I walked in. "Welcome back, Sheriff. And good job on getting Rory back. She's called for you a number of times . . . as have a few judges."

I rolled my eyes and held out my hand for my messages.

"They're on your desk," Betty said, arching her brow. "I'd start with Judge Wentworth."

It took me about an hour to work through my calls and get everybody placated. I left the hardest call till last.

"Rory, it's Hardin. I'm back in my office."

"Hardin! Damn, I'm glad you're back. Is everybody okay?"

I got up and walked over to my office door and closed it. "Ochoa has Wes and Buck . . . and Yazov."

"Oh, my God," Rory said, almost in a whisper.

"There's a good chance I can save Wes and Buck. But I'm afraid Ochoa won't deal when it comes to the Russian."

"I see," Rory said, her voice thick with emotion. "I know I shouldn't feel bad for Alexsie, but I do. He treated me well." She paused for a moment. "And I don't mean just at the end. He could have made my life hell, but he chose not to. And for that I'll always be grateful. But that's all, Hardin. That's as far as it goes. Do you understand?"

I lit a strike-anywhere kitchen match against the sole of my cowboy boot and fired up a cigar.

"Hardin. Are you listening?"

I took deep pull on the cigar and blew a perfect smoke ring, which I cut in half with the index finger of my left hand. "Yeah, I'm still here, Rory. And I'd like to see you . . . tonight."

"My place at seven," Rory said. "And Hardin . . ."

"Yes?"

"Thanks for understanding."

I'd no more than hung up when Betty knocked on my door and stuck her head in.

"Sheriff, there's a Mr. Jack Thompson waiting to see you."

I nodded. "Send him in, Betty."

A moment later, Tommy stepped into my office.

I motioned to one of my side chairs. "Take a load off. Cigar?"

"Yeah, thanks, Hardin."

I handed Tommy a cigar, match and cutter. He prepped the cigar and fired it up.

"Are we good to go?" I asked.

Tommy took a couple of quick puffs to be sure he had ignition. "Yeah, plane's fueled and flight plan's filed." He took a longer drag and exhaled. "Funny, ATC seemed eager for me to be departing their airspace."

I chuckled. "Yeah, I'll bet."

"So, Hardin, how the hell are you and I going to pull this off?"

I exhaled a lungful of white cigar smoke and watched the downdraft from the ceiling fan disperse it. "With help from Deputy Chief Inspector Amos Kincaid. Grand Cayman's finest."

"Have you talked with him?"

"I called him and gave him a general overview of our little operation."

"And?"

"And he asked if the DEA was involved."

"Are they?"

"Not yet. But I have a plan."

Tommy smiled and rubbed what was left of his right ear. "Oh, good. I feel a hell of a lot better now."

At seven sharp, I pulled into Rory's condo on South Padre Island. And yes, I'd had a couple of pre-function shots of Jose Cuervo, who, as the song says, "is a friend of mine." I figured this "post-commie coitus" reunion might be a little uncomfortable . . . for both of us.

Rory opened the door and I took one look at her and it was as if none of the bad stuff had happened. She looked great. We managed to get through an awkward hug and kiss.

"Hungry?" I asked, taking a half step back.

Rory looked up at me and smiled. "Famished. But let's not go out. I've got steaks and salad. If it's okay with you, I'd like to eat here. I want to hear how we're going to get Wes and Buck back."

"*We*?" I said.

"You heard me, Hardin," Rory replied, taking me by the hand and leading me toward the kitchen. "You may need a woman's help, if you're going to do what I think you're going to do."

"And just what do you think I'm going to do?"

Rory bent down and pulled a bottle of Marlborough Bay Sauvignon Blanc from her built-in wine cooler. "Pour us each a glass, will you, Hardin?"

I nodded and raised my eyebrows. "Well?"

"I think you're going after the men in Cuba who bought Ochoa's cocaine."

I poured the sauvignon blanc into two wine glasses and handed one to Rory. "And if I am, how could you be of help?"

Rory took a sip of her wine, stepped back and motioned with the open palm of her left hand at her body. "They're men, are they not?"

She had a point.

Over a supper of ribeyes and tossed green salad I told Rory everything that had happened in Mexico, including Ochoa's demands for the release of Buck and Wes. And then I explained my plan.

She pushed her empty wine glass in my direction and tilted her head toward the wine bottle. "Well, we actually have several things working in our favor."

I filled her glass about half full and handed it to her. "Really?"

Rory took the glass and nodded. "Yes. You don't have to grab the two men in Cuba, which, by the way, would be next to impossible. You have your connection in the Caymans, you have Tommy's seaplane, and you have me."

I laughed. "And here I thought this might be tough."

Rory looked over at me and wrinkled her brow. "Oh, I never said it would be easy, Hardin. I just said you had a number of items in your favor."

At that moment, two things became very clear to me: Rory was going with Tommy and me to the Caymans, and, secondly, I was in love with her. Even if her name wasn't June or Margaret.

Chapter 27

The bad thing about flying east at sunup . . . is the damn sun in your eyes. But as soon as we'd cleared the Texas coast, Tommy brought the Grumman to a heading of 110 degrees and we put the giant yellow orb to our port side.

In about eight hours—the Grumman was everything but fast—we'd land back at the Barcadere, where the whole Yazov ordeal had started.

I'd called Deputy Chief Kincaid and confirmed our arrival and asked if he'd meet us at the old Hyatt Hotel. I could tell from his tone he wasn't a hundred percent on board. And I really couldn't blame him. Kidnapping two Cuban nationals, when your closest neighbor is Cuba, probably wasn't on the top of his to-do list.

Tommy set us down just past two in the afternoon. We tied up to the same buoy as before, and as before Oscar was waiting in his Zodiac.

In ten minutes we were at a taxi stand hailing a cab.

"Grand Cayman Beach Suites," I said to the cabbie as the three of us piled into the cab.

The cab driver, an older, white-haired, very dark-skinned gentleman nodded. "Yes, sir. Used to be the Hyatt. You know they made a movie there?" The cabbie looked into the rearview mirror and smiled. "Tom Cruise sat right where you're sitting."

"When they were filming *The Firm*?" I asked.

"Yes, sir. Mr. Hackman, too. Real nice fellows. And big tippers," the cabbie replied with a chuckle.

I laughed. "Well, I'm afraid we're not in their league, but we'll do the best we can."

"Yes, sir. Thank you, sir."

Deputy Chief Amos Kincaid was waiting in the hotel lobby.

"Hardin, glad to see you made it okay," Kincaid said, glancing at Tommy and Rory. "This is it? This is your crew?"

I looked at Kincaid. "Yes. And don't worry, they're more than up to the task."

"Uh-huh. Well, no offense, Hardin, but several of my best and most trusted men will be participating in this *little* operation." Kincaid said, shaking his head. "You know, Hardin, this is a fairly dicey situation—abducting two Cuban nationals. I don't suppose you have any kind of warrants?"

I shook my head and dug copies of the photos Ochoa had given me out of my backpack. "These are my warrants, Amos," I said, handing the photos to Kincaid. "Look, Amos, these fellows are two of the worst drug dealers in the Caribbean. And if we don't deliver them to Ochoa, two Americans are going to be murdered."

Kincaid studied the photos for a moment. "Johny Mosqueda and Javier Estrada. Yes, you're right of course, they're a bad lot, indeed. Especially Mosqueda. But bloody hell, Hardin, this kind of operation is totally off the books. Do I make myself clear?"

"Crystal. Are they on-island yet?" I asked.

"Yes, they arrived via private jet this morning. They're staying at a rented villa on Seven Mile Beach. My men have them under surveillance."

I nodded. "Good. I want to grab them tonight and be well out of your jurisdiction by daylight."

Kincaid chewed on his lower lip for a moment. "I assume you have some sort of plan?"

"I do," I said, taking the photo of Mosqueda from Amos and turning it over. "Evidently, Ochoa has had his eye on these two for some time. He's noted the names of their bank, their favorite restaurants, bars, etcetera."

Kincaid took the photo from me and read over Ochoa's notes on the back. He tapped his finger on one of the items. "Hemingways. It's a restaurant and bar, and it's right next door," Kincaid said, gesturing in the direction of the restaurant.

I nodded. "That'll work."

Kincaid looked at me and lowered his voice. "Are you armed?"

I shook my head. "No. I was sort of hoping you could help us in that regard."

Kincaid rolled his eyes. "There is no *us*, Hardin. Only you may have a weapon."

Kincaid waited in the bar while the three of us got checked in and cleaned up. Tommy had reserved a two-bedroom suite. He took one of the bedrooms and Rory and I took the other.

I put our bags on the king-sized bed, opened my suitcase and started to lay out some fresh clothes.

"You want to shower first?" I asked.

Rory came up behind me and put her arms around my waist. "How about we share a shower?"

I turned and put my arms around her. "How about that?" I said, kissing her deeply.

Thirty minutes later, we made it to the shower.

"Hey, shake a leg, you guys," Tommy said, pounding on our bedroom door. "The deputy chief inspector awaits."

"Okay, Tommy, we'll be there in a minute," I said, smiling and winking at Rory.

Rory smiled back but I could see a look of concern in her eye.

"What is it, babe?"

She hesitated a moment. "Don't take this wrong, Hardin, but I can't help thinking about Yazov. Isn't there something we can do to get him out of Ochoa's hands?"

"Funny you should mention him. I was more or less thinking the same thing. And not because you and he had a brief tête-à-tête. The big lug does kind of grow on you. Course, Wes might disagree since Alexsie tried to shoot him down—twice."

Rory laughed. "Yeah, he is a piece of work—Alexsie, I mean."

I smirked. "He's all of that. Kinda fits right in with our little group."

Rory smiled. "Isn't there something we can do?"

I thought about it while I finished getting dressed. "Didn't you say Alexsie met with a Russian in Tampico?"

"Yes," Rory said and chuckled. "He sold Ochoa's Huey to a Russian he called Vasily."

I nodded. "Look, Rory, we've got our hands full right now kidnapping the two Cubans." I paused and rolled my eyes. *Jesus. Farther down the rabbit hole, and no end in sight.*

Rory read my mind. "It is getting a bit out of control, isn't it?"

I laughed. "Oh, I don't know. A Texas county sheriff selling drugs to pay for a trip to Cuba to rescue his girlfriend. During the course of said rescue he kills several Cuban nationals. And then later flies to the Caymans to abduct two Cuban drug dealers whom he intends to hand over to the leader of the worst cartel in Mexico. You see any problems with any of that?"

Rory smiled. "Off the top of my head, maybe just one or two small ones."

I smiled and nodded. "Okay, then. Let's grab the Cubans and get Wes and Buck out of purgatory." I paused for a half-second, "And I'll think about Vasily and his brand-new, second-hand Huey."

We grabbed Tommy and went down to the bar to meet Deputy Chief Kincaid and finalize our plans.

"Amos . . . any news?" I asked as we joined Kincaid at his table.

Amos stood until Rory was seated and then sat back down in his chair.

"Yes. My men have had eyes on the Cubans since they deplaned. So far the Cubans have not left their beachside villa. But they've run through a herd of hookers." Amos looked at Rory. "Pardon me, Rory."

Rory smiled and nodded.

"They haven't been to a bank?" I asked.

Amos shook his head. "No. Not yet."

I looked at Tommy. "That means, if Ochoa's intel is any good, which I suspect it is, they haven't deposited their cash."

Tommy raised his eyebrows. "Interesting."

Amos looked at Tommy and me. "Now wait just a minute, gentlemen. It's bad enough doing what we're proposing to do; don't add robbery to the list."

I leaned in toward Kincaid. "Amos, we're talking about drug money. I say we grab it if we can. You can give it to local charities. I don't care. No offense, Amos, but if it gets into the local banking system . . . it's gone."

Amos rubbed his chin and thought about it for a moment. "Possibly. If the opportunity presents itself . . ."

Before Amos could finish, his cell phone rang. He listened for a few moments and hung up.

"My men grabbed one of the hookers," Amos grimaced and cut a quick glance at Rory. "She said the Cubans are going to Hemingways at seven."

I looked at my watch. It was nearly six. "Okay, we'll let them eat and get good and liquored up." I paused and looked at Rory. "And then Rory will make a move on Mosqueda. Once she gets him outside, we'll grab him."

"What about Estrada?" Amos asked. "How do we take him down?"

"After we have Johny-boy secured, you approach Estrada and tell him you're with the police and that Mosqueda has been in an accident. When you get him outside, we'll nab him."

"And what about my men?" Amos asked.

"Strictly backup," I replied. "Your people need to keep as low a profile as possible."

Amos rolled his eyes. "Bloody right."

I paused and looked at Rory. "You good to go with this?"

Rory nodded and winked at Amos. "Bloody right."

Kincaid chuckled at Rory's comment, then leaned forward and tapped me on the side of my right leg.

I looked at Amos and he cut his eyes downward. I reached under the table and took a small automatic from his left hand.

"Beretta .380," Amos whispered. "Don't use it unless it's absolutely necessary."

I pocketed the Beretta and glanced over at Tommy. He looked uncomfortable. "Everything copacetic, Tommy?"

Tommy glanced around the crowded bar. "Wouldn't it be better to grab them at their villa?"

I started to say something but Amos cut me off. "The villa they've rented is a damned fortress," Amos replied. "Eight-foot wrought-iron fencing and gates it would take a big truck to knock open. It could turn into a protracted firefight."

Tommy nodded. "I see. Okay, we grab them here. Hell, they may not even be armed."

"Possibly," Amos said. "But don't count on it. Especially with Mosqueda. He didn't get this far being careless."

We spent the next hour nursing club sodas and waiting for Amos's men to call. At ten after seven, Amos's cell phone rang. He answered, listened for a moment and hung up.

"They're at Hemingways," Amos said looking around the table at each of us. "And they're drinking Cuba Libres like there's no tomorrow."

I smiled. "Apropos."

"Uh-huh," Amos said. "And just to double up, one of my men slipped the bartenders $20 each to be sure their drinks are strong."

*****

At eight o'clock, we deployed. Rory went into the bar at Hemingways and took a seat as near as she could get to the Cubans' table.

Tommy and I waited in an unmarked police car near the entrance to the restaurant. Amos positioned himself in the foyer of the restaurant, which was packed with diners waiting for their tables.

By 8:30, Rory's frequent admiring glances had caught Johny Mosqueda's eye. He leaned forward and whispered in Spanish. "Excuse me, Javier. I believe a young lady at the bar would like to meet me."

Javier half-turned and looked in Rory's direction. "The dark-haired beauty?"

Mosqueda patted Javier on the shoulder as he stood up. "Yes. And don't wait up."

Mosqueda walked over to Rory. "*Buenas tardes, senorita.*"

"Good evening," Rory replied, flashing a killer smile.

"Oh, you are an American," Mosqueda said, switching to English and sliding on to a barstool next to Rory.

"Texan, actually," Rory replied.

Mosqueda laughed. "Is it not the same thing?"

Rory chuckled seductively. "No, sir, it is not."

"I see," Mosqueda said, extending his hand. "I am Johny Mosqueda, from Havana. Is it permissible for a Texan to have a drink with a Cuban?"

Rory shook his hand. "Rory Roughton. And yes, I believe it is. Crown Royal, on the rocks, please."

Mosqueda motioned to the nearest bartender. "Two Crowns, on the rocks."

Rory looked at the dark-haired, very tan Cuban. He was quite good-looking and tall for a Latin. "So what brings you to the Cayman Islands, Mr. Mosqueda?"

"Please, call me Johny. May I call you Rory?"

"Of course," Rory replied.

"Excellent. Well, Rory, I have banking business on the island, but not until tomorrow."

"I see," Rory said, smiling at Mosqueda. "Sounds terribly intriguing."

Mosqueda laughed. "Hardly intriguing, more like mundane."

Rory nodded and watched the bartender deliver their drinks. "So, *Johny*, are you staying at the Cayman Beach Suites?" she asked, gesturing with her drink in the direction of the hotel.

"No. My associate and I," Mosqueda tilted his head toward Estrada, "have rented a villa a bit further up the beach. Would you care to see it?"

Rory took a sip of her drink and paused for a moment. "Yes, I believe I would."

Amos Kincaid had a clear view of the bar and watched as Mosqueda and Rory moved toward the exit. He quickly stepped outside and flashed a small penlight three times.

I elbowed Tommy. "There's the signal. Let's move."

As Rory and Mosqueda exited Hemingways, Deputy Chief Kincaid sidestepped slightly into their path, just enough to bump into Mosqueda.

"Excuse me, sir," Amos said, catching Rory's eye. "Entirely my fault, sir."

Mosqueda snorted and looked at Amos. He looked like a local civil servant of some kind. Probably a banker. Mosqueda nodded. "No harm done, señor, but you should be more careful in the future."

Amos nodded and bowed slightly. "That I shall, sir." *And so should you, my friend.*

Mosqueda continued walking with Rory toward the street and waiting taxis, but something made him turn and look back. Something didn't quite feel right. And Johny Mosqueda always trusted his instincts.

While he was looking in Amos's direction, I thrust the barrel of the Beretta into his lower back. "Just keep walking, Johny, and nobody gets hurt."

Mosqueda glanced at Rory, who had stepped away and toward me. "My compliments, señorita. Very well done, indeed."

Tommy joined me and we escorted Mosqueda to our waiting car. To a casual observer, it looked as if we were helping a friend who'd had too much to drink.

At the car, Tommy looped a plastic tie around Mosqueda's wrists and helped him into the back seat. I turned to go back to the bar and saw Amos walking Estrada toward the car. Amos was slightly behind and off to Estrada's left, which told me Amos had him covered with a handgun.

"Nice work, Amos," I said, sidling up to Estrada's right side.

Amos glanced around and nodded. “Yeah, so far so good. But I’ll feel better when you and the Cubans are airborne . . . and out of my jurisdiction.”

“Ditto, pardner,” I said, taking a firm hold of Estrada’s right arm. “And one more thing, Inspector,” I said. “Be sure to search their villa. I think these two upstanding Cuban gentlemen would like to make a rather large cash donation to local island charities.”

Estrada turned and glared at me. “You should be careful who you steal from, Yankee.”

I smiled and winked at Estrada. “As should you, *mi amigo*.”

Tommy had arranged for Oscar to have the Zodiac standing by. Amos rode with us out to the tethered Grumman and kept the two drug dealers covered.

Tommy popped the hatch and I climbed in ahead of our two guests. I pulled out the .380 Amos had given me and motioned for Mosqueda and Estrada to climb aboard. With their hands bound behind them, it took a bit of help from Amos and Tommy to push them through the hatch. They both landed rather unceremoniously on the floor of the Albatross.

“Welcome aboard, fellas,” I said, gesturing down the cabin. “By the way, this is a U.S. registry aircraft, so consider yourselves on U.S. soil . . . and under arrest.”

Tommy helped Rory get aboard and then pulled himself through the hatch. Once Tommy was clear, Amos pushed the Zodiac away from the Grumman.

I leaned out to close the hatch and threw a salute to the Deputy Chief Inspector. “Thanks, Amos. I owe you one . . . a big one.”

Amos smiled and nodded. “Aye, Hardin, that you do. Keep me posted on how this all . . .” Amos paused. “On second thought, I never want to hear another word about this little operation.”

Chapter 28

I was riding shotgun in the copilot's seat and I should have been happy, but I wasn't. Two hours into the flight, I turned and looked at Tommy and back at Rory. "I can't do it," I said. "Change course, Tommy, and head for Brownsville."

Tommy looked at me. "Are you sure, Hardin? What about Buck and Wes?"

I grimaced and looked back at our prisoners. "If I deliver these two scumbags to Ochoa, I'm no better than he is. There's got to be another way. Bring her around, Tommy."

Rory leaned forward and nodded. "It's the right thing to do, Hardin. You'll figure something out." Then she winked at me and mouthed, "I love you."

It didn't solve my immediate predicament, but it did make me feel better.

One hour out of Brownsville, I had Tommy contact ATC and request that DEA agents meet the plane. I had yet to tell the local DEA office about Lee Fairchild's death in our failed attempt to grab Ochoa. I'd have a bit of explaining to do, but I figured when I was done, there'd be plenty of volunteers for what I had in mind.

Tommy landed and taxied up to the private aircraft terminal and shut the Grumman's engines down. Two rather large men in suits were waiting along with the usual cadre of local immigration and customs officers.

I looked out Tommy's side window. "The two big fellows in suits . . . got to be DEA."

Tommy nodded. "I'll let you deal with them." He looked again at the two men. "I think I've had some *dealings* with the one on the left."

"Great," I said, shaking my head.

I walked aft and popped the hatch. One of the airport workers rolled a stairway up against the side of the Grumman.

I stuck my head out of the open hatch and held out my badge. "I'm Sheriff Hardin Steel. I have a couple of drug dealers you may be interested in talking to."

I neglected to mention they were Cuban nationals, and that we'd kidnapped them. What the hell. These guys were Feds; they could figure it out.

The two DEA agents took us back to the Brownsville field office. They put Mosqueda and Estrada in a holding cell and herded Tommy, Rory, and me into a conference room. One of the agents stayed in the room with us.

A few minutes later, a tall, well-groomed man wearing a dark-gray Brooks Brothers suit walked into the conference room and took a seat at the head of the table. He had the demeanor of one in charge.

"I'm Special Agent Bill Rand, from the agency's Houston office. I'm acting agent-in-charge until Agent Fairchild gets back from special assignment."

I took out my badge and ID and handed them to Agent Rand. "The special assignment Agent Fairchild was on was my operation. We tried to grab Frederick Ochoa, and Lee was killed in the attempt."

I didn't sugarcoat it. I wanted it to hit him hard, because I wanted him mad. Mad enough to do something about it.

It took an hour of explaining, but Special Agent Rand finally got his arms around what had gone down.

"Ms. Roughton, you're free to go," Rand said, gesturing to the other agent in the room. "Agent Garcia will give you a ride home. Sheriff, I'd like a few minutes with you and Mr. Thompson."

I looked over at Rory. "I'll call you later."

Rory nodded and walked out of the conference room with Agent Garcia. Once the door closed behind her, Special Agent Rand got up and walked around the conference table. He sat on a corner of the table nearest me.

"So, Sheriff, I'm listening."

I rubbed my hands together and nodded. "Okay, since I don't have Mosqueda and Estrada to trade for

Wes and Buck, I'm going to need two of your agents, preferably Hispanic, to stand in."

Agent Rand crossed his arms and looked at me like I was nuts. "You want two of my agents to pose as Mosqueda and Estrada?"

"Only long enough for us to grab Ochoa . . . and rescue Bateman and Stoddard."

Agent Rand snorted softly and shook his head. "You ever see the movie *Charlie Wilson's War*?"

I had—about ten times. "Yes, and I know what you going to say."

Agent Rand nodded. "Uh-huh. The same thing the Jewish guy said when Wilson asked him to provide arms to the Pakistanis—'I only see one or two small problems.'"

It was past 6:00 when Agent Rand finally saw the light. He drummed his fingers on the conference table and nodded. "The two agents who met you at the plane, Garcia and Rodriquez, were brought into the agency and mentored by Fairchild. And they were friends with the two agents killed by Ochoa's people. I'll run it by them. If they agree, and by *agree*, I mean volunteer, I'm on board."

By 6:45, we had our stand-ins. Now I just needed to address the one or two small problems.

Agent Rodriquez dropped Tommy and me at the Sheriff's Department. I checked in with the night shift and looked at my messages. There were quite a few. I grabbed the most pressing ones and got a deputy to run me and Tommy to my place.

"Fire up the blender, Tommy," I said, pointing to the bar. "I've got to return a few of these calls, and then call Rory."

I hated to call judges after hours, but I didn't have a hell of a lot of choice. Especially if I was planning to leave again, which I was.

Once I explained to the judges that I was working a kidnapping case—Ochoa kidnapping Buck and Wes, not me kidnapping the Cubans—and that drugs were involved, they all cut me some slack.

All that remained was for Tommy and me to contact Ochoa and set up a prisoner swap. It didn't sound like a big deal . . . if you said it real fast.

When I finally hung up the phone, Tommy came over and handed me a margarita. "Everything copacetic?"

I nodded. "Yeah, more or less. But I still have to call Rory. And we need to contact Ochoa and set up a meeting."

Tommy laughed. "What meeting? We don't actually have Mosqueda and Estrada."

I took a drink of my margarita. "True enough. Any ideas?"

"You have a cigar?" Tommy asked, looking around my humble abode.

"Yep," I said, reaching into my shirt pocket. "I took these off the Cubans."

I handed Tommy one of the four cigars I'd confiscated.

"Montecristos," Tommy said, rolling the cigar in his fingers. He trimmed the end of his cigar with a small pocket knife, fired it up and inhaled deeply. "Damn good," Tommy said. "You know . . . I actually think better with nicotine in my system."

I laughed. "Well, take a couple of good drags, pardner, 'cause we've got some serious shit to figure out."

Tommy nodded and took another pull on his cigar. He exhaled and blew a perfect smoke ring. "Do you have a way to contact Ochoa?"

I watched the smoke ring dissipate and walked over to my backpack and pulled out the photos Ochoa had given me. I flipped Mosqueda's photo over and looked at the notes Ochoa had written. At the bottom was a phone number.

"Could be," I said, looking at the number. "But before I call, we need a plan."

Tommy took his drink and cigar and sat in one of my well-worn leather chairs. He appeared deep in thought.

"Earth to Tommy," I finally said.

"Patience, Hardin. I'm working on it."

"Could you work a little faster?"

"Is grabbing that little Nazi-loving bastard absolutely necessary—this go-round?"

I set my nearly depleted margarita on a side table and looked at Tommy. "No. It would be nice . . . but top priority is getting Wes and Buck back."

"I agree," Tommy said, rolling his cigar between his thumb and index finger. "So here's what we do."

*****

Tommy and I worked through the shank of the evening fine-tuning our plan. It was almost ten when I remembered I needed to call Rory.

"Rory, it's Hardin. Sorry so late, but Tommy and I have been working on the best way to rescue Wes and Buck."

There was a pause on the line. I knew what was coming next.

"What about Alexsie?"

I took a deep breath and exhaled. "If the opportunity presents itself, we'll grab him too."

"I don't want to see him again, Hardin, it's just I can't bear to think about what Ochoa is doing to him."

"Yeah, I know, kiddo. I have the same problem."

We talked a few more minutes and I told her I would keep her posted. I was about to hang up, when she cut in.

"Hardin, I just want you to know how much I appreciate what you've done for me. And for what you're about to do for Wes and Buck. I love you, babe." And then she hung up.

I put my cell phone on the table, refilled my glass and looked over at Tommy. "You ever have any *dealings* with a Russian by the name of Vasily?"

Tommy nodded. "Yeah. Some. He works out of Tampico, mainly for the Ambrosio Cartel. Why?"

"Can you get hold of him?"

"Probably. What's on your mind, Hardin?"

"An air-mobile assault on Ochoa's compound."

Tommy smiled. "Tied in with our prisoner swap?"
"Exactly."

Chapter 29

Tommy managed to get hold of Vasily Yagobov and, after a bit of explanation, handed the phone to me.

"Here, Hardin," Tommy said, passing me his cell phone. "His English is quite good . . . and he hates Ochoa."

I took the phone. "Vasily, this is Hardin Steel. Do you understand the situation?"

"I do indeed, Sheriff Steel."

I glanced over at Tommy and arched my eyebrows. "You're quite well informed, sir."

Vasily snorted. "Which is why *I'm* not the one being held by that Nazi pig, Ochoa."

"So you'll help us get Alexsie out of there?"

"It will be a pleasure to save Comrade Yazov and—what is it you Americans say?—'blow up Ochoa's shit'."

I grimaced. "Yeah, that's what we say. But remember, Vasily, we'll have two operations going on. There's no telling where Ochoa will be."

Vasily paused for a moment. "The bastard will either be at his compound, in which case I will deal with him, or he will be at the prisoner exchange, in which case you can deal with him. In either case, he's a dead man."

"On paper," I said, under my breath.

"What?"

"Nothing. I just hope you're right. Ochoa is nothing if not cunning. And he's lucky."

"That son of a whore's luck is about to run out," Vasily snarled. "I've modified his old Huey with side-mounted machine guns and rocket pods. That German prick is about to get a personal lesson on Russian revenge. Tommy has my private cell number. Keep me posted."

The line went dead and I looked over at Tommy. "Jesus. I'd hate to be Ochoa if Vasily does catch up with him."

Tommy smiled. "My gut feeling is Ochoa will be at the exchange. His ego won't allow him to miss an event like that. He'll want to be the first person Mosqueda and Estrada see when they land in Mexico."

I shook my head. "It would be better for us if he stayed in his compound."

"Don't count on it, pal. He'll be at the exchange."

The next morning I called the number on the back of Mosqueda's photo.

"Sheriff Steel, I was beginning to get a bit concerned."

I recognized Ochoa's voice from our little get-together on the beach.

"Yeah, well, plucking two Cuban nationals off Grand Cayman Island took a bit of doing."

"I would imagine. So you have them?"

"I do. Both of them."

"How soon can we do the exchange?"

"We can head south as soon as I get proof of life."

Ochoa paused. "You wish to speak to Stoddard and Bateman?"

"You bet your ass."

"Very well, wait one."

A couple of minutes later, Wes was on the phone.

"Hardin, it's Wes. I'm okay."

Before I could say anything, Buck was on the line. "Stainless, it's Buck. I'm okay, too."

Again, before I could speak, Buck was gone.

"Satisfied?" Ochoa asked.

"Yes," I replied, then I took a chance. "And Yazov?"

"He's alive, but not part of this conversation," Ochoa replied, his tone sending a shiver up my back.

"I see."

"So, will you land as before and raft in to the beach?"

Tommy and I had studied maps of the Mazatlán area most of the previous night. "No. I want to do the exchange in a more *controlled* environment. We'll land in El Cid Marina. Do you know it?"

"Yes, I know it," Ochoa replied.

"Good. There is a long L-shaped pier just south of the Marina Mia Bar. We'll taxi to the far end of the pier, tie up, and make the exchange."

"When?" Ochoa asked.

"Tomorrow at 10 a.m."

"I look forward to it," Ochoa replied.

"Uh-huh. Just one other item. It will just be Tommy and myself on the plane. Plus Mosqueda and Estrada. So I'll expect to see only you and one other man, plus Stoddard and Bateman. If I see anyone else . . . the deal is off."

"I understand. What about the money the Cubans were to deposit in the Caymans?"

Boy, this guy doesn't miss a trick. "I gave it to charity."

Ochoa actually chuckled. "You do have *cajones*, my friend."

"So I've been told. Tomorrow at ten."

At four the next morning, Tommy and I met Agents Rand, Rodriquez, and Garcia at the Brownsville airport. I'd briefed Special Agent Rand after my call to Ochoa. I hoped his men were ready.

They were. Rodriquez and Garcia were dressed identically to the two Cubans. Plus they'd added Panama straw hats to the ensemble. From a distance they could easily pass for Mosqueda and Estrada.

"Good job, Agent Rand," I said, looking at the two stand-ins. Are they armed?"

Rodriquez and Garcia each pulled up their pant legs, showing .25 autos in ankle holsters.

I nodded. "Very good. Tommy and I each have Glock 9mm pistols. If the exchange goes south, the bad guys will know they were in a gunfight."

Agent Rand pulled me aside. "Look, Sheriff, the main thing is to get your two friends out of there. If you can grab Ochoa, or put a couple of bullets in him, it's a bonus. But it's secondary. Agreed?"

I looked at Agent Rand for a long moment. "Agreed."

Rand nodded. "And if at all possible, please bring my two agents back . . . in one piece."

I looked at Rand and glanced at his two agents. "I'll do my level best."

I'd neglected to mention Vasily's air-mobile operation. I figured it was on a need-to-know basis, and right now Agent Rand didn't need to know.

On the flight to Mazatlán, Agents Rodriquez and Garcia and I worked out the final details of the operation. The two agents would deplane first with me in the rear covering them with my Glock. I wanted my weapon out and up just in case.

The two agents would have their hands bound behind them with break-away ties. We'd approach whoever was on the dock with Buck and Wes—I still had my doubts if Ochoa would show—and act out the prisoner swap.

We'd make our move as soon as an opportunity presented itself. When it did, the two agents would break their bindings and go for the guns in their ankle holsters. If Ochoa was present, I was supposed to cover him while the agents took out the hired help. However, with apologies to Special Agent Rand, if I got the chance, I intended to shoot the sawed-off psychopath twice in the chest and once in the head—Corleone-style.

At 9:30 a.m., El Cid Marina was dead ahead. Tommy swung the Grumman out over the Gulf of California and made a low sweeping turn back toward the marina. He hadn't bothered filing a flight plan with Mazatlán air traffic control. The Mexican authorities would never approve a water landing. Planes like the Grumman were at the top of every drug smuggler's wish list, and *approved* water landings were rarely granted.

Tommy did a low fly-by over the marina. We could see Wes and Buck, and two of Ochoa's men. They were waiting near the end of the dock.

I looked over at Tommy and back at the two agents. "Y'all see anybody besides those four?"

They all shook their heads.

"Okay, unless they have frogmen, it looks like we're a go," I said. "Keep those Panamas pulled down low and look down as much as you can."

Tommy held up his hand. He was getting a radio message. I figured it was Mazatlán ATC asking why we'd dropped off radar.

"That was Vasily," Tommy said, grinning. "He's commencing his attack."

The two agents leaned forward. "What attack?"

Chapter 30

Vasily came in low out of the east with the morning sun behind him. He was piloting the Huey and had twelve heavily armed men with him.

Vasily hit the compound's guard turrets first. He triggered the side-mounted 7.62mm machine guns and took out two turrets and their gunners in the first pass.

He swung the chopper hard about and came out of the west, hitting the second two turrets. The Huey took a few rounds of return fire, before reducing the structures to splinters.

Vasily keyed his mike. "*Se preparó, señores.*"

He made a quick pass over the open courtyard and cut down any men who were returning fire. He then put two 2.75-inch rockets into the garage area. The one-kilogram, composition B-4, high-explosive warheads demolished the parked vehicles.

Vasily landed in the middle of the open courtyard. Smoke from the burning vehicles spun off the Huey's rotor blades, forming ghostly concentric circles.

Cutting power to the turbine engine, he grabbed his AK-47 and joined his men as they deployed.

In his subterranean prison, Yazov slowly regained consciousness. He thought he heard gunfire and explosions, but he couldn't be sure. The beatings had left his head pounding, and the ringing in his ears was so loud he had trouble placing sounds.

He glanced around the room with his one good eye. His left eye was swollen shut. He was naked and still chained to a steel chair, but he appeared to be alone. He looked down at his body and grimaced. The blonde bitch was very good at her trade. His body was a mass of cuts and bruises. He was pretty sure his time with Ochoa was about over. They were very close to breaking his will to live.

Vasily caught the tall blonde trying to sneak out of the compound.

"Where is he?" Vasily yelled, squeezing her right arm in a vise-like grip.

"Who?" the blonde shot back, trying to pull away.

"The Russian, you Nazi whore. And for your sake he'd better be alive."

Vasily could see the fear in the Amazon's eyes. He pulled a knife from a sheath on his pistol belt and put the point under the woman's chin. "Where is Comrade Yazov?"

The woman hesitated, and Vasily pushed the tip of the knife deeper, drawing blood.

The Amazon cut her eyes toward a doorway.

Vasily nodded. "Show me."

The woman led Vasily through several hallways, and finally down a stairway to a series of rooms.

"He's there," she said, pointing to a door.

Vasily tried the doorknob. It was locked. Two vicious kicks managed to shatter the doorjamb.

Yazov looked up, blinking his one good eye, trying to comprehend what was happing. Vasily grabbed a handful of the blonde's hair and threw her into the room.

"Alexsie, it's me, Comrade Vasily." He looked at Yazov and swore in Russian. "I see the pig, Ochoa, gave you a very tough time."

Yazov shook his head and cut his good eye toward the blonde, now curled up in a corner.

Vasily glanced at the woman. "What? She did this to you?"

Yazov nodded.

Vasily took a step toward the woman. "Where are the keys to his handcuffs?"

She pointed to a small desk in one corner of the room. "In the middle drawer."

"Get them and unlock my friend," Vasily snapped, his voice charged with anger.

The blonde retrieved the key, unlocked the cuffs, and stepped away from Yazov.

"Where are his things?" Vasily asked.

"In the wardrobe," the woman replied, pointing.

"Yazov, can you get dressed?" Vasily asked, grimacing as he watched his friend get up.

"Yes, I think so," Yazov said, his words slurred due to his cut and swollen lips. He glanced at the KA-

BAR knife hanging on Vasily's web belt. "May I borrow your knife?"

Vasily nodded and handed the KA-BAR to Yazov, butt first. Yazov took the knife and smiled. Vasily could see that a number of his teeth were missing.

Yazov stepped over to the cowering blonde and pulled her roughly to her feet. He moved behind her and cupped her chin with his left hand, pulling her head back. "Take your clothes off," Yazov whispered, his breath sharp as the knife's edge.

The blonde unbuttoned her blouse and shrugged out of it. She had small, firm breasts and wasn't wearing a bra. "Now the rest," Yazov said, placing the razor-sharp KA-BAR under her chin.

She unbuckled her jeans and kicked them off.

"That will do," Yazov said in a whisper.

In a quick, violent move he stabbed the KA-BAR deep into the woman's lower belly, just above her pubic bone. The force of the blow caused her eyes to bulge and her mouth to gape open, but the only sound was air rushing from her lungs. And then Yazov opened her up until he hit her ribcage.

Yazov pulled the knife out and released the woman. She collapsed at his feet, clutching the incision with both hands, desperately trying to keep her intestines from spilling onto the hard tile floor. Dark-red blood was oozing from between her fingers.

Yazov watched her for a moment and then nodded at Vasily. Vasily nodded back, took a half-step toward the dying Amazon, raised his AK and shot her between the eyes.

Vasily helped Yazov get dressed, and then half-carried his friend out of the dungeon and back to the Huey. When Vasily's men saw him with the obviously wounded man, they ran to his aid and helped get Yazov into the chopper.

One of Vasily's men shouted over the Huey's idling turbine. "We killed everyone in the compound, but there's no sign of Ochoa."

Vasily nodded. "The Americans will have to deal with him." He took a quick look around the compound and signaled for his men to get aboard the Huey.

"You lose," I said, looking over at Tommy. "Neither of the men with Wes and Buck is Ochoa. He's not here."

Tommy wrinkled his brow. "Don't count on it."

I looked at him and nodded. "Yeah, I have the same feeling," I said, taking one more look at the dock. "Set her down, Tommy. Let's get this over with."

Tommy made a wide, low turn and brought the Grumman down near the long pier.

I looked over my left shoulder at the two DEA agents. "Okay, boys, it doesn't look like the big man is here. Ochoa's men on the dock probably don't know what Mosqueda and Estrada look like, so we may have caught a break. As soon as there's an opening, we take them out and get Stoddard and Bateman, and ourselves, back on the plane. Clear?"

Both agents nodded.

Tommy eased the Grumman along the end of the dock and I popped the hatch. The look of relief on Wes's and Buck's faces put a big smile on *my* face. Ochoa's men, however, weren't smiling; in fact, they looked very nervous.

"Mosqueda, Estrada, let's go!" I yelled.

As the two agents passed by me, I whispered, "Something's wrong. Be ready."

Rodriquez and Garcia stepped on to the dock, with me close behind. I had not drawn my Glock. Something told me to keep it holstered.

I looked at Ochoa's men. I figured they were armed, but they didn't have their weapons out either. I motioned for Wes and Buck to step forward, and pushed the two agents ahead. Once Wes and Buck were clear of the two agents, I yelled, "Now!" and drew my Glock.

The two agents dropped to a knee and drew their automatics from their ankle holsters. One of Ochoa's men dove off the dock and swam under the wooden structure.

I fired and took down the remaining bad guy.

Agent Rodriquez jumped to his feet and pointed up the marina. "Speedboat's coming. And coming fast."

I looked to where Agent Rodriquez was pointing. It was either the authorities, or more of Ochoa's men. Either way, it was trouble. "On the plane . . . now!" I yelled, turning and running for the Grumman.

I half dove through the open hatch. "Tommy, we've got company!" I yelled.

Tommy leaned forward and looked out the copilot's window. "I see them," he said. "Get everybody on board. We're out of here!"

I ran aft and made sure Wes, Buck, and the DEA agents were aboard, and that the hatch was secured.

Wes slapped me on the back. "Very smooth, Stainless."

Buck smiled and nodded. "Nice shot, Hardin."

"Uh-huh," I said. "Get strapped in. There's liable to be more shooting."

Ochoa and three of his goons were in the speedboat and they were fast closing the gap. I heard a round hit the fuselage.

Tommy looked at me. "Change places with Wes. I may need him."

I climbed out of the copilot's seat and Wes slid in.

Tommy looked over at Wes and grinned. "Welcome back from your little vacation. Now give me full flaps, this is going to be a downwind take-off. The folks shooting at us have the wind behind them."

I head a couple more rounds tear into the plane. "Anytime from now would be good, fellows. Let's see some of that pilot shit!" I yelled.

Tommy pushed the throttles ahead and glanced at Wes. "Here we go."

To say the roar of the engines was deafening would be an understatement. It was the shortest takeoff, I'd experienced since flying with Tommy.

Wes looked over at Tommy, who winked and pointed due west. "Let's get twelve miles offshore, and then we'll fly up the coast. There's liable to be some seriously pissed-off Mexicans back there."

Wes grinned and nodded.

"Take it a minute, Wes," Tommy said, leaning forward to change radio frequencies. "I have an idea."

Tommy keyed his radio and spoke for a few minutes. Then he turned and looked back at me. He had to yell to be heard over the engines. "I managed to get hold of Vasily. He's got Yazov. He's in pretty bad shape, but looks like he'll make it. I told him about the speedboat ambush. He's going to drop over to the El Cid Marina. He said he still has a bunch of rockets left. If the big dog is in the speedboat, maybe we'll get him yet."

I rolled my eyes. "They're going to lock me up and throw away the key."

Agent Garcia leaned over. "No, they aren't, Sheriff. Hell, my partner and I are going to recommend you for a decoration."

I looked at Garcia. "*What*?"

Agent Garcia nodded and winked at me. "Order of the Coca Leaf."

Chapter 31

Ochoa had just pulled up to the dock and was retrieving his men—the dead one, and the one who'd swum under the dock—when he heard the chopper. At first he thought it was the Mexican Army, but then he recognized his Huey . . . and knew he was in serious trouble.

Vasily dropped the nose of the chopper and fired off four rockets. Ochoa ran for his life down the dock. At the last second, he dove off and swam hard for the bottom.

The concussion of the rocket explosions nearly knocked him out, but he managed to hug the bottom by holding on to one of the dock pilings. When he ran short of air, he pushed off hard from the bottom, bursting through to the surface, gasping.

The Huey, *his* Huey, was well past the dock and turning hard to the northwest. Ochoa surveyed the damage. The last twenty feet of the dock were in splinters and only the stern of his speedboat was visible. All four of his men, or what was left of them, were floating near the destroyed dock.

Tommy keyed his radio and listened for a minute.

"Good shooting, amigo. Watch your six. Out."

Tommy turned to me and yelled out, "I just got a sitrep from Vasily. Ochoa was on the speedboat, but he can't confirm if he was KIA'd or not. Four men are floating face down in the bay, and the speedboat is at the bottom of El Cid Marina."

"Damn, I hope he nailed that son of a bitch," I said, looking around the cabin at my motley crew. "Take us home, Tommy, I need a drink—a goddamned big one."

Special Agent Bill Rand was at the Brownsville airport when we landed. He walked over to the Grumman as Tommy shut down the big radial engines.

"Damn, you boys stirred up a friggin' hornet's nest down south."

I grimaced. "I'll bet. Did we get Ochoa?"

Rand frowned and shook his head. "No. Our contacts say he's back at his compound, or what's left of it. You want to tell me about that part of the operation?"

I couldn't help but chuckle. "Yeah, but another time. Okay?"

"Okay. You can buy and I'll listen," Rand said, grinning. "And I must admit you're a bit sneakier than

I gave you credit for." Rand laughed. "I think there could be a place for you in our organization."

I snorted and shook my head. "Sorry, Agent Rand, I already did my time."

Rand smiled. "Yeah, I guess you did at that. Well, the good news, other than getting everybody back safe and sound, is that the Mexican government thinks the attack on Ochoa was by a rival cartel."

I looked at Rand. "The Ambrosio Cartel?"

Rand nodded. "That's what they think. And we're going to feed them some fake intel to keep them thinking along those lines."

"No harm, no foul," I said, watching Tommy securing the Grumman.

Rand shoved his hands in his pants pockets and dug the toe of his right shoe into the asphalt. "Well, there may be one foul."

Wes and Buck had joined me. The three of us looked at Agent Rand and waited.

"We're going to have to kick Mosqueda and Estrada loose."

I put my hands on my hips, leaned back and took a deep breath. "Why?"

Rand raised his eyebrows and pursed his lips. "Well, during the initial arraignment, the judge had a big problem with how we, that is to say, y'all, arrested them. And he mentioned something about Miranda."

"He let them go?" I asked.

Rand nodded. "More or less. He ordered them deported, *post haste*, to Cuba."

Buck leaned forward. "Jesus. Are we in trouble?"

Agent Rand looked around for a moment and then smiled. “No. Judge Friedman hates drug dealers.” Rand chuckled. “But, if I were y’all, I’d stay out of Cuba—for the foreseeable future—and leave clandestine operations to us.”

Chapter 32

Over the next few weeks, things pretty much got back to normal. Depending on your definition of normal.

Tommy said it had been *stimulating*, but he had to get back to the charter-flying business. Buck slipped back into his private-eye work, while Wes looked for a new line of employment. And I got back to my duties as county sheriff, and my relationship with Rory.

Down south, Ochoa was re-staffing and repairing his compound. And thinking a lot about getting even.

In Cuba, Mosqueda and Estrada were thinking along the same lines.

Rory and I met up with Wes and Lacey one Friday evening at Bluebeards for dinner. We ordered drinks and some calamari for a starter. It was the first time I'd seen Wes since our invasion of Mexico.

I wiped the salt off the rim of my margarita, took a sip and looked at Wes. "So, any prospects, pard?"

Wes nodded. "Yeah, I'm getting a lot of charters from oil companies. Flying the Eagle Ford Shale trend. Giving the oil execs a bird's-eye view of new drilling. And I'm getting some charters from Brownsville to Corpus and San Antonio, and back.

"So, all in all, not too bad. Not too exciting . . . but not bad." Wes said, putting his arm around Lacey and pulling her close. "And I get lots of time with Lacey, and I haven't had to dodge any SAMs."

I laughed. "Yep, once you've had a Strela on your butt, it's pretty much downhill from there."

Wes scratched his right earlobe with his middle finger. "Uh-huh. So what's new on the law-dog side of things?"

"It's been strangely quiet," I replied. "I mean just normal sheriff stuff. Nothing from the DEA boys on our two friends back in Cuba. Or our buddy Ochoa."

Wes laughed. "Yeah, he's probably still rebuilding his compound after Vasily worked it over." Wes paused, "Any word on Yazov?"

I shook my head. "Haven't heard a peep."

Rory cleared her throat, and I looked at her. "Or maybe we have?"

Rory leaned forward, putting her elbows on the table and clasping her hands together. "I did get an e-mail from Alexsie."

I arched my eyebrows at her. "An e-mail?"

Rory nodded. "Yes. He said he wanted to let me, and y'all, know he was recovering. And how much he appreciated what we did for him."

"Anything else?" I asked, glancing over at Wes.

"Just that he's going to get back to Ochoa."

"*Get back to him*?" I asked.

Rory shrugged. "That's what he said."

After dinner, Rory and I said goodbye to Wes and Lacey and retired to Rory's condo. It had been a good while since we'd, or I should say, since I'd, had sex. I tried not to think about Rory and Yazov. But I'll admit I was a bit nervous. If Yazov's dick was as big as the rest of him, I'd be in trouble.

I was glad when Rory offered me a drink. Sometimes, as you'll recall, she tends to monitor my drinking. So I figured the offer of a drink indicated she was a tad nervous as well.

"Yeah, I'll have a Cuervo on the rocks, but just a small one," I said.

Rory nodded and chuckled. "A little nervous, big boy?"

I raised my eyebrows and nodded. "Yeah, I guess I am. And you?"

Rory smiled and began unbuttoning her top. She wasn't wearing a bra. "Not so much," she said, dropping her blouse on the floor.

I never did get that shot of tequila.

The next morning, my nerves calmed, I managed to sleep till almost eight. I looked over at Rory. She rolled away from me, pulled the sheet over her head and said, "*No más*."

I laughed, swatted her lightly on the backside, and got up and went to the kitchen to make some coffee.

My cell phone was on the granite countertop and it starting jumping around. I glanced at my watch; it was eight sharp. As it was a Saturday morning, I was a bit irritated at being called this early. I looked at the caller ID; it was Wes.

This can't be good, I thought, picking up the phone.

"Mornin', Wes."

"Morning, Hardin. Sorry to call so early, but I've got a charter and I needed to give you a heads-up before I leave."

From his tone, I knew my first instinct had been right. "Something up?"

"Tommy's dead."

"What? How? Where?" I said, feeling like I'd just been kidney-punched.

"His plane exploded shortly after takeoff from Grand Cayman."

"Mechanical or . . . ?"

"Not sure at this point, Hardin. I thought maybe you could get some info from your contacts on the island."

"Deputy Chief Kincaid?"

"He'd be the one."

"I'll call him. How'd you hear about it?"

Wes paused. "You don't want to know, but my source is good."

"Wes, you're not back in the *import-export* business . . . are you?"

"Hell, no. But I still have contacts, and I thought you'd want to know."

"You're right . . . and thanks."

"Check it out, Hardin. I doubt it was mechanical."

"Will do, Wes. I'll get back to you as soon as I know something."

Rory walked into the kitchen as I was ending the call.

"Who was that?" she asked, pouring herself a cup of coffee.

"It was Wes. Tommy's plane went down. Some kind of explosion."

All the color drained from her face. "One of those Strela things, like they shot at Wes?"

I hadn't thought about a surface-to-air missile. "Wes didn't have any info on the cause, just that the Grumman went down."

"And Tommy?"

I shook my head. "Wes said he didn't make it."

Rory's hand trembled slightly and she set her coffee cup on the counter. "You think it's the Cubans?"

I shrugged. "Could be, or it could've been Ochoa, or it could have been mechanical. The Grumman was an old plane."

"Where did it happen?"

"Wes said he was just departing Grand Cayman."

Rory grimaced. "It was the Cubans."

Never disregard a woman's intuition.

*****

I waited until Monday and then managed to get hold of Deputy Chief Amos Kincaid.

"Amos, Hardin Steel. Have you got a minute?"

"I was expecting your call, Hardin. From all indications it was some kind of bomb."

"Could it have been a SAM?"

"No. The explosion came from inside of the aircraft. And he was still on our radar. ATC would pick up a missile."

"Are our two Cuban pals in town?"

"Not officially. But they could be here. We're an island, Hardin, with very porous borders."

"Just like Cuba," I said under my breath.

"What?"

"Nothing, just thinking out loud."

"Look, Hardin, I'm pretty busy, so if there's nothing else . . . ?"

"No. Nothing else. I appreciate your time, Amos. And watch yourself. If it was the Cubans, and I'm betting it was, they won't forget you made a generous contribution to charity—using their money."

"Uh-huh. And who's bright idea was that?"

He had me there. "Thanks for the intel, Amos," I said and hung up.

Chapter 33

Ochoa's contacts were better than Wes's. It had been a bomb and the hit had been sanctioned by Johny Mosqueda.

Ochoa leaned back in his custom-made chair and looked out the window at the contractors scurrying around, finishing the repairs to his compound.

One down, three to go, he thought. Maybe the Cubans would take care of all the Yankees for him. In any case, his first priority was to hit the Ambrosio Cartel.

If he didn't hit them, and hit them hard, he'd be perceived as soft. And that perception could be fatal.

Yazov spent the next week at Vasily's compound recovering from his torture-inflicted injuries. Most of the damage would heal with time. His broken or missing teeth could be repaired or replaced by a dentist. The only permanent damage appeared to be the loss of sight in his left eye.

Vasily walked out into the courtyard of his house. Yazov was reclined on a chaise longue, enjoying the sun and a Bloody Mary.

"Good morning, comrade," Vasily said, pulling up a chair. "How are you feeling this morning?"

Yazov turned his head. He had a black patch over his left eye. "Much better. Thanks to you, my friend."

Vasily smiled and nodded to a servant. "Bring another Bloody Mary." He pulled his chair closer to Yazov. "I think it is time you left Mexico. At least for a while."

Yazov swung his legs to the side of the chaise longue and sat facing Vasily. "Ochoa?"

Vasily nodded. "Yes. It is most unfortunate that he survived the rocket attack at the Marina." Vasily paused and smiled, thinking how close he'd come to getting the little Nazi. "My informants tell me he's planning to retaliate."

Yazov patted his old friend on the knee. "I should stay and help you kill that sadistic pig."

Vasily shook his head. "No, my friend. I think you should go to your dacha in Tortola. You need to rest and finish healing up. I will take care of Señor Ochoa."

Yazov tentatively touched his eye patch. "Perhaps you are right, comrade. When you kill him, please send me his testicles in a jar."

Vasily laughed. "If he actually has any—I will."

Two days later, Yazov was on a flight to Tortola. The following day, Ochoa's men attacked the Tampico compound of Ernesto Ambrosio, head of the Ambrosio Cartel. After heavy fighting, Ochoa's men were able to take the compound, killing everyone inside, including Ambrosio's dogs.

A second smaller force reclaimed Ochoa's Huey and flew it to a small compound on the outskirts of Tampico.

Vasily heard the distinctive sound of a chopper approaching. He stepped into his enclosed courtyard in time to see the Huey's pilot lower the nose and fire off a fusillade of 2.75-inch rockets. Vasily managed to give the pilot the finger before he was torn apart by the explosions.

I was having lunch with Buck at Red's BBQ joint when Special Agent Bill Rand walked in. Rand looked around like he was looking for someone. That someone turned out to be me.

"May I join you fellows?" Rand said, pulling out a chair.

I nodded. "You look like a man on a mission, Agent Rand."

Rand nodded and sat down. "Actually, your office said you'd be here."

"Okay, you found me. What's up? Are the Cubans in town?" I said, cutting a quick glance at Buck and winking.

Rand looked at me like I was being a smart-ass, which I was. "No. Not yet. But Ochoa's people were in Tampico yesterday. They paid a little visit to Ernesto Ambrosio and your friend Vasily."

My shoulders sagged along with my attitude. “Did they get Vasily?”

Rand nodded. “Yeah. Ochoa’s boys recovered his Huey and used it to blow up Vasily’s compound . . . with him in it.

“Ambrosio?”

“KIA, along with everybody in his compound . . . even his dogs.”

I took a deep breath and blew it out. “Jesus, the chickens are coming home to roost . . . aren’t they?”

Rand arched his eyebrows. “Yes, I’m afraid they are. The bad guys are squaring accounts.”

Buck leaned forward. “Did they get Yazov?”

Rand shook his head. “No. Our sources tell us he flew to Tortola, in the BVI, the day before the attack.”

“Damn, that was good kismet,” Buck said, looking at me.

I nodded. “Yeah, well, after his *stay* with Ochoa, he probably deserves a bit of luck.”

The waitress came by and we all ordered the lunch BBQ plate and sweet tea. When she left our table to turn in our order, I leaned closer to Agent Rand. “What about the Cubans?”

Rand looked around the café. “Our sources are telling us Mosqueda was behind the bombing of Jack Thompson’s plane. They’re also telling us Mosqueda has a contract out on a Cayman Island immigration officer, one Deputy Chief Amos Kincaid. We’re not sure why he has such a hard-on for Kincaid.”

I looked at Buck and rolled my eyes.

Rand caught my glance at Buck. “You have some information you’d like to share, Sheriff Steel?”

I nodded. "When we grabbed Mosqueda and Estrada on Grand Cayman, Kincaid was with us."

Rand shook his head. "That doesn't seem like enough reason to put a contract out on a senior immigration officer?"

I clasped my hands together and put my elbows on the table. "Well . . . there's a bit more to it."

Rand nodded. "There always is. Let's have it."

I put my index fingers together and tapped on my upper lip. "Mosqueda and Estrada were in the Caymans to make a little cash deposit."

Rand nodded. "Uh-huh. Go on."

I looked at Buck and then back at Agent Rand. "Well, we didn't want the drug money to get into the Cayman banking system, so I suggested Kincaid grab the money and donate it to charity."

Rand laughed. "Very noble. Now I understand Mosqueda's interest in the good deputy chief."

"Glad I could clear that up, Agent Rand," I said, feeling quite righteous.

"Yeah, well, don't get too cocky," Rand said, looking at me. "There's also a contract out on you."

Ochoa and the Cubans laid off killing anybody for the rest of the week. The only excitement was when Robert Lee had some kind of seizure. But he was now out of the hospital, and Rory was staying at the ranch to keep an eye on him.

Around seven Friday evening, I heard the distinctive rumble of Wes's Corvette as he pulled into my drive. I walked over and opened the front screen door. Buck was in the Vette with Wes.

"Howdy, boys," I said, watching the two, pretty good-sized men climb out of the low-slung Corvette. "How *the* hell are you going to get out of that rig when you get old?"

Wes laughed. "I'll have 'em roll the wheelchair up real close to the door."

I smiled and nodded. "Uh-huh. Well, when y'all get your big backsides out of that teeny plastic car, I have margaritas and cigars waiting."

Buck smiled and raised his eyebrows. "Cuban cigars?"

"Very funny, Buckmeister," I said, giving him a middle-finger salute.

We adjourned to my den-living area bar, and I poured a round of margaritas. "Here you go, boys," I said, handing my two partners in crime a drink. I picked up the remaining glass and nodded toward Wes and Buck. "Here's to firm-breasted, bowlegged women." I took a healthy drink of margarita and gestured toward a wooden humidor on the bar. "Help yourselves to a cigar, gents."

"I'll get 'em," Buck said, walking over to the humidor. Buck put a cigar in his shirt pocket and tossed another to Wes.

Wes studied the paper ring on his cigar. "Herrera Esteli. I *am* impressed."

I nodded. "Yep. Ten bucks a pop. They're what all us *contractees* smoke."

Wes and Buck both laughed.

"Well, maybe we ought to *smoke* the contractor," Wes said, clipping off the end his Esteli.

I took another sip of my margarita and grabbed a cigar. "Same thought crossed my mind. Should we adjourn to the smoking deck?"

I had three folding chairs on my small wooden patio, which overlooked my weathered dock.

We sat on the deck and watched the boats running up and down the Intercoastal. For a few minutes nobody said a word.

"What about Mosqueda?" Wes said, breaking the silence.

I watched a couple of good-looking young women paddle by in their kayaks. "Well, a return trip to Cuba is out of the question."

Wes nodded and waved to one of the kayakers. "What about the Caymans?"

I puffed on my Esteli and thought for a moment. "You mean some kind of sting operation?"

"Exactly," Wes said. "I'm sure Deputy Chief Kincaid would get onboard. Hell, Mosqueda has a contract out on him, too."

I looked over at Buck, who was nodding in agreement. "What would we use as bait?"

Wes laughed. "Hell, Stainless, the same thing you law enforcement types always use—dope or cash."

I studied the ash on the end of my cigar for a couple of seconds. "Well, seeing as how we've depleted our supply of dope, it'll have to be cash. And I think the good deputy chief might be of considerable assistance in that regard."

Buck stood up and walked over to the deck railing. "You know, it just might work. Outside of the three of us, only Agent Rand and Kincaid know what happened to Mosqueda's cash."

I interrupted Buck. "And Ochoa. I told him we gave Mosqueda's dough to charity."

Buck nodded. "Yeah, well, I wouldn't worry too much about that. I doubt Ochoa and Mosqueda exchange e-mails."

I laughed. "I guess you're right about that. So as far as Mosqueda knows, Kincaid grabbed his drug money and kept it."

"Yeah," Wes chimed in. "Hell, it's perfect, Hardin. Kincaid can get word to Mosqueda: Drop the hits on you and him, and he'll return the cash."

I took a drink of my margarita and looked at Wes. "Might just work at that. But how do we get Mosqueda to the Caymans?" I asked, grinning at my two friends. "As I recall, he and his buddy, Estrada, were kidnapped on their last trip to George Town."

Wes smiled and turned for a moment, looking out across Laguna Madre. "That's easy, Stainless. We meet in a neutral spot."

"Got one in mind?" I asked.

"Tortola, British Virgin Islands," Wes said, grinning wickedly.

I wagged my cigar at Wes. "I like the way you think, pardner."

"Uh-huh. And I think I know how to contact our Russian friend."

*****

The next morning, after the tequila haze dissipated, I managed to get hold of Deputy Chief Kincaid. I explained *most* of our plan, which, even sober, didn't sound too farfetched.

"It's doable, Hardin," Kincaid said when I finished my pitch. "But, I really did give Mosqueda's money to charity. All of it."

I started to reply, but Kincaid jumped back in. "However, we've got a hell of a bunch of counterfeit $100 bills. And they're good, Hardin. Best we've ever seen. Mosqueda won't know the difference."

"Don't worry, Amos," I said. "If all goes according to plan, he won't have long to examine the currency."

Chapter 34

I signed out for a week of vacation and we put our plan in motion. Kincaid used his contacts to get word to Mosqueda. The Cuban was understandably reticent, but doing the deal on neutral ground brought him around, abetted by his greed and ego.

As Wes's King Air didn't quite have the range to reach Tortola, we told Kincaid to take a commercial flight to Cancún. We'd pick him up when we refueled.

Bright and early Monday morning, Buck and I met Wes at the airport. We were wheels up just as the sun peeked over the eastern horizon. After a quick stop in Cancún for fuel and to pick up Kincaid, we flew on to the Tortola airport, which is actually located on Beef Island and connected to Tortola by the Queen Elizabeth II Bridge.

Kincaid had ten stacks of *funny money*, 100 hundreds per stack, hidden under the false bottom of an aluminum briefcase he'd appropriated during a drug bust.

I hoped the hundred grand would be enough bait. And I hoped we wouldn't run into an overzealous customs officer. A hundred thousand in counterfeit U.S. currency would be hard to explain. Even for a deputy chief inspector.

Customs turned out to be a breeze. island tax havens, it seems, aren't in the habit of going through potential depositors' luggage. We cleared Customs without opening a bag—welcome to the British Virgin Islands.

We rented a car and took the QE-II Bridge over to Tortola Island. We had two days before our meeting with Mosqueda.

Wes was driving and leaned toward me. "I googled Yazov's vacation villa before we left . . . You're not going to believe it."

Kincaid leaned forward from his seat in the back. "Whose villa?"

Wes glanced over his shoulder at Kincaid. "We have a friend on the island. He's agreed to help us with some of the finer points of our little operation."

Kincaid sat back and looked at Buck who was sitting next to him. "Bloody good. It's always best to use locals when one can. Especially in operations of this type."

Wes glanced over at me and rolled his eyes.

*****

We drove through Parham Town and followed Waterfront Drive for about ten miles. The views of the bluish-green Caribbean waters and nearby islands was close to breathtaking.

Wes slowed and took a left. We followed the private lane to the crest of a rounded hilltop and stopped at a closed gate. Wes reached out his open window and pushed a button on an intercom mounted on a painted steel pipe.

"Yes?" the voice was deep and heavily accented.

"Alexsie, it's your friends from the Hotel Ochoa."

There was no reply, but the twin white gates swung open with barely a sound.

I shook my head. "Hotel Ochoa?"

Wes nodded. "Yeah, I figured he'd get a kick out of that."

Wes pulled through the gate, drove a couple hundred yards and parked.

Alexsie Yazov stood waiting at the front of his hilltop villa. Hands on hips, wearing khakis and a bright tropical shirt, a black patch covering his left eye, looking every bit the rascal pirate.

We all climbed out of the rental car and walked toward Comrade Alexsie.

"Welcome to Tortola, gentlemen," Yazov said, extending his arms with his palms open.

I stepped forward and shook hands with the big Russian. His facial bruises were pretty well faded and, except for the eye patch, he appeared to be in good shape.

"Good to see you again, Alexsie," I said, glancing at his eye patch and grimacing. "And more or less in one piece."

Alexsie laughed, exposing a couple of missing teeth. He lightly touched the patch covering his left eye. "Yes, more or less intact, except for the eye and a few teeth I need to get replaced." Alexsie looked at Kincaid with his one good eye. "And who is your English-looking friend?"

Kincaid stepped forward and extended his hand. "Cayman Islander, actually. Deputy Chief Amos Kincaid, at your service."

Yazov tilted his head in my direction. "An awful lot of law in this group."

I nodded. "Yes, well, don't worry, Alexsie, this little operation is strictly off the books."

Yazov grinned. "Good. This way, gentlemen. I'll get you quartered."

Yazov's house was at least 6000 square feet with six bedrooms and six baths. Each room was painted in a different pastel color. The high vaulted ceilings were constructed of darkly hued tropical woods, nicely complimenting the cool off-white tile floors. There were two pools, one on either side of the house, each overlooking a different picturesque bay.

Alexsie showed us to our rooms. "Drinks and hors d'oeuvres by the north pool in twenty minutes."

I was quartered last. Yazov opened the door to my room and gestured for me to enter. I walked into the large bedroom, put my travel bag on the bed and looked around. The room was painted a very light blue, with incredible views of the water. "Damn, Alexsie, you do know how to live."

He looked at me and smiled. "My life does have its moments."

I wasn't too sure what he meant by that. I guess I was still getting past the fact he'd kidnapped and then seduced the third love of my life.

Before I could respond, Alexsie said, "Come out to the north pool when you're ready. We have much to discuss."

I took a quick shower and changed into Bermuda shorts, a Tommy Bahama linen shirt, and flip-flops. I could go *islander* with the best of 'em.

I finally found the *north* pool. I'd never known anybody with north and south pools. And I guess I was late, or they were all early. Everybody was having a drink and chowing down on fried conch, grilled shrimp, and fresh-baked bread.

A gorgeous girl with dark hair and skin the color of roasted coffee beans asked for my drink order. She was wearing a bikini top and had a sarong wrapped around her trim waist.

I knew immediately where I was going to retire. "Tequila, straight up, please."

My concerns of Yazov still lusting for Rory were diminishing.

I joined my co-conspirators at the buffet table. "I say again, Alexsie . . . you *do* know how to live."

Alexsie nodded and passed me a china plate heaped with grilled shrimp and fried conch. He winked at me as I took the plate. "The best revenge is to live well . . . don't you agree?"

I watched the Caribbean beauty return with my drink. "Yes, comrade, I do indeed."

Satiated, we retired with coffee and cigars to deck chairs near the pool. The cigars were Cuban, courtesy of our host.

I fired up my cigar and took a long drag. I exhaled and admired the cigar.

"Like it, my friend?" Alexsie asked.

I nodded. "Extraordinary. Very smooth."

Alexsie smiled. "They're Cohibas. Fidel's favorite. The smoothness comes from a third fermentation of the tobacco."

I took another draw on the cigar. "Do you have a room I could rent?"

Alexsie laughed. "If we survive our little undertaking, you *all* are welcome to stay, or return, as you wish."

Wes set his drink on a small table and leaned forward. "I briefed Alexsie on our plan." He looked at our host. "Perhaps you have some comments?"

Alexsie took a deep drag of his cigar, leaned his head back and exhaled a plume of white smoke. "My people in Cuba tell me Mosqueda is planning to depart on schedule."

"Is Estrada coming with him?" I asked.

Alexsie nodded. "Yes. Along with two assassins."

Buck choked on his coffee. "Assassins?"

"Yes," Alexsie replied. "Two of Mosqueda's best."

I looked at Alexsie. "Damn, I thought we killed off Mosqueda's shooters during our little gunfight in Cienfuegos."

Alexsie shook his large bald head. "No, my friend. Those were second-tier street thugs. Mosqueda hadn't counted on you and your friends being there." Alexsie paused and snorted softly. "Nor had I."

Damn. He'd brought Rory back into the equation. Albeit indirectly, or maybe I was being over-sensitive.

Alexsie smoked his cigar for a moment and then continued. "The two men accompanying Mosqueda and Estrada are very good at their trade. We will need to be at the top of our game." Alexsie paused. "May I see a sample of the counterfeit money?"

Deputy Inspector Kincaid pulled his wallet out of his back pocket, removed a $100 bill and handed it to Alexsie.

Yazov took the bill and rubbed it between his thumb and fingers. Then he held it to the light. "Very good work—I know the makers."

Kincaid looked shocked. "You know the makers?"

"Yes," Alexsie replied, still examining the bill. "They're Iranian. Best counterfeiters on the planet. These will certainly fool Mosqueda and damn near anyone else, for that matter. How many of these bills do you have?"

Kincaid hesitated.

"Tell him, Amos," I said. "We're all on the same team here."

Kincaid nodded. "All together, we confiscated 15,000 $100 bills. Coincidently, the exact amount I seized from Mosqueda's villa in the Caymans."

I could see Alexsie doing the math.

"One million five," Alexsie said.

Kincaid nodded.

Alexsie laughed. "That's a good deal of money. Where is it?"

"One hundred thousand is in my briefcase," Kincaid replied. "The rest is still in police custody in the Caymans."

Alexsie looked disappointed, so I jumped in. "Amos will use the hundred thousand as bait. He'll tell Mosqueda the rest is at a villa he rented—your villa. We get him and his crew up here, and, well, you know the rest." I paused and glanced at Amos. "And you can keep the hundred grand in funny money."

Kincaid visibly blanched, but went along.

Alexsie nodded. "Okay, my friends, just so everybody's clear: Mosqueda tried to have me killed in Cuba." He paused and looked directly at me. "And his men would have raped and killed Rory. Therefore, I intend to execute them." Alexsie looked at each of us in turn. "You may participate or not, as you wish. Understood?"

It's one thing to kill a man in the line of duty; it's quite another to kill in cold blood. I wasn't sure if I could do it, but I nodded and said, "Understood."

I looked at Wes and Buck, both of whom also nodded. I was worried about Amos. I knew from my

DEA days that he was tough. I just wasn't sure if he was up for this. But when I glanced at him, he also nodded.

"It's a bad business, fellows," I said. "But if we don't take out Mosqueda and his crew, we'll be right back where we started. And Wes and Buck will likely be added to the hit list."

Two days later, at four in the afternoon, Amos got the call.

"Deputy Chief Kincaid, do you know who this is?"

"Yes. I recognize your voice, Señor Mosqueda. Have you arrived?"

"Yes. I am at the airport on Beef Island. Where do you wish to meet?"

"Who's with you?"

"My associate, Señor Estrada. Should we rent a car? Do you have the funds with you?"

Kincaid looked at Alexsie and held up two fingers. Alexsie shook his head and frowned, and held up four fingers.

Wes, Buck, and I were listening to the conversation and watching Alexsie's reactions.

"A rental car?" Kinkaid paused and looked at Alexsie, who nodded. "Yes, that would be fine. And yes, I have the money with me."

"Excellent," Mosqueda replied. "Shall we say 7:00? And I will require directions."

Kincaid spent the next two or three minutes giving the Cuban directions to Yazov's villa. Hopefully, they would be Mosqueda's *final* instructions.

Kincaid closed his cellphone and looked at me. "Did you get the gist of the conversation?"

I nodded and looked at Alexsie. "Yeah, 7:00 tonight, and Mosqueda lied about how many men he has with him."

"It's perfect," Alexsie said, rubbing his two large hands together. "As you probably noted driving in, I have no neighbors. And steep cliffs drop away from both sides of the villa into deep water. The current, and the sharks, will take care of the bodies."

Even though we were about to execute—I prefer *execute* to *murder*—four men, we were all in good appetite. We enjoyed an early meal of grilled fish, salad, and a very fine sauvignon blanc. Actually, three bottles of the sauvignon blanc. I didn't say we weren't nervous. We were. All of us except Alexsie. He seemed totally at ease, but then assassinations were a significant part of his résumé.

After the meal, Alexsie dismissed his cook and house servants for the evening. "Gentlemen, if you would be so kind as to join me in my study."

We followed Alexsie into his wood-paneled study. I was expecting an after-dinner, pre-execution brandy. I was wrong.

Alexsie walked over to his mahogany desk and ran his hand under the right edge of the desk, just above the drawers. He evidently pushed a control, because a portion of one wall began to open.

Behind the wall was what could only be described as an armory.

Alexsie came around from behind his desk and strode over to the walk-in gun storage. He motioned for us to join him. "Gentlemen, tonight's weapon of choice . . .," Alexsie paused to pick up a small automatic with an attached silencer, "will be silenced .22 automatics."

Mosqueda, Estrada, and the two shooters stopped at Yazov's front gate. Estrada was driving and pushed the intercom button.

"Yes?" Kincaid said.

Estrada glanced at Mosqueda, grinned and turned back to the intercom. "Señores Mosqueda and Estrada to see Señor Kincaid."

"This is Amos Kincaid. You may pass."

As soon as their car had cleared the gate, Mosqueda turned to the two men hunched down in the backseat and nodded. Estrada slowed the vehicle to a crawl and the two shooters slithered out of either side of the backseat like deadly serpents.

Wes and I were on the north side of Yazov's villa. Buck was positioned on the south side. Alexsie had taken up a position inside the house. Amos was waiting at the door.

I watched as the two men slid out of the backseat of Mosqueda's car. I keyed my hand-held two-way radio and whispered into the mic. "Mosqueda and

Estrada are in the vehicle. The two shooters are trailing on each flank."

Amos acknowledged, followed by Alexsie and Buck.

Estrada parked the rental car, and he and Mosqueda walked down the tree-lined entry. Amos met them at the front door.

"Gentlemen. Welcome to my humble dwelling. Come in," Amos said, casting a quick glance around the entryway.

Mosqueda noticed the glance. "Not to worry, señor. We are alone."

Smooth as a Cohiba, Amos thought. "Of course. Come gentlemen, *mi casa es su casa*. May I get you a drink?"

Both men nodded. "Cuba Libre," Mosqueda said, taking in the grandeur of the villa. Kincaid looked at Estrada, who nodded.

"I had no idea a deputy chief could afford such a place," Mosqueda said, arching his right eyebrow.

Kincaid laughed and stepped over to the well-stocked bar. "Well, there are certain perks that come with the job."

Mosqueda nodded. "*Sí*, like seizing cash from Cuban nationals?"

Kincaid snorted and prepared three Cuba Libres without replying. He handed Mosqueda and Estrada their drinks, and then picked up his own.

"Gentlemen," Kincaid said, holding up his glass, "here's to dirty money."

*****

Outside, Mosqueda's two assassins had worked their way to the open French doors off the pools. The man on the north side of the villa was just about to go inside when Wes and I stepped out of the shrubbery. My silenced .22 was pointed directly at the man's right ear-hole.

The man jumped back a half step when he saw me, but any thought of action was dismissed when Wes put the barrel of his .22 against the back of the man's neck.

I held my left index finger to my lips and whispered, "*Silencio*."

On the south side of the villa, Buck had tried the same move. But his man had spun, trying desperately to bring his Glock 9mm to bear on Buck.

No one, not even the dead guy, heard the small pop from Buck's .22. The 36-grain, hollow-point bullet took Mosqueda's goon through his right eye.

Inside the villa, Mosqueda finished his drink and set his glass down on a side table. "You have our money, señor?"

Kincaid cupped his drink in his right hand and looked at Mosqueda. "I have $100,000 in my briefcase, there by the bar," Kincaid said, gesturing with his free hand. "The rest is in a safe deposit box at FirstCaribbean National Bank, just up the island in Road Town."

Kincaid saw the flash of anger in Mosqueda's eyes. "I thought the exchange was to be made here . . . tonight?"

Kincaid snuffled. "And what would stop you from killing me after I turned over all the funds?"

Mosqueda cut a quick glance at Estrada and then looked back at Kincaid. "I do not care for surprises."

Kincaid cut him off. "Yeah, well, I don't care for a bullet in the back of the head. You get the hundred grand tonight, and tomorrow we'll meet at the bank and you'll get the rest; inside the bank, where I doubt even you aren't dumb enough to start shooting."

Kincaid could see the color rising in Mosqueda's cheeks. But there was something else—a hint of nervousness.

"Something wrong, Señor Mosqueda?" Kincaid asked. "You seem nervous." He paused. "If you're worried about your two men—don't be."

Mosqueda started. "My compliments, señor. I have underestimated you."

Kincaid smiled and gestured for the two Cubans to look behind them. "Indeed."

Wes and I pushed Mosqueda's shooter through the open French door into the living room. We followed close behind—guns up and out.

A moment later, Buck stepped into the living area from the south side of the villa. I looked at Buck, wondering where the second shooter was. Buck looked at me and shrugged.

One down, three to go.

Kincaid was savoring the moment. He walked over to the bar and picked up his aluminum briefcase.

"Come into my study and I'll give you the hundred thousand."

Wes, Buck, and I covered the Cubans as we all followed Amos into the study.

Kincaid turned to Mosqueda as soon as he entered the study. "I know you said you don't like surprises, but I'm afraid I have one more for you."

Yazov's high-backed desk chair was facing away from our little entourage. Slowly the chair swiveled around to face us.

"Yazov!" Mosqueda yelled, his knees buckling.

Alexsie put his feet up on his desk. The .22 automatic and silencer very visible in his right hand.

"Comrade Mosqueda, Comrade Estrada, we meet again."

Wes and I pulled plastic ties from our pants pockets and bound our three prisoners' hands behind them. I pulled Mosqueda's cinch extra tight. He flinched.

I leaned forward and whispered in his ear. "That's for Tommy, you son of a bitch."

Mosqueda sneered. "The Grumman pilot with the deformed ears?"

I handed my pistol to Buck, cupped both my hands and popped Mosqueda hard on both ears. He dropped like TV interviewer John Stossel when pro-wrestler David Schultz *eared* him. Stossel got more than 400 grand in the settlement. I didn't see a settlement in Mosqueda's future.

"They're called cauliflower ears, dickhead," I said, jerking Mosqueda to his feet. "He got them wrestling."

Alexsie looked at me and smiled. “Where is the other shooter?”

Buck handed my pistol back to me and looked at Alexsie. “He’s by the south pool. He won’t be joining us.”

Kincaid walked over to Alexsie’s desk and placed his aluminum briefcase on it. He popped the latches and took out ten bundles of $100 bills. He placed the bundles side by side on the polished mahogany desk. “There’s the 100 grand, Señor Mosqueda. Take a good look; it’s as close as you’re ever going to get.”

Kincaid winked at Alexsie and closed his briefcase. He turned and looked at Wes and me. “Gentlemen, I believe that concludes our business here, does it not?”

Alexsie tapped the silencer of his .22 automatic against the palm of his left hand. “Yes. I believe I can take it from here. Unless any of you would care to stay?”

Chapter 35

A low-pressure zone trying to get its act together over the Caribbean made the flight back to Cancún pretty rough. But probably not as rough as what Mosqueda and company were facing on Tortola.

We landed in the Yucatan and topped off the tanks for the final leg into Brownsville. And said goodbye to Deputy Chief Amos Kincaid.

Wes stayed with the refueling crew while Buck and I walked Amos over to the commercial terminal. Wes was damned particular about what went into the King Air's tanks. No argument there.

"Well, Amos, as you like to say, 'Very well done, indeed'," I said, patting him on the back.

Amos turned and shook hands with Buck and me. "Yes, all's well that ends well . . . I suppose."

"Second thoughts, Amos?" I asked.

Amos shook his head. "No, not really. But I would have preferred to put the Cubans in jail—for a good long time."

I glanced at Buck and then nodded. “We wouldn’t have been able to hold them, Amos. And don’t forget they blew up Jack Thompson’s plane—and put contracts on you and me.”

Amos grabbed his bag and his aluminum briefcase. “Yes, yes, I know. But still, it rather goes against the grain, if you know what I mean.”

“I do,” I said, putting my hand on his shoulder. “But two bad actors are off the board, and you and I can quit looking over our shoulders.”

Amos smiled and started to walk toward his gate and his flight to Grand Cayman. He took a step and then half-turned and looked back at me. “Can we?”

The flight from Cancún to Brownsville was smoother, at least weather-wise. But the turbulence in my head wouldn’t clear. I kept thinking about what Amos had said. Were we in the clear? I couldn’t shake the feeling that we probably weren’t. And by *we,* I meant Wes, Buck, and me.

The 800-pound gorilla in the room was named Frederick Ochoa. I didn’t think Amos was in any direct danger from the cartel leader, but I was pretty damned sure *we* were.

“South Padre Island dead ahead, boys,” Wes said, pointing out the cockpit window.

I was sitting in the copilot’s seat and reached back across the aisle to grab Buck’s knee. “Wake up, big fella, we’re just about wheels down.”

Buck yawned and stretched. "Boy, that was fast."

I shook my head. Buck could sleep through just about anything. It was a gift I wish I had.

We cleared Immigration and Customs without a hitch. I was, after all, still the county sheriff.

Wes decided to stay with his plane to do some maintenance. Buck's truck was at the airport and he gave me a ride to my place. Technically, I still had a few days of vacation time left and I was in no hurry to check in with my office.

"Thanks for the lift, pard," I said, shaking hands with Buck.

Buck held my grip for a second and looked at me. "Not a problem, Stainless. Why don't you give Rory a call? Take her out and have some fun. Forget about the goddamned Cubans, Russians, and that Nazi runt south of the border. At least for a while."

I climbed out of Buck's truck, grabbed my gear from the bed and leaned back into the open passenger window. "Sounds like good advice, Buckmeister. You should call Dotty and do likewise."

Buck chuckled. "By God, I believe I will."

Duty got the better of me and I called Betty at the office. Ochoa's men hadn't parachuted into Brownsville and assaulted our building, so I told her I'd see her on Monday.

I hung up and called Rory. She picked up on the fourth ring. "Hey, babe, I'm back."

"Hardin! I'm so glad you're back. Is everybody okay?"

I wondered if *everybody* included Alexsie, but decided not to ruin the moment. "Yeah, everybody's okay." I paused to see if she'd ask. She didn't.

Rory exhaled softly. "Thank God. And is the problem with the Cubans taken care of?"

A line from *The Godfather* ran through my head. "*Oh, Paulie . . . won't see him no more.*" But I didn't use it. "Mosqueda and Estrada are in good hands. They won't bother us again."

"Good," Rory replied.

Before she delved any deeper, I jumped in. "Listen, how about dinner on the island?"

"Sounds good. I'm at the ranch; can I meet you at your place?"

"Sure, we can have a drink and watch the sun go down. And I brought you something from Tortola."

"Better not be the Cubans' ears," Rory said with a chuckle.

"Hmmm. Okay. I'll keep those for my collection. But I do have a little something else."

"I'll be there at six."

"Perfect. Hey, how's Robert Lee?"

"He's fine, Hardin. It was a small stroke. No lasting side effects. And he'll be glad to hear you're back."

"Good, glad to hear that. And by the way, Alexsie is doing fine. His left eye suffered a bit of damage and he's wearing an eye patch, but it just adds to his character."

There was a pause. "Thanks for telling me, Hardin."

I stoked up the blender at a quarter past six. Rory was always fashionably late. At 6:20, I heard the crunch of tires on ground-up oyster shells. I turned and looked out my front screen door. Rory's black Land Rover was pulling into my driveway.

I hit purée and walked to the door. I watched her climb out of the high-riding Land Rover. She was in her beach togs: khaki shorts, blue denim shirt, and flip-flops. Damn, she looked good.

I pushed the screen door open and held it for her. She stopped in the doorway and gave me a hug.

"I'm so glad you back safe and sound," she said, looping her right arm around my waist. "And I'm so glad this mess is over."

She saw the look on my face. "It is over, isn't it?"

I nodded and guided her to the blender. I needed a drink. "The Cuban problem has been resolved, thanks in large part to Deputy Chief Kincaid." I paused. "And in no small part to Alexsie."

Rory grimaced. "Did they hurt him badly?"

"Well, they didn't kill him. But they would have if Vasily hadn't showed up."

Rory looked stunned. "Vasily was involved? The same Vasily I met in Tampico?"

"One and the same. He put Ochoa's old Huey to good use. And to answer your question, yeah, they gave Alexsie a pretty bad time."

I left out the part about Vasily and his boss later being killed.

Rory arched her perfect eyebrows and nodded. "You left the Cubans with Alexsie?"

"Why don't we have a margarita and watch the sun go down," I replied, pouring us each a drink.

Rory took her drink. "You're not going to tell me about it, are you?"

I smiled. "Someday, after we're married and you can't be made to testify against me, I'll tell you all about it."

"*Married*?"

I chuckled. "Come on, let's go out on the deck. It's the best time of the day. And I brought you a little something from Tortola," I said, handing her a small gift-wrapped box.

"What is it?" Rory asked, still rattled from my *married* comment.

I chuckled. "Don't worry, babe, it's not an engagement ring. Open it."

Rory pulled off the small bow and tore off the gift wrapping. She opened the small jewelry box. "It's beautiful, Hardin . . . what is it?"

I laughed. "It's a necklace."

Rory punched me in the shoulder. "I know that, silly. I mean what kind of stone is it?"

"It's called Larimar. They dig it out of volcanic rock on some of the islands in the Caribbean."

Rory took the necklace out of the box and held the cabochon-cut, light bluish-green stone in her hand. "It's the color of the Caribbean Sea. It's beautiful."

I took the necklace from her hand and fastened it around her neck. “Yeah, looks pretty damn good . . . and so do you.”

We decided to skip driving over to South Padre Island. We ordered pizza, emptied the blender, and enjoyed each other’s company.

The next morning, I scrambled some eggs while Rory showered. My cell phone was on the counter, next to the stove. I jumped when it rang and flipped some egg on the backsplash.

Caller ID showed it was Wes. “Ochoa better be in a landing craft invading Padre Island.”

Wes laughed. “Not yet, but you’re not far off.”

I lowered the heat to simmer. “What’s up?”

“One of my old contacts in Matamoros called—this guy hates Ochoa even more that we do.”

“Uh-huh. And?”

“And word is the little Nazi-loving SOB is moving a large shipment of coke.”

“He’s a drug dealer, Wes. That’s what drug dealers do.”

“No shit, Stainless. Is that how it works?”

I paused for a second and wiped the egg off the backsplash. “Sorry, Wes. I didn’t mean to be flippant. What have you got?”

“My contact says the dope is coming into the U.S. at La Paloma. And that Ochoa himself is going to oversee delivery.”

La Paloma is a small town on the U.S. side of the Rio Grande, about sixteen miles upriver from Brownsville. And, for a change, in my jurisdiction.

"Okay, you've got my attention," I said, giving the eggs a quick stir. "Have you ever known Ochoa to accompany a shipment?"

Wes thought about it for a couple of seconds. "Not since he was a young up-and-comer."

"Kind of makes you wonder, don't it," I said.

"Think it's a setup?"

"Could be, pard. I mean, why would Ochoa take a chance like that? And why La Paloma? Which happens to be just up-river from three guys he'd like to see dead."

"So what're you going to do, Hardin?"

I added a little salt and pepper to the eggs. "Well, pal, it's an FIYD situation."

Wes laughed. "A what?"

"FIYD. Fucked if you do, and fucked if you don't."

Rory walked in as I was explaining the FIYD principle to Wes. She looked at the eggs and then at me. "Who's fucking who, babe?"

I pointed to my cell phone and mouthed the word, "Wes."

Rory smiled. "So Wes is fucked?"

I rolled my eyes and covered the phone with my free hand. "Have some eggs."

"Hardin, you still there?" Wes asked.

"Yes. Sorry. Rory just walked in. Listen, get all the info you can on when the drop is going down. And get back to me."

Chapter 36

Rory and I spent all day Saturday relaxing and doing very little but each other. Sunday morning I called Buck to see if I could borrow *my* boat for a little fishing. He said I could if I cleaned and fueled it when I was done.

Buck savored opportunities to remind me that without his intervention, Margaret, the life-sucking ex-wife from whom there is no escape, would've taken my boat—like she had everything else.

Having acceded to Captain Buck Bligh's demands, Rory and I loaded my Jeep with fishing gear and headed for Rick's Marina. High tide was at three p.m., and I liked to fish the small coves and inlets on the incoming tide.

By 3:30, we had three eating-sized reds and one nice speckled trout. More than enough for supper.

When we got back to Rick's, Buck was waiting on the pier.

"Come to oversee the refueling and cleanup?" I asked, only half in jest.

I threw Buck a line and he tied off the bow.

"Not entirely. We need to talk, Hardin."

I could see he was serious. "Okay. Just give me a minute to tie off the stern and help Rory with our gear and catch."

Buck looked in our cooler. "Wow. Y'all did pretty good."

Rory smiled and nodded. "Yeah, we've got plenty. Follow us over to my condo and we'll grill up some fillets."

"Thanks, Rory, but I'll have to take a rain check. Dotty's waiting for me in town. But I need a minute with Stainless."

Rory grabbed an armful of gear and poles and winked at me. "I'll wait for you at the Jeep, babe."

I smiled and winked back and waited for Buck to get to it.

"Sorry to bother you on a Sunday, Hardin, but Wes has been trying to get hold of you."

I nodded. "I left my cell phone on the charger. So what's up?"

"Wes said to tell you he has solid confirmation that Ochoa will be in Matamoros this coming Friday."

"Did he tell you about the dope going into La Paloma?"

Buck nodded. "He did. And I don't like it, Hardin. It smells like a big-time setup to me."

"Yeah, I think the deal is as fishy as those reds we just caught. But La Paloma is in my jurisdiction. If that little SOB comes across the ditch, I intend to nail his sorry ass."

Buck grunted. "I figured that was the plan. Call Wes when you get a chance, will ya?"

"Yep, just as soon as I get this here boat fueled and hosed down."

Buck laughed. "I was kidding about that, Hardin. I have a kid who'll take care of the boat. You just take care of yourself and Rory." Buck paused for a moment. "Of course, I'll be going along."

I grabbed the rest of my gear from the boat and stepped onto the dock. "Going where?"

"La Paloma."

I smiled and looked at Buck. "I never thought otherwise, amigo."

Later that evening, after Rory and I polished off a couple of grilled redfish fillets, I called Wes. "Hey, pard, it's Hardin. Sorry I missed your call. I was out fishing with Rory. But I ran into Buck at Rick's and he filled me in."

"Good. So what do you think?"

"I think if Ochoa gets past the middle of the river, I'm going to take him down."

"DOA?" Wes asked.

"I think it best."

"That's pretty much what I figured," Wes said, pausing. "Just promise me one thing, old buddy . . ."

"If I can."

"Don't cross the river. Don't go into Mexico."

"You think it's a setup?"

"Don't you?"

I didn't say anything for a couple of seconds. "You can't be in on this, Wes."

"Uh-huh. Well, you and Buck and your deputies work your side of the street and I'll work mine."

"Meaning?" I said, my tone a bit sharper than I'd intended.

"Meaning, if Señor Ochoa doesn't cross the river, and I get the chance, I'll put him down for you."

Monday morning, I was in my office before seven a.m. I looked at my desk and shook my head. It's flat amazing how much damn paperwork can pile up.

At a quarter till eight my cell phone buzzed. I looked at Caller ID. It was an incoming international call. Area code 284, wherever the hell that was.

I hit Talk. "Sheriff Steel."

"Good morning from Tortola, Sheriff."

I recognized the voice immediately. "Alexsie. How did you get this number? No, check that . . . is everything copacetic?"

Alexsie chuckled. "Yes, yes. No problems in paradise. Our Cuban friends recently departed on an extended sea voyage and everything is back to normal. However, I think you may have a small problem on your end."

"Ochoa?"

Alexsie didn't reply for a moment. "You are on your game, Hardin. How did you know?"

"Wes Stoddard. He still has good connections south of the river."

"Ahhh, yes, I should have guessed," Alexsie said. "It's a setup, Hardin. Ochoa lost a good deal of face because of you, and he's looking for payback."

"That seems to be the consensus of opinion up here as well."

"Do you have a plan?"

"Yes. I plan to stay on my side of the river."

Alexsie laughed. "Good plan." The Russian paused for a moment. "Perhaps I could be of service?"

"Possibly. God knows you've earned a shot at that SOB."

"Indeed. And he had my friend Vasily killed. A man to whom I owed more than my life."

I thought about Alexsie's offer for a long moment.

"Hardin?"

"Yes, I'm still here. Listen, I'm going to give you Wes's cell number. Coordinate with him." I paused. "Alexsie, do not, under any circumstances, cross into the U.S. Do you understand me?"

"The DEA agents?"

"Yeah, Alexsie, the DEA agents—the dead ones."

"An unfortunate situation, Hardin," Alexsie said, pausing for a moment. "I took out the men responsible. Doesn't that count for anything?"

"Not much," I said.

"Understandable," Alexsie replied. "Give me Wes's number. If you don't get Ochoa on your side of the river, I'll do my best to take him down on our side. Fair enough?"

"Only after the delivery is made," I said. "I want the coke. And remember what I said about crossing the river."

*****

By Wednesday, I had a new and improved plan. I called Buck and told him to be at my office in an hour. While I waited for Buck, I did some paperwork and called Wes.

"Wes, Hardin. Did our Russian friend show up?"

"Yeah, he's here with me now."

"Good. Anything new on Ochoa?"

"Alexsie and I have been working our contacts. Ochoa will be in Matamoros tomorrow. The shipment is due to cross at La Paloma, Friday at dawn. They're ferrying it across on an airboat. Those things are fast, Hardin, and can run across a mudflat."

"Roger that. Good work, Wes. And don't worry, I'll be ready."

Wes paused for a couple of seconds. "Listen, Hardin, there's a slight chance Alexsie and I might have an opportunity, while Ochoa's in Matamoros to . . ."

I cut Wes off. "No. I want the coke, too. If you take out Ochoa beforehand, the drop won't happen."

"Understood," Wes said, but I could hear the disappointment in his voice. "Okay. The big Ruskie and I will be on Ochoa's six. If you don't get him, we'll give it our best shot—no pun intended."

I'd just hung up with Wes when Betty buzzed me. "Buck Bateman is here to see you, Sheriff."

"Send him in, Betty."

Less than a minute later, there was a tap on my office door and Buck walked in.

I stood up from behind my desk. "Raise your right hand."

Buck smiled and looked at me like I'd sprung a leak. "*What*?"

"You heard me. Raise your right hand and repeat after me."

I swore Buck in as a deputy sheriff. "Have a seat, deputy."

I pulled open the middle drawer of my desk, grabbed a badge and flipped it to Buck. "Here, wear this. And get a couple of uniform shirts and a hat from supply before you leave."

Buck was grinning like he'd won 100 bucks on a scratch-off lottery ticket.

"It's a temporary appointment, Buck. Just until we take Ochoa off the board."

Buck nodded. "Or until he takes us off the board."

I smiled at my newest deputy. "Whichever comes first."

Chapter 37

Ochoa was no fool. He figured Wes would hear about the upcoming cocaine shipment. But just to be absolutely sure, he had one of his lieutenants leak details of the delivery to a couple of Wes's contacts.

Ochoa knew Wes would pass any information on to me. What he didn't know was that Wes and Yazov would be on his six, and I'd be on his front. And I had a few surprises for his flanks.

Dawn comes in a hurry on the Rio Grande. Buck and I, along with two of my best *real* deputies, Rodriquez and Allen, had been in position since 3:30 a.m.

Daybreak was lighting up the horizon to the east, exposing a misty fog rising from the tepid, opaque waters of the Rio Grande.

I looked over at Buck and keyed my two-way radio. I whispered into the mike, "Get ready."

Buck and I were concealed on a low bluff just downstream from a well-used trail. A route that'd been used by smugglers for more than 100 years. Deputies Allen and Rodriquez were well hidden on the opposite side of the rocky path.

Buck had a pair of binoculars and was glassing the far bank. He nudged me and passed me the binocs. He tilted his head toward the far bank and whispered, "Showtime."

I took the binoculars and sighted in on the opposite bank, where the old trail came down to the river. A pickup truck with no lights on was backing a boat and trailer into the shallow river. It was, as Wes had foretold, an airboat.

The men floated the boat off the trailer and pulled the craft close ashore and began loading black packages, each about the size of two Brownsville phonebooks, into the airboat.

On our side, a crew-cab pickup towing an aluminum horse trailer appeared at the top of the trail. The driver found a well-used wide spot, turned the truck and trailer around, and began slowly backing down the old trail toward the river.

I keyed my mic and whispered as low as I could. "Wait until they start off-loading the dope."

I watched the men across the river loading bundle after bundle into the airboat.

Buck half-turned his head and whispered, "Do you see Ochoa?"

I barely shook my head. "Not yet . . . wait one."

A smallish figure stepped out of the pickup across the river and walked down to the airboat. It was still false dawn, but in the half-light it looked like Ochoa.

I slid the binocs to Buck. “The little guy by the airboat.”

Buck squinted in the low light. “Yeah. It’s our pal Ochoa. And he’s getting in the boat.”

Rather than fire up the airboat, the smugglers elected to paddle the flat-bottomed boat across the river.

I looked at Buck. “Think they’re worried about noise?”

Buck shrugged. “Could be. Those damn airboats are loud.” Buck hesitated. “Notice anything else, Hardin?”

I took the binocs back from Buck and watched the smugglers rowing hard against the current. “No.”

“Look again, Stainless,” Buck whispered. “I don’t see any weapons.”

I took another look. “You’re right. I don’t see even a pistol.”

“You ever come across an unarmed drug smuggler?” Buck asked.

I shook my head. “Not recently.”

Buck nodded. “Uh-huh. Me neither. Something stinks.”

By now the airboat had made it across the Rio Grande and the smugglers were busy unloading the dope. I keyed my radio and called two deputies I had waiting downstream in one of the sheriff’s department’s patrol boats.

It was time to cover the flanks and move on the smugglers. I keyed my mic again and called Rodriquez and Allen. “Move in.”

Buck and I moved down a game trail that paralleled the old smugglers route. When we were opposite the horse trailer, I pulled a small flare gun from my backpack and fired off a red flare. A second later, Buck and I rushed the *contrabandistas*. At the same instant, Deputies Rodriquez and Allan burst out of the brush just upstream and closed on the smugglers.

“*Manos arriba! Ahora!*” I shouted as Buck and I ran toward the small group of men.

The smugglers froze and raised their hands. They all turned toward the river as they heard our patrol boat approaching.

I glanced across the river and watched the driver of the pickup drop the boat trailer and haul ass.

Buck grabbed Ochoa and pulled him roughly out of the airboat. “We’ve got a little problem, Sheriff,” Buck said, holding up Ochoa’s right hand. “This ain’t Ochoa.”

“What?” I said, looking at the diminutive man. “He looks like him to me.”

Buck shook his head. “No burns on his hands. No gloves. This is a goddamned doppelganger.”

I looked at the man Buck was holding. “*Sprechen sie deutsch*?”

The frightened little man looked at me like I was speaking an alien language. “*¿Como se llama*?” I asked.

"Santiago Ramirez," the man replied, never taking his eyes off the big gringo holding his right arm.

I looked at Buck and frowned. "You're right, Buck. That sure as hell isn't the most feared cartel leader in all of Mexico."

Buck nodded. "We've been had, pardner."

I motioned for Deputies Rodriquez and Allen to come forward. "Y'all cover the munchkin and his helpers." I tilted my head toward the boat. "Buck, let's check out the cargo."

Buck released Ochoa's double and told him in Spanish to stand over with his buddies.

Buck looked at me. "Are you thinking what I'm thinking?"

"Uh-huh. Six will get you ten, there's no dope on this old scow."

Buck snorted. "Scow is right. This tub has been gutted. There's no engine. No propeller. It's a damn shell."

I stepped over to the boat. "Which explains why they rowed it across the river." I pointed to one of the black plastic bundles neatly stacked in the bottom of the boat. "Toss me one of those, Buck."

I caught the bundle, squeezed and hefted it. "Feels right," I said, pulling out my pocketknife.

I slit the black plastic wrapping from end to end, and pried open the packet. And then I laughed.

"You hungry, Buck?" I said, tossing him the bundle.

Buck caught the package and tore it open. "Tortillas! Are you friggin' kidding me?"

I smiled and shook my head. “As you said, amigo, we’ve been had.”

I walked over to my two deputies. “Any weapons on these boys?”

Deputy Rodriquez shook his head. “No, sir. They are unarmed.”

I looked at Buck and shook my head. “Okay, Alex, cut ’em loose.”

Deputy Rodriquez looked at me. “Don’t you want to know who hired them?”

I took a cigar from my shirt pocket, trimmed the end and fired it up. I inhaled, blew out a perfect smoke ring, and watched it drift toward the river. “I know who hired them, Alex. Kick ’em loose. And let them keep the tortillas.”

Chapter 38

The local papers dubbed it the "Great Tortilla Raid," and I took a lot of ribbing. Most of it good-natured. But I was still waiting for *the* call.

A few days after the headlines, I got the call I'd been expecting. Caller ID said "Unknown," but I knew who was on the other end.

"Señor Ochoa, I presume?" I said, answering the phone.

Ochoa actually chuckled, sort of. "Very perceptive, Sheriff."

There was a brief pause on the line and I knew what was coming.

"Sheriff Steel, I understand you made a significant bust down on the river the other day."

I was ready. "Yes, sir. My deputies and I seized a load of contraband tortillas that would have flooded our local markets and caused irreparable damage to consumers."

This time the little Nazi bastard actually laughed. "Good for you, Sheriff. And did you learn anything from your experience?"

"Yes, sir. I learned you're a sneaky little bastard. And I want you to know, I've moved you to the top of my most-wanted list."

Ochoa snorted. "Have you, indeed? And how do you plan to get me, Sheriff?"

"Any way I can."

"So am I to assume the *game* is on?"

"You may assume the last thing you'll see will be me pissing on your dying carcass."

"Bravo. Well said, Sheriff. I look forward to the contest. And by the way, is Comrade Yazov still in Matamoros, or is he back on Tortola?"

Boy, this guy knows which buttons to push. "Who?" I said.

Ochoa almost chucked, again. "You may tell Alexsie that both you and he are at the top of *my* list."

I started to lose it, but reined in my temper. "I'll be seeing you, Ochoa. And I'm going to do my best to arrange a little *face time* for you with Der Führer—if you get my drift."

I hung up before the little prick could reply.

I took a cigar from the humidor on my desk and fired it up. It took both hands to hold the damn match steady.

When the nicotine overpowered the adrenaline, I called Wes. "Wes, Hardin. You'll never guess who just called me."

"Gruma?"

"*Who*?"

"Gruma. They're the largest manufacturer of tortillas in the world."

I took a long drag on my cigar and put my feet up on my desk. "Very funny, amigo. No, it wasn't Gruma; I have a conference call with them in the morning. No, this was a call from your favorite inn-keeper down Mazatlán way."

"Ochoa called you?"

"Yeah."

"What did he . . ." Wes laughed. "The tortilla bust?"

"That, and to tell me Yazov and I are on the top of his hit parade."

"He knew Yazov was in Mexico?"

"In Matamoros, to be more specific," I replied. "And he knows about Alexsie's place on Tortola."

"Jesus, is there anything that guy doesn't know?"

"Not much."

"So, I assume you have a plan?"

I paused for a moment and knocked the ash off the end of my cigar into an ashtray. "Yeah. Get Ochoa . . . before he gets us."

"*Us*?"

"Yes, *us*. You think he doesn't know Alexsie was with you?"

"Good point, Hardin. Should I call Yazov, or do you want to do it?"

"Is he back on Tortola?"

"Yeah."

"You get your ass back to Brownsville. Be at my place at seven. We'll call Yazov then."

"What about Buck."

"I'll round him up."

Wes chuckled. "I sense a *reckoning* is about to happen."

"A what?" I wasn't used to Wes using high-powered English.

"A reckoning. A final settlement of accounts."

"Could be, Wes, could be. I'll see you at seven."

Ochoa's ranks had been decimated by Vasily's attack on his compound and the strafing at El Cid Marina. He was in the process of recruiting additional men. But for the Yazov sanction, he decided to go outside the local labor pool and bring in a pro.

Ochoa opened the upper right-hand drawer of his desk and retrieved his satellite phone. He walked out of his study onto the balcony overlooking the Mar de Cortéz. From memory, he punched in the country code for Argentina, the city code for Buenos Aires, and a private number very few people knew.

Ludwig Duerr answered his private line. "*Ja*?"

Ochoa replied in fluent German. "Ludwig, it's Frederick. I am in need of one of your best specialists."

Buck and I had the blender in overdrive when Wes pulled up to my place. He parked his Corvette, walked to my front screen door, opened it slightly, and tossed in a package of tortillas. "Don't shoot, I'm unarmed."

I looked at Buck and shook my head. "There's always a smart-ass in the crowd."

Buck nodded and called out, "Come around to the back. We don't take deliveries at the front of the house."

I handed Buck a margarita. "Well said, amigo."

We could hear Wes laughing. "I'm coming in. Hold your fire."

"Come ahead," I said, pouring a margarita for our humorous friend.

Wes strode in, stopping to scoop up the package of tortillas. "Sorry, boys, I just couldn't resist."

I held out a margarita.

Buck gave him the finger.

Wes laughed and took the margarita. "So, I understand we're at the top of Ochoa's *hit* list?"

I took a swallow of my margarita and nodded. "So the little runt says. But my guess is he whacks Yazov before he messes with us."

Wes set his drink down on my coffee table and pulled out his cell phone. "Should I make the call?"

I nodded. "Get him on the line, then let me talk to him."

Wes tapped in the numbers. "It's two hours later down there." He paused. "Alexsie, you old commie bastard, it's Wes, Buck, and Hardin. Hold on a sec, Hardin needs to speak to you."

Wes grinned and handed me his cell phone.

"Alexsie, Hardin."

"Evening, Sheriff. Don't tell me you have another Cuban problem?"

I shook my head and glanced at my two friends. "No, it's not Cubans."

Alexsie could tell by my tone this wasn't a social call.

"Ochoa?" he asked.

"Uh-huh. The little bastard called me. Congratulated me on the tortilla bust, and informed me he was going to take us out."

"*Us*?"

"Yeah. You and me. And I doubt Wes and Buck will get a pass."

I could hear Alexsie take a deep breath and exhale. "I see. But from what I remember of Vasily's airborne assault, he did a damn good job of shooting up Ochoa's crew."

"That could be a double-edged sword, Alexsie," I said.

The Russian paused for half a second. "You think he'll go outside his normal group, or what's left of it?"

"I would," I replied. "I'd find an unfamiliar face. A pro that's not well known in the west."

Alexsie paused again. "Buenos Aires."

I hadn't thought about Ochoa's reputed connection to ODESSA. "Damn, Alexsie, the war's been over a hell of a long time. You think they're still active?"

Alexsie laughed. "Go down to Argentina and start asking questions about former Nazis."

"Understood," I said, glancing at Buck and Wes. "So how would you recommend we proceed?"

"From my end, it will be difficult, Hardin. As you can imagine, Russians aren't too well regarded in Argentina, especially by those of German descent."

"I *can* imagine," I said. "I don't have any contacts in that area of the world, either," I added, looking over at my two compadres to see if either had his hand up. Neither did.

"Well, forewarned is forearmed," I said. "See what you can dig up, and we'll do likewise. Let's touch base again in two days. And Alexsie . . ."

"Yes?"

"Watch yourself. Whoever Ochoa uses, they will be off the radar and deadly."

Chapter 39

The assassin Ludwig Duerr procured for Ochoa was known only as *Adawulf*, which in Old High German meant "Nobel Wolf."

Adawulf was the perfect for the job. He had no distinguishing features, was neither good-looking nor ugly, of average height, and fluent in half a dozen languages. He melded into the population, passing easily through Customs and Immigration, looking like a common, ordinary businessman. In short, the perfect assassin.

Adawulf preferred to work in Europe and South America. But Duerr had prevailed on him to take this job. Ochoa was, after all, a major contributor to the cause.

Ochoa put a together a detailed dossier on Yazov: photos, background information, everything he had on the Russian. He had one of his men take the package to the DHL office on Av. Camarón Sábalo in

Mazatlán. Duerr would have the dossier in two days and would see that it got delivered to Adawulf.

The DHL office was near El Cid Marina, which seemed only fitting to Ochoa.

Two days later, as agreed, I called Yazov. It rang a long time and I was about to hang up when Alexsie answered. "Hardin?"

"Yes. Everything okay?"

Alexsie chuckled. "I was in the pool . . . giving a young lady a swimming lesson."

Obviously the big Russian wasn't too worried about lurking assassins. "Anything to report?"

"Sorry, Hardin. As I told you, it is very difficult for me to obtain information from that region."

I rubbed the day-old stubble on my chin. "Same here. Even Wes has no contacts that far south. But I guess no news is good news."

Alexsie grunted. "I doubt it. My gut feeling is Ochoa is moving ahead. Unfortunately, we won't know it's going down until one of us is shot in the head."

Not what I wanted to hear. "Roger that," I said, feeling like things were spiraling out of control. "Watch yourself, and stay in touch. And I'll do likewise."

Alexsie was right, of course. The following Friday, Adawulf was on a private jet, making his way to Tortola. The plane was a three-engine, French-made,

Dassault Falcon 7X, with a range of more than 5900 miles. Buenos Aires to Tortola was a bit more than 3600 miles.

Adawulf smiled as he watched the plane's track on a TV screen mounted on the front bulkhead. The plane belonged to a consortium of high-level Nationalist-Socialist industrialists, which is to say, a bunch of rich Nazis.

This particular Falcon had been modified. There were a number of hidden compartments where contraband could be stored. For this trip, Adawulf had stowed an aluminum case holding his favorite sniper rifle in one of the larger compartments. He wasn't overly concerned about Customs inspections in Tortola. But young assassins got to be old assassins by being careful.

Ludwig Duerr and his group maintained close relationships with a number of the larger banks in the BVI. And this particular Falcon was well known by airport authorities. Along with the fact that the pilots were most generous when they paid their landing fees.

Adawulf took a sip of his club soda, slipped off his Santoni calfskin oxfords—top-quality shoes were the one indulgence he allowed himself—and reclined his seat. He was looking forward to a few days in the islands, and to dispatching the Russian.

After my conversation with Alexsie, I spent the balance of the week busy with the duties of a county sheriff. I was relieved when quitting time rolled around on Friday.

It had been a relatively quiet week, as sheriffs' weeks go. No shootings, no fatal stabbings, not too many drunk drivers plowing into something, or someone. Just a normal run-of-the-mill week . . . for a change.

And no calls from Alexsie, which I decided to take as good news. I should've known better.

The minute hand of the 100-year-old Regulator wall clock hanging in my office grudgingly slipped the final notch, and the official workday and week were over.

I went home, shucked my uniform, took a shower, put on some jeans and a T-shirt, and called Rory.

"Hey, babe. Any plans for the weekend?"

"Just seeing you."

"Sounds good. Where are you?"

"I'm at the condo. Why don't you come over and join me?"

She didn't have to ask twice. "Be right there."

On my way over to South Padre Island, I stopped and bought some fresh shrimp and a half-case of beer. As I was putting both on ice in my cooler, I was tempted to pop a top and have a cold one on the way to Rory's. But I figured it wouldn't look too good if the county sheriff got arrested for DWI. Especially after the tortilla raid. Although most of my constituents would look on the DWI as the lesser offense.

It was a hot mid-summer late afternoon, but the steady on-shore breeze from the Gulf took the edge off. As I crossed the causeway from Port Isabel over to Padre Island, I could see lots of boaters and fisherman out on Laguna Madre.

Through my polarized sunglasses, I could easily see the channels and clumps of sea grass. Up ahead loomed the condos and hotels and the sandy beach fronting the Gulf. And Rory. For the moment, life was very good.

I pulled into Rory's place about fifteen minutes later. The island was jumping. It always was on a summer weekend.

Rory was out on her dock trying out a new fly rod.

I grabbed my overnight bag and my cooler with the shrimp and beer. "Any luck?" I yelled when she noticed me.

Rory waved. "Put your gear in the house and come on out. I just had a big red follow my fly all the way to the dock."

I put the shrimp and all but two of the beers in the fridge, and headed out the patio door.

Rory's fly rod bent nearly double. "Hardin, get out here! I've hooked something."

Beers in hand, I sprinted down the dock. I got a quick glimpse of the fish's tail and saw a black spot. "It's a red, babe. And a damned big one."

Rory turned and tried to hand me her rod. “Here, Hardin, you take it.”

I stepped back, opened one of the beers and took a long drink. “Hell, no. You can land him.”

“Well, at least give me a drink of beer.”

I smiled and nodded and held the open beer to her mouth. Most of it spilled and ran down the front of her shirt. I put down the beers, took out my trusty bandana, and wiped off as much as I could. Especially over her breasts.

Rory shot me a look. “Forget about the beer and my tits and grab the damn net. I think this big boy’s about done in.”

I grabbed the long-handled net and got down on my knees on the edge of the dock. “Keep his head up and slide him toward the net.”

Rory guided the big red toward me, and I slid the net under the fish, but I kept the net and the fish in the water. “It’s probably a big female,” I said, glancing up at Rory. “What do you want to do?”

“Can you get the fly out?”

I looked at the fish. “Yeah. She’s hooked on her upper lip.”

“Save my fly and let her go, Hardin. She needs to lay her eggs.”

I reached down and pushed the fly out of the big red’s mouth. “Okay, she’s free.”

Rory knelt on the deck beside me and watched the redfish working its gills, pumping oxygen back into its depleted system. “Wow! It’s a magnificent fish. And on a fly, too.”

I nodded. “Yep, you did good, babe. It’s a hell of a fish.” I glanced at Rory. “I think she’s revived. You ready?”

“Yes, let her go.”

I lowered the net deeper into the warm bay water. The red watched us for a moment and then with a flick of her tail was gone.

I handed Rory her beer. “Feels good, doesn’t it?”

She took a long pull on her beer, then looked at me and winked. “Yeah. I think there’s something to this catch-and-release stuff.”

I laughed. “Agreed, but let’s release a few of the smaller ones into a frying pan.”

Adawulf stepped off the plane at the Tortola airport and retrieved his suitcase from the copilot waiting at the bottom of the stairway. “I have an additional piece of luggage, an aluminum case, in one of the onboard compartments, which will require *special* handling,” Adawulf said, glancing at the copilot. “Please see to it that it is delivered discreetly to my hotel as soon as possible.”

The copilot snapped off a salute. “Yes, sir, I will handle it personally. Customs is just over there, sir,” the copilot said, pointing to a small terminal building. “And where shall I deliver your case, and in what name?”

“Surfsong Resort, here on Beef Island. The name is Hollinberry.”

“Very good, sir. I’ll have the case to you this evening.”

Adawulf nodded. "Be very careful with the case."

"Yes, sir. I will take every care."

"See that you do."

The copilot nodded. He sensed Mr. Hollinberry was a lot more dangerous than he looked.

Adawulf made his way to Customs and Immigration. He presented a forged British passport to the immigration officer.

The officer looked at the passport and then at Adawulf. "And what brings you to Tortola, Mr. Hollinberry?"

"A bit of business with one of your financial institutions," Adawulf replied, using his near-perfect British accent.

The immigration officer nodded. "Are you a fisherman, sir?"

Adawulf tried to hide his irritation at the questioning. "Not really. Why do you ask?"

The immigration officer arched his right eyebrow. "Your passport says you're from Stockbridge in Hampshire."

"Yes?"

"Well, I thought you might be a member of the Houghton Fishing Club?"

Adawulf shook his head. "No. I'm afraid I don't have time for fishing."

The immigration officer flipped to the back pages of Hollinberry's passport and stamped an entry visa.

"That's a shame, Mr. Hollinberry. The Test River, which runs through your village, is world renowned for trout fishing."

Adawulf nodded. "Perhaps when I retire, I shall look into joining the club."

The immigration officer handed back Adawulf's forged passport. "Good luck to you, sir. And enjoy your time on Tortola."

Adawulf smiled at the nosy officer, picked up his suitcase and headed toward Customs.

The customs officer gave the approaching *suit* his normal once-over. "Anything to declare, sir?"

Adawulf shook his head and handed over his customs declaration. "No, sir. Not this trip."

The officer took the declaration, checked to be sure it had been signed, and motioned for Adawulf to proceed.

Bloody imbeciles, Adawulf thought as he exited the terminal and waved down a cab.

As there were no commercial flights due in for several hours, the immigration officer left his post and walked over to Customs. "That bloke who came in on the Dassault, did he seem okay to you?"

"A bit curt, but I figured you'd pissed him off."

The immigration officer smiled. "Maybe. He seemed a little irritated when I asked him about fishing."

"Fishing?"

"Yes. His passport said he's from Stockbridge, in the U.K."

"So?"

"So, the Test River runs right through the town of Stockbridge, and it's a world-class trout stream."

"Well, maybe the gentleman is too damned busy to fish."

The immigration officer wrinkled his brow. "Maybe, but I think there's something *fishy* about our British visitor."

The customs officer laughed. "Hell, this is the BVI. A lot of our visitors won't pass the smell test."

Adawulf checked into Surfsong Hotel. His room was ground-level, with sliding-glass doors opening to the beach and a breathtaking view of Well Bay.

He unpacked his suitcase and hung up his business clothes. His "field" clothes, consisting of camouflage military fatigues, black T-shirt, black baseball cap, and black sneakers, went into a drawer.

The flight from Buenos Aires had taken nearly seven hours. Adawulf wanted a shower, a drink, and something to eat. In precisely that order.

After grabbing a quick shower, he changed into khakis, a dark-blue polo shirt and a pair of Johnston & Murphy slip-ons.

He hailed a cab in front of the hotel and crossed the Queen Elizabeth II Bridge to Tortola Island. The cabbie had suggested the Red Rock Restaurant. It was close by, had a good bar and excellent food.

Normally, Adawulf's first order of business would've been to recon his target: look for possible shooting locations, ingress and egress, etcetera. But it was getting late and the sun would be setting shortly.

He preferred not using headlights when he was reconnoitering a target.

The cabbie dropped him at the quaint bayside restaurant.

"Can you return and pick me up in an hour and a half?"

"Certainly, sir. *Bon appetit.*"

Adawulf nodded and walked into the lobby of the restaurant. A very pretty dusky-hued girl approached him. "Dinner or drinks, sir?"

Adawulf smiled. "A bit of both."

The girl flashed him a killer smile.

Perhaps another time, he thought, following the curvy young lady to a table overlooking the bay. "Thank you, miss. And would you please bring me a tall gin and tonic?"

"Right away, sir," the girl replied, handing him a menu.

While he perused the menu, he couldn't help but overhear a rather large, bald-headed gentleman talking and laughing. The man and a lady friend were seated about three tables down. When the bald man turned to signal a waiter, Adawulf got a good look. The fellow bore a striking resemblance to the photos of his target, except for the black eye patch.

A moment later the waitress returned with his gin and tonic. "Excuse me, miss. The large, bald man at the third table down. He looks familiar to me. Do you happen to know who he is?"

The girl turned and looked, and then giggled. "Why, yes, of course. Everybody on the island knows Alexsie. I think his last name is Yazov?"

Adawulf nodded. “I see. No, he’s not who I thought.” He reached into the right front pocket of his slacks and handed the girl a five-pound note. “But thank you for your very kind assistance.”

Yazov always paid attention to his surroundings, one of the reasons he’d survived this long. He’d seen the European-looking gentlemen enter the restaurant, but had written him off as just another businessman mixing a little offshore banking with a short holiday.

But he thought he noticed the man occasionally glancing in his direction. Or was it just his imagination? Perhaps a lifetime of being suspicious of everything had left him a bit paranoid.

Maybe it was the alcohol, maybe the distraction of his date’s ample cleavage, or maybe he was just tired. Whatever the case, Yazov made a rare mistake and blew off the preppy European as just another meddlesome tourist.

Adawulf enjoyed his meal of grilled Mahi-mahi, and allowed himself one additional gin and tonic. Without being too obvious, he watched the Russian. Yazov seemed totally at ease. And why not? The buxom blonde seated with him was hanging on his every word.

Adawulf finished his meal and motioned to a nearby waiter. “Check, please.”

He glanced at the bill and slid enough British pounds under the side of his plate to cover the meal and a generous tip. Getting up, he noticed the Russian glanced, more or less, in his direction.

Adawulf smiled. *The Russian is good, but they're never good enough.* He stepped out into the balmy tropical evening. True to his word, the cabbie was waiting.

Just before nine p.m., the Dassault copilot called from the hotel lobby. "Mr. Hollinberry, it's First Officer Grace. I have the rest of your baggage, sir."

"Very good," Adawulf said, "I'll be right there."

Ten minutes later, Adawulf was back his room. He placed the rectangular aluminum case on his bed, rotated the four dials on the lock, and opened it.

Inside was a disassembled Ruger Mini-14 .223 caliber rifle with steel folding stock and custom pistol grip.

Also in the case was a four-power rifle scope, two ten-round magazines and twenty rounds of precision, hand-loaded ammunition. Adawulf preferred 55-grain, hollow-point bullets for their velocity and devastating fragmentation.

The only thing not in the case was a silencer. Adawulf preferred not to use one, as they reduced muzzle velocity. Instead, he would slide a condom over the muzzle and tape it to the barrel. The condom acted as a small buffer to the sound, but didn't affect the velocity of the bullet.

If all went according to plan—and Adawulf was nothing if not extremely self-confident—the Russian's bald head would disintegrate like a very large, ripe pomegranate.

Chapter 40

They say bad news rides a fast horse . . .

My cell phone went off just as I tossed my keys on my office desk. The area code was one I recognized.

"Alexsie, still dodging assassins?" I said with a chuckle.

There was a pause on the line. "Mr. Steel? Mr. Hardin Steel?"

It wasn't Alexsie, but the call was from the BVI. "Yes, this is Hardin Steel. Who's calling?"

"Mr. Steel, this is Winston Daltry. I am Mr. Yazov's attorney. Or at least, I was."

"*Was*?"

"Yes. Unfortunately, I now represent Mr. Yazov's estate, which is the purpose of my call."

"Slow down, pardner. What happened to Alexsie?"

"I'm sorry, Mr. Steel. I assumed you knew."

"Knew *what*?"

"Well, as a significant beneficiary to Mr. Yazov's estate, I assumed you'd been contacted by a relative or the police."

"Beneficiary?"

"Yes, sir."

"What happened to Alexsie?"

"I am sorry to be the one to tell you, Mr. Steel. Mr. Yazov was shot and killed last week."

I walked over to one of my office windows and looked out. It had the makings of a perfect summer day—until now. "Is anybody in custody?"

"No, sir. No one heard or saw a thing. Mr. Yazov was shot through the back of the head while he was sitting poolside at his villa."

"North pool or south pool?"

Daltry hesitated a moment. "I believe it was the pool on the north side of the house."

I knew there wouldn't be any clues, but I asked anyway. "Any shell-casings, footprints. Anything?"

"According to the police report, sir, nothing related to the shooting was found in or around Mr. Yazov's villa."

I took a deep breath and steadied up. "I see. So what can I do for you, Mr. Daltry?"

Daltry cleared his throat and got back on point. "Well, sir, Mr. Yazov had entrusted me with two documents. One document is a letter addressed to you, to be opened only upon his death. The other document is his last Will and Testament."

I stepped over to the humidor on my desk and took out a Cuban cigar, one Alexsie had given me on

Tortola. I trimmed the end and fired it up. "I'm listening, Mr. Daltry."

"Yes, well, my instructions are to read the letter to you before we get into the will."

I took a deep drag and exhaled a plume of smoke. "Fire away."

Alexsie's lawyer cleared his throat again and started reading:

Hardin, if my attorney is reading this to you, it means Ochoa got the better of me. That being the rather unfortunate case, and as I have no living heirs or surviving friends, I have left the bulk of my estate to you (exluding my holdings in Cuba, for obvious reasons).

Consider it a 'dowry'. If you plan to marry into the rich and powerful Roughton clan, you'll need more than a tin star.

My attorney will explain the terms of the will when he finishes this letter.

For better or for worse, I had a hell of a run. Now I'm off to find Stalin and kick his sorry ass.

I do have one small final request. If at all possible, find the prick who whacked me and return the favor. Same goes for Ochoa.

Long life and happiness, comrade.

—Alexsie.

Daltry paused when he finished. "Well, I must say that is one of the more interesting letters I've read during my career, and certainly begs a number of questions.

"But that aside, I should tell you that Mr. Yazov had me amend his will shortly before he was killed. Basically, Mr. Steel, Mr. Yazov left you all of his holdings in the British Virgin Islands."

I'll admit I was shocked. And being human, the next thoughts that popped into my mind were: *How much and how dirty?* I decided to concentrate on the former. "What kind of holdings?"

"Cash and property, Mr. Steel."

Not wanting to appear too greedy, I changed tack. "So how do we proceed?"

"It would be best if you could come to my office in Tortola. Our probate laws are not all that dissimilar to U.S. law. But there are steps that must be followed and certain documents provided to the court.

"As attorney for Mr. Yazov's estate, I will handle the details. But I think it best if you come down in person. There will be property deeds to execute and bank deposits to transfer. When would be convenient?"

I looked at my calendar. I had to be in court several days this week. And half the local judges were already mad at me. "I can fly in this coming Sunday, and be in your office on Monday morning."

"Excellent. If you will kindly give me your e-mail, I shall have my secretary send you my coordinates."

I gave him my e-mail address and added, "Thanks for letting me know about Alexsie."

"I'm sorry to have been the one to tell you. Murder is a dirty business. I look forward to meeting you on Monday. Good day."

*****

I sat at my desk, pondering what I'd just been told, until my cigar had burned about halfway down. I gently tamped it out in my ashtray and saved the rest for another day. Then I called Buck.

"Morning, Hardin. What's up?"

"Yazov's dead."

I could hear Buck suck in a deep breath. "Holy shit. Ochoa wasn't kidding, was he?"

"Doesn't appear so. There's more."

"Always is. Let's have it."

"Yazov left me the bulk of his estate."

"*What*?" Buck said, choking a bit. "How much?"

I laughed. "Same question popped into my head, pard, along with how dirty."

"Screw the dirt, Stainless. You can run it through a laundromat."

"Buck, you're talking to an officer of the law."

"Yeah, well, you know what I mean."

"Uh-huh. You feel like another run down to Tortola?"

"You picking up the tab?"

I laughed. "Yes. I just hope my *inheritance* will cover it."

Buck snorted. "Oh, I think you'll probably be surprised."

"Hell, I'm already surprised."

At 1:30 p.m., Wes called me. "We'll take the King Air."

I laughed. "*We*?"

"Yeah. Buck filled me in over lunch. And last I heard, I was also on Ochoa's hit parade."

"Yeah, well, money's pretty tight, Wes."

"Like hell. Buck said you inherited millions from Yazov."

I shook my head. "Wes, I'm in his will and that's all I know at this point."

"Not a problem, podjo. I still have a little of the *missing* kilo money left over from our trips with Tommy. Hell, Stainless, all we're talking about is fuel. And besides, you may need to smuggle in a little 'hardware'."

I rolled my eyes, wondering how many *keywords* had just tripped a government computer listening in to our conversation. "Wes, be careful what you say on a cell phone."

"Relax, Hardin. My cell has FIPS 140 encryption."

I should have known. "Okay. I have to be in Tortola Sunday. I'm meeting with Yazov's lawyer Monday morning."

"Hey, pal, you're talking to Sky King here."

"Okay, Wes. Thanks. Just keep in mind whoever got Yazov has our names, too. And he could still be on the island."

"Don't worry, I haven't forgotten. I'm turning over every rock looking for information. But so far, nada. Whoever Ochoa is using, he's from way off the reservation. And I'll tell you something else, Hardin."

"What?"

"Whoever this guy is, he's very, very good."

I nodded. “I’ll see you Sunday, bright and early.”

Chapter 41

I spent the rest of the week testifying at various trials, mostly domestic violence and drunk-driving cases. During some of the testimony, I began to wonder if alcohol shouldn't be banned and drugs, at least pot, legalized. I'd never had a case where someone got stoned and then beat the crap out of his wife. Maybe I should run for the Texas State Legislature.

By Friday, Ochoa's assassin and Tortola were starting to look pretty good.

I hadn't talked to Rory since I'd found out about Alexsie. She'd been in Austin all week, doing a little lobbying of her own. She was due back today.

I waited until a little past five and called her cell phone. "Hey, babe. Are you back in town?"

"Hi, Hardin. Yes, I flew in around three. What's up?"

"Have you got a minute?"

My tone is always a dead giveaway.

"What is it, Hardin?"

"It's Alexsie. He's been murdered."

There was a long pause before Rory replied.

"Where?"

"At his villa on Tortola."

"Did they catch the guy?" Rory asked, her voice catching just a bit.

"No. And I doubt they ever will."

"Ochoa?"

"Not personally, but one of his retards."

"Are you going down there, Hardin?"

"Yes, but not to look for the shooter."

"Then why?"

I was a bit embarrassed. "Well, turns out Alexsie left me all his holdings in the BVI."

"You're kidding."

"No. He left a note, too. It said if I was going to marry a rich and powerful woman like you, I should have a decent dowry. Or words to that effect."

Rory was silent of a long moment. "Hardin, I don't know what to say."

"Say yes."

Rory laughed. "*Yes*?"

"Okay. Let's set a date."

"Whoa, pardner, I was saying I didn't know what to say to Alexsie's letter."

I chuckled. "Oh. So you don't want to marry me?"

"One thing at a time, big boy. Don't you think you should take care of Ochoa and his assassin—and probate the will—before we get too far ahead of ourselves?"

"I do. No pun intended. Pick you up at seven?"

*****

Rory and I spent Friday and Saturday at her condo on South Padre Island. When I left at six Sunday morning, she was sleeping soundly.

I stopped at the Taco Shack and got a half-dozen breakfast tacos and three large coffees. I ate one of the tacos in the parking lot, and then headed for the airport to meet Buck and Wes.

I got to the airport around seven a.m. Wes and Buck were standing by Wes's Corvette waiting for me.

I pulled up next to them. "Morning, fellas," I said. "I've got coffee and tacos there in the bag on the passenger seat. Help yourselves."

"Thanks, Stainless," Buck said, reaching through the open passenger window. He grabbed a taco and one of the coffees, and handed the bag to Wes.

"*Por nada, amigos*," I said, pulling my AWOL bag from the back of my Jeep.

Wes finished a taco and threw the wrapper in a nearby trashcan. "I was out here yesterday afternoon. We're fueled and ready. We can leave any time y'all are ready."

As before, we flew to Cancún and refueled. But in no rush this trip, we took a cab into town and had lunch at La Cantinita. After chowing down on excellent Mexican food, we headed back to the airport for the final leg.

We lifted off runway 12R and headed for the Caribbean. We had a little more than four hours flying time to Tortola.

Once we cleared the Mexican coastline, Wes turned the plane to a more easterly heading of 95 degrees. I was sitting in the right seat, and he glanced over at me. "We'll be going right by El Fidel's island, in case you want to stop for cigars."

I looked back at Buck who was seated in the first row of the cabin. "Wes wants to know if we'd like to stop in Cuba for cigars."

Buck grimaced and gave me the finger.

I looked over at Wes. "Buck says no."

We had a smooth flight all the way to Tortola. Wes set the King Air down with barely a squeak of the tires.

I looked over at him. "I think you're beginning to get the hang of this."

Wes nodded and said something to the tower. Twenty minutes later, we'd secured the plane and were clearing Immigration and Customs.

"You all together?" the immigration officer asked.

I nodded. "Yes, sir."

The officer motioned us forward. "Passports, please."

We handed over our passports and waited for the officer to review them.

"Business or pleasure, fellows?"

I glanced at Buck and Wes and spoke for the group. "A bit of both, sir. I have a meeting in the morning with a local attorney. After that we'll sightsee a bit, and then fly out on Tuesday."

The officer nodded and stamped all three of our passports and handed them back. "Enjoy your time in the British Virgin Islands, gentlemen."

We took our passports and started for the Customs area. I stopped, turned back to the officer, and took a long shot. "Sir, I'm a law enforcement officer from Texas," I said, producing my badge and ID. "The man, Yazov, who was shot on Tortola a week or so ago, was working with my office and the DEA on a case. And I was just curious if anybody had come through Immigration recently who didn't seem to be what they claimed."

The officer looked at my badge. "Sheriff, is it?"

"Yes, sir," I replied. "And formerly DEA."

"Well, Sheriff, this is one of the offshore banking capitals of the world. We see a little bit of everything."

I nodded. "Yes, I guess you do at that. Well, thanks anyway."

I started to walk away.

"Wait just a second, Sheriff. There was one guy who bothered me."

I motioned for Buck and Wes to hold up. "Yes?"

"Yeah, his passport said he was from Stockbridge, Hampshire, England. But he didn't know a damn thing about trout fishing."

I looked at Buck and Wes and then at the immigration officer. "Trout fishing."

The officer nodded. "Stockbridge sits on the Test River. Some of the best fly fishing in England. When

I mentioned something about it to this bloke, he looked like he didn't know what the hell I was talking about."

I set my AWOL bag down. "Really? Have you got a name?"

"It's in our files, but I wrote his name in my log book, for future reference. Hang on a minute."

The officer pulled a small black notebook from a drawer in his desk. "Kind of a diary, really. I jot down names, information, things I want to remember."

He thumbed through the pages. "Yes, here it is. Hollinberry. William Hollinberry, from Stockbridge, U.K. I made a note to check his passport through Interpol."

"Anything come back?" I asked.

The officer frowned. "Afraid I haven't gotten around to it. But I'll do it first thing in the morning. Where are you staying, Sheriff?"

"We're staying at the Surfsong. Our pilot," I pointed at Wes, "doesn't like to get too far from his plane."

The immigration officer raised his eyebrows and checked his notes. "That's where Mr. Hollinberry said he was staying."

"Can you remember how he looked?"

"The guy looked average. Average height, weight, medium-length dark hair. Really, nothing stood out about this guy." The officer paused. "Except for his shoes. He was wearing expensive-looking shoes. Probably Italian."

"Is he still on the island?" I asked.

"Couldn't say, Sheriff. Once we check them in we sort of lose track."

"Would his airline check his passport when he boarded to fly out?"

"Yes, just to be sure he had one. And his ticket, of course. But Hollinberry came in on a private jet."

"You get many flying in on private planes?"

"Yes, sir, we do. But not many on a Dassault."

I glanced at Wes.

"It's a French three-engine job," Wes said. "Very expensive, very fast, with a hell of a range."

I nodded and handed the immigration officer one of my cards. "My numbers are on the card. I'd appreciate a heads-up if Mr. Hollinberry returns."

We cleared Customs and caught a cab to our hotel. Wes looked around as we pulled up to the front of the Surfsong. "Wow! I see why Hollinberry chose this place."

I paid the cabbie and grabbed my bag. "Yeah, sits right on Well Bay. Close to the airport, in case you need to adios in a hurry. And only twenty minutes from Road Town."

"Is that where you're meeting Yazov's attorney?" Buck asked, joining me at the curb.

"Yeah. Ten in the morning." I replied, glancing at my watch. It was 3:30, local time.

I'd booked a three-room suite for two nights. When I saw the rate, I hoped Buck was right about my inheritance.

When we finished checking in, I asked the desk clerk if he remembered a guest by the name of Hollinberry. The clerk hesitated so I took a hundred from my wallet and slid it across the desk. "It's important."

The clerk looked around and deftly palmed the C-note. "Yes, sir. Mr. Hollinberry was here about a week ago. Stayed one night and checked out."

"Did he pay by credit card?"

The young clerk smiled and shook his head. "No, sir. He paid cash. Along with a nice gratuity for the staff."

I nodded. "Did he happen to say where he was going?"

The clerk looked at me like I was nuts and shook his head. "No, sir. He did not."

I sensed I'd exhausted the hundred. "Thanks for your time."

Our suite was much more accommodating than the desk clerk.

"This'll work," Buck said, looking out through the sliding glass doors at the white sand beach and crystal clear water. "Anybody for a swim?"

He didn't have to ask twice. For the next couple of hours, we swam and dozed on the beach until we were totally rejuvenated.

"Anybody hungry?" I said, getting up from my beach towel.

Wes jumped up. "Yeah, I'm starved."

"Me, too," Buck chimed in.

"Okay. There's no restaurant in the hotel, but we can get a cab over to Tortola and grab a bite. We're free until tomorrow at ten."

We grabbed quick showers, climbed into shorts, polo shirts and flip-flops, and headed to the front of the hotel to catch a cab.

There were three taxis parked near the front entrance. We hailed into the first one in line, and the three of us managed to squeeze into the backseat.

The cabbie turned and looked over the seatback. "Maybe one of you fellas should ride up front . . . just to balance the load."

I laughed and volunteered. "Good idea."

The driver nodded and waited until I'd climbed into the front passenger seat. "Where to, fellas?"

"Is there a good place to eat close by?" I asked.

"Red Rock is the closest, and the food's very good."

I looked at Wes and Buck, who both nodded. "Red Rock it is, pal."

We drove past the airport, crossed the QE-II Bridge and went a short way down the south coast of Tortola Island.

"Here we are, gentlemen," the cabbie said, pulling into the restaurant's parking area. "That'll be ten dollars. And would you like me to come back in a couple of hours?"

I nodded. "We'd appreciate it," I said, handing him a ten and three ones.

Adawulf hadn't gone far. He had the *company* jet drop him at nearby Saint Thomas, in the U.S. Virgin Islands. He instructed the pilot to fly back to Buenos Aires. He intended to stick around for a while to see if anybody of interest showed up to say goodbye to Comrade Yazov.

From Saint Thomas, Adawulf took the short ferry ride from Red Hook Bay over to Saint John. Hurricane season was not the high season in the Caribbean, and he was able to rent a very spacious townhouse overlooking Cruz Bay.

Before departing Tortola, First Officer Grace had introduced Adawulf to a young aircraft mechanic who had very good connections with the local authorities. Adawulf had paid the fellow one hundred pounds and given him one of his business cards, with instructions to call should anyone show up asking questions about Yazov.

He'd heard nothing in more than a week. He was beginning to think his hunch was wrong.

Sunday afternoon he got the call. "Mr. Hollinberry?"

"Yes?"

"Sir, this is Michael at the Tortola airport."

"Yes, Michael. You have something for me?"

"Yes, sir. At least I think so."

"Go ahead. And take your time."

"Yes, sir. Well, I have a friend at Customs. He said three Americans flew in today. One was some kind of police officer. He had a badge."

"I see. Go on."

"Well, they asked one of the immigration officers a lot of questions. And my friend thought he heard your name mentioned."

"Indeed."

"Yes, sir. And they said something about meeting with a lawyer in Road Town on Monday."

"Did they fly in on a commercial flight?"

"No, sir. They flew in on a King Air 350."

"Do you know where they are staying?"

"Yes, sir. I checked with the airport cabbies. One of them said he'd taken them to the Surfsong Hotel. Do you know it?"

Adawulf smiled. "Yes, I know it. Any idea how long they plan to stay?"

"The cab driver heard the one of them say they were flying out on Tuesday."

"Anything else?"

The man thought for a moment. "No, sir, that's about it."

"Well, Michael, you've done very well indeed. I will be back on Tortola tomorrow, and there'll be another hundred pounds for you."

"Thank you, Mr. Hollinberry. Are you flying in?"

Adawulf paused just long enough to let the young man know not to ask such questions. "I'll see you tomorrow. And Michael . . ."

"Yes, sir?"

"Keep our conversations confidential. Understood?"

"Yes, sir. I'll see you tomorrow."

Adawulf hung up and smiled. *Carnivores or cops . . . there's nothing like a dead body for bait.*

Chapter 42

The next morning we took a cab from our hotel to the financial district in Road Town. Aside from being the capital of the British Virgin Islands, Road Town is home to scores of offshore corporations, some little more than a post office box and phone number.

A good number of local lawyers oversee the corporate filings, board and shareholder meetings, and generally keep the myriad companies compliant with BVI rules and regulations. A like number of banks and bankers handle the money—compliant or otherwise.

The cab driver pulled over in front of a white three-story, colonial-looking office building. "Here we are, gentlemen."

I'd asked Wes and Buck to accompany me. I had a little surprise in mind for them, depending on my inheritance.

I paid the cab fare and we walked into the historic office building. I checked the registry and found

Winston Daltry's name. "Third floor, boys. Room 310."

We located the elevator and stepped in. Buck was just about to punch the button for the third floor when a very large, very dark-skinned woman wearing a bright flower print dress and matching hat joined us.

"Three, please," she said.

Buck pushed the button for the third floor, and the elevator doors slowly closed.

As we passed the second floor, I noticed a strong odor in the elevator. I looked at Buck and Wes to see if they'd broken wind. They both shook their heads and rolled their eyes toward the big gal standing off to one side and slightly behind us.

I cut a quick glance in her direction. She was holding her handbag in front of her with both hands. I think she was blushing, but her skin was so dark it was hard to tell.

She smiled and raised both her eyebrows. "Sorry 'bout dat. I t'ought I had me a better grip on it."

I couldn't help myself, I cracked up. Buck and Wes weren't far behind. I hadn't laughed so hard in years. When I finally caught my breath, I said, "Not a problem, ma'am. And I believe this is your floor."

She nodded and stepped out and turned to the left. Wes, Buck, and I piled out, still chuckling, and went to the right. We walked down the hall until we found number 310.

I took a deep breath to regain some semblance of composure. "Well, here goes nothing," I said, opening the door.

Mr. Daltry's receptionist greeted us. "Mr. Steel, I presume?"

"Yes, ma'am. And my associates, Mr. Stoddard and Mr. Bateman. Here to see Mr. Daltry."

"Have a seat, gentlemen. I'll tell Mr. Daltry you're here."

The receptionist was a rather heavy-set black gal. She stepped into Mr. Daltry's office and closed the door behind her.

A minute later she opened the door and held it for us. "Please come in, gentlemen."

Winston Daltry, Esq., got up and came around his large desk to greet us. He looked to be of English derivation and was maybe five-six and probably weighed around 220 lbs. He was wearing a well-cut suit and had a grip like a moray eel.

"Mr. Steel, gentlemen. Very nice to meet you all. Please have a seat. May we get you anything . . . tea, Coke?"

"A Coke with ice would be great," I said, glancing at Wes and Buck, who nodded in agreement.

"Sorry, gentlemen. No ice, but the bottles are quite cold." Daltry nodded to his receptionist. "Four Cokes, please, Sallie."

Daltry returned to his desk chair. I sat in one of two chairs in front of Mr. Daltry's desk. Wes and Buck sat on a sofa, off to the side.

"I hope you don't mind if my two associates sit in on this," I said, tilting my head toward Buck and Wes.

"No, not at all," Daltry replied. "Yazov's will will be of public record, once you and I are through."

I nodded. "I see."

Daltry had the will in a manila folder on his desk. As he pulled it out, Sallie returned with four bottles of Coca-Cola. We each took one.

"Thank you, Sallie. Please hold my calls until Mr. Steel and I have concluded our business."

Sallie nodded "Yes, sir." She turned to the rest of us as she walked out. "Gentlemen."

Daltry held up his bottle of Coke. "Health, wealth, and happiness."

We all held up our bottles and then took a drink of the less than ice-cold Coca-Cola.

"Okay," Daltry said, setting his bottle on a coaster. "Down to business. "I'll read Yazov's will. It won't take long, and I think you will find it very straightforward."

Two minutes later, I couldn't have agreed more. Yazov had left me three million U.S. dollars. The money was in a local bank and was POD (payable on death). He'd also left me his villa on Tortola, the one where we'd dealt with the Cubans.

"Any questions, Mr. Hardin?"

I glanced quickly at Buck and Wes, who both looked flabbergasted . . . as was I.

"No," I replied. The *no* was barely audible. I took a breath, cleared my throat, and said it again. "No."

Daltry nodded. "Very good. I will accompany you to the bank as soon as we are done here. We'll present the necessary documents and get the account transferred to you. Once the will has been probated, I will prepare a simple deed transferring Yazov's real estate to you as well. The house is free and clear of any liens, but you will have to pay local property taxes."

I looked at Daltry and shook my head. "I can't believe it."

Daltry smiled. "Occasionally, I have a day when I get to make someone happy," he said, raising his bottle of lukewarm Coke. "This, gentlemen, is one of those days. *Salud.*"

Twenty minutes later, we were in the office of the senior vice president of FirstCaribbean National Bank. It took about thirty minutes of paper-shuffling, notarizing of signatures, a copy of the original death certificate, and stamping of numerous documents, but Daltry got the funds transferred into my new account.

Daltry shook hands with the bank officer and prepared to leave.

"Just one or two more details, gentlemen," I said, looking at Daltry and my new best friend, the senior VP of FCNB. "I want to make two transfers of $750,000."

I could see my new best friend was crushed. "Not to worry, sir. I want you to set up accounts for Messieurs Stoddard and Bateman," I said, gesturing toward Buck and Wes.

"Hardin, you don't have to do that," Wes said, looking and sounding stunned.

Buck didn't know whether to nod or shake his head, so he kind of did both.

I laughed. "No arguments, boys. It's a done deal. You've earned it. And besides, the fat lady ain't sung yet."

Daltry and my greatly relieved new best friend looked at me like I'd lost it. But I knew Buck and Wes understood. We still had an assassin—one resourceful enough to take out Yazov—loose on the reservation. And maybe worse, the guy who hired him.

When we finished up at the bank, Daltry said he'd be in contact regarding the deed to the property and should anything unforeseen come up.

"Just one more thing, Mr. Steel," Daltry said, fishing around in his pants pockets. "Here, you may as well take these."

He handed me an electronic gate opener and a set of keys.

"These open the front gate and the doors to Yazov's villa. Feel free to use the place as you see fit. I doubt anyone will object."

I took the keys. "Thank you, Mr. Daltry," I said, grinning at Buck and Wes. "Since we're recently *cashed up,* maybe we'll stay a few extra days and kind of get a feel for the place."

Buck and Wes both nodded.

"You should do just that," Daltry replied, handing us each a card. "If I can be of further service, gentlemen, please call me."

I shook Daltry's hand. "What about your fee?"

Daltry shook his head. "Mr. Yazov kept an escrow account with me. It will cover my fees. Good day, gentlemen."

While we celebrated our windfall at the Mid-Town Bar and Grill, Adawulf was getting off the ferry from Saint John.

With only a backpack and small suitcase, Adawulf looked like every other tourist on the ferry. He breezed through the minimal Immigration and Customs inspection at the ferry landing.

Out on the street he waved down a passing taxi and climbed in. "Surfsong Hotel."

Twenty minutes later he was checking in.

"Mr. Hollinberry. So good to see you back again, and so soon," the over-eager desk clerk said, remembering Hollinberry's very generous gratuity.

Adawulf looked at the young hotel employee. "Yes. A bit of unfinished business, I'm afraid." He paused. "I left a piece of luggage, an aluminum case, with the hotel on my last visit. Would you be so kind as to retrieve it and have it delivered to my room?"

"Yes, sir. Right away," the clerk replied.

Adawulf nodded and handed the clerk his bag claim tag and a ten-pound note. "Thank you."

*****

After our celebratory lunch and a couple of cold beers, the three of us piled into a cab and headed back to the Surfsong.

As we entered the lobby, I noticed a fellow who'd evidently just checked in. As the man walked across the hotel lobby, something about him caught my eye.

I nudged Buck and tilted my head in the man's direction and whispered. "Take a look at the guy who just checked in."

Buck watched the fellow cross the lobby. "Yeah. What about him?"

"Pretty average-looking guy. Run-of-the-beach clothes," I replied.

Buck looked past me. "Yeah? So what?"

"Check out his shoes."

The desk clerk had disappeared through a door into a luggage storage room behind the front desk. We were standing at the front desk when he returned a few minutes later. He was carrying a well-traveled, oversized, aluminum briefcase.

"Sorry, gentlemen. I had to retrieve a piece of luggage for a guest,"

On a hunch, I said, "Did Mr. Hollinberry forget something?"

The clerk looked surprised. "This is the second time you've asked about Mr. Hollinberry. Are you friends of his?"

"In a manner of speaking," I said. "We have, or rather, had, a mutual acquaintance."

The surprise worn off, the clerk quickly regained his innkeeper demeanor. “Was there something I can do for you gentlemen?”

I glanced at Buck and Wes and hoped they’d play along. “Yes. We were scheduled to leave tomorrow, but I was wondering if we might be able to extend our stay a few more days?”

The clerk relaxed and smiled. “Let me check,” he said, typing some information into his computer. “Yes, your suite is available through Friday. Would that be satisfactory?”

I smiled back. “Perfect. Just one more thing,” I said, pulling out my sheriff’s ID. I opened and closed the leather wallet before the kid could get a good look at my badge. “I’ll need Hollinberry’s case.”

The clerk started to object, but backed off when Buck started around the desk. “We’d hate to arrest you for obstruction of justice,” I said, holding up my hand, signaling Buck to wait.

“What will I tell Mr. Hollinberry?” the clerk asked, visibly shaken.

“Tell him you haven’t been able to locate his case, that it may have been misplaced, or possibly stolen. And that the hotel is doing everything it can to locate it,” I paused and glanced at Buck and Wes. “Offer to pay him for the case and its contents.” Buck and Wes both smiled. “And don’t worry, kid, Hollinberry won’t go to the police.”

Case in hand, I looked at Buck and Wes. “I could use a real drink.”

They both nodded. I could see they were dying to find out what in the hell I was up to.

We adjourned to a small bar overlooking the beach and took a table off to the side. I slid Hollinberry's case under the table.

A good-looking young barmaid came over as soon as we sat down.

"Rum and coke, please." I said, glancing at Buck and Wes. They both nodded. "Make it three."

We sat quietly with our thoughts until the barmaid returned with our drinks.

Buck took a large drink of his rum and coke and set his glass on the table. "That little pipsqueak was Hollinberry?"

I leaned forward. "That little *pipsqueak* took out Yazov, and I'm betting the murder weapon is in the aluminum case. And there's one more thing—he's looking for us."

Wes looked at me. "Hell, Hardin, we were damn near face to face in the lobby."

I nodded. "I know. I don't think he knows what we look like. He probably got a tip some fellas were making inquiries about Yazov's murder, and he's put two and two together."

Buck leaned in. "So he's here to take us out?"

I took a drink of my rum and coke. "That's my guess, and why I extended our stay." I winked at Buck. "Plus, we can all afford it now, thanks to Alexsie."

Buck shook his head. "The money won't do us much good if we're dead."

I smiled and took another drink. "I've got a plan."

Wes chuckled and glanced at Buck. "A plan would be good."

They both looked at me and waited.

I took another sip of my drink and watched a topless gal run down the sandy beach and dive into the crystal clear water.

I tilted my glass toward Wes. "Wes, you go over to the airport and check on the plane. Make sure she's fueled and ready to leave. And bring back our *hardware*."

Wes's King Air was, to say the least, *modified.* The plane had more secret compartments than a pirate ship. Which, come to think of it, was exactly what it was. For this operation, he'd smuggled in three small .22 caliber Beretta automatics.

"Buck and I will go up to Yazov's villa, get the place squared away for the party, and open Hollinberry's case."

Wes was in the middle of a drink and nearly choked. "What party?"

I watched another topless gal join her friend in the gentle surf. "A housewarming party," I said, taking out a pen and writing a *special* invitation on a cocktail napkin. I folded the napkin and motioned to the barmaid. "And we're going to see to it that Mr. Hollinberry gets an invitation."

Chapter 43

While Wes checked on the plane and recovered our weapons, Buck and I went up to Yazov's villa. We managed to get Hollinberry's case open without too much trouble.

Inside the case, as I'd expected, was a weapon. A disassembled Ruger Mini-14.

Buck looked at the rifle and whistled. "Think it's clean?"

"As Nixon's tapes," I replied. "The only thing tying Hollinberry to this weapon is the hotel claim-check, and our friend the desk clerk."

"I doubt the clerk will cooperate," Buck said, rolling his eyes.

I nodded. "You're probably right, but I may have an idea."

Wes showed up about an hour later. We hid the Berettas and Hollinberry's case, and headed into Road Town to hit a few of the local bars.

Between the three of us, we managed to invite a couple dozen good-looking women to a party: Wednesday night at Yazov's villa. And we told them to bring friends.

As we exited the last bar on our tour, I took Buck and Wes aside. "There's just one small problem, fellas."

"What's that, Stainless?" Wes said, smiling at nothing in particular.

I took a deep breath and exhaled. "I don't think I can shoot Hollinberry in cold blood."

Buck snorted. "Hell, Hardin, he'll probably shoot us first."

I nodded. "Yeah, that's a distinct possibility. Maybe we should just turn him over to the local authorities and take our chances."

Wes grimaced and shook his head. "All they'll have him on is traveling under a fake passport. He'll claim we stole the case and planted the rifle. And we'll be right back in the shitter."

I nodded. "Maybe I can come up with something short of killing the SOB, and better than turning him over to the locals."

By the time our barmaid passed my written invitation to Hollinberry, he'd already heard about the party at Yazov's villa.

He also knew there would be no chance of a hit at the party. There would be way too many witnesses and semi-innocent bystanders. And besides, there was the added problem of the hotel not being able to locate his case. But the party would give him the chance to identify his targets, and perhaps glean some small tidbit of information he could use in planning their demise.

Wednesday was hectic. The three of us spent the day laying in food and drink for the party. I made good use of my brand-new FCNB debit card.

By six p.m. we were ready, and we still had two hours before the festivities were scheduled to begin.

I opened a Red Stripe and plopped into an easy chair. “I don’t know about you two, but I going to finish this beer, take a short nap, and then shower and get ready. It should be one hell of an interesting evening.”

Buck and Wes both laughed.

“You want a beer, Buck?” Wes asked, heading for the kitchen.

Buck nodded. “Yeah, thanks.”

Wes was gone a couple of minutes. When he returned he had two Red Stripes wedged between the fingers of his right hand. In his left hand, he was carrying a brown paper bag. He handed Buck one of the beers, set the other on a table, and opened up the paper bag.

“Gentlemen,” Wes said, reaching into the bag and tossing Buck and me each an ankle holster holding a .22 Beretta, “these are for tonight. Wear slacks and come heeled.”

The first guests showed up at eight sharp. And once they started arriving, they came in droves. Nothing like free food and booze at a murdered Russian's villa to draw a crowd.

By 8:30, the party was in full swing. There were topless women in both the north and south pools, and booze was flowing like Prohibition had just ended.

I was mixing drinks for a couple of latecomers when Buck and Wes came over. Both were grinning like they'd won the lottery, which in effect they had.

I handed drinks to the two partygoers and glanced at Buck and Wes. "Any sign of *Fancy Shoes*?"

Buck motioned in the direction of the front door. "Uh-huh. I believe Mr. Hollinberry has arrived. And in very good company."

I looked past Buck. Hollinberry was here alright, looking like he'd just stepped out of a Tommy Bahama catalogue. And he had a gorgeous, very tan, Caucasian woman on each arm.

Wes winked at me. "Well, you said it would be interesting."

"Take over, will you?" I said. "Just tell everybody to help themselves. I want to go greet our newly arrived guests."

I wiped my hands on a bar towel and headed for Hollinberry

"Evening, y'all," I said, extending my hand to Hollinberry. "I'm Hardin Steel, your host for this evening's festivities."

I noticed just the slightest flicker in his eyes when I said my name. *Damn, this guy is one cool customer*.

Hollinberry shook my hand with a firm, dry grip.

"I'm William Hollinberry. I received your invitation and took the liberty of inviting my two friends Amber and Chris. I hope you don't mind, old chap."

"Not at all. Everyone is welcome. The bar is over yonder," I said, gesturing toward where Buck and Wes were standing. "My two associates will get you started. Enjoy the evening."

Hollinberry smiled and put an arm around each *Playboy* centerfold wannabe's waist. "I don't see any way around it, Mr. Steel."

Damn. A man after my own heart. Now I knew I'd have a hard time shooting the SOB.

I watched as Hollinberry and company strode up to the bar. I could see they were exchanging small talk with Buck and Wes. When they got their drinks and moved off to join the party, Wes looked over at me and rolled his eyes. Buck never took his eyes off the two *Playboy* wannabes.

It's a surreal feeling to socialize with a man who's been hired to kill you. But by two in the morning, nobody'd been shot and the party was still going strong.

Standing there watching the drunken revelers, I suddenly had a first-order epiphany. Usually when that happens, I just have another drink. But this time I decided to act on it.

I came up behind Hollinberry, who was watching his two lady friends frolic naked in the south pool. It was obvious they'd lost all interest in *Tommy Bahama* and the male species in general.

"There's just no accounting for taste," I said, watching Amber slide down Chris's belly, until her head was under water. "Coffee, Mr. Hollinberry?"

Hollinberry nodded, watching Amber's friend suddenly shudder. "She must have hit a nerve."

I laughed. "Looks like. Come on, I just put on a fresh pot."

Hollinberry followed me into the kitchen. I took two clean cups from a cabinet and poured the coffee. "Cream, sugar?"

"No. Black is fine."

I nodded and handed him his cup. For a moment neither of us said anything.

I took a sip and looked at him over the top of my cup. "So, Mr. Hollinberry, should I just shoot you now and save us both a great deal of trouble? Or would you be interested in a deal?"

Hollinberry was in the middle of sipping his coffee. He didn't even flinch.

"What type of deal, Mr. Steel?"

I made a sweeping gesture with an open palm. "This type of deal."

"The villa?"

"Yep. It's worth millions and it's yours on two conditions."

Hollinberry took another sip of his coffee. "The villa is yours to give?"

I nodded and smiled. "Yazov left it to me in his will."

The corners of Hollinberry's mouth turned up just a fraction. "And what would those conditions be?"

"You forget about me and my two associates . . . and you kill Ochoa."

Hollinberry arched both his eyebrows. "I see. And what guarantees would I have?"

I opened a cupboard under the sink and took out Hollinberry's case. "I guarantee I won't turn this over to the authorities. I'm sure a bullet fired from the rifle in this case will match the one that went through Yazov's brain. I understand the authorities dug that bullet out of a wall by the north pool."

There was no bullet found, but I was guessing Hollinberry didn't know that.

"Further, I have an attorney here in Tortola. I will instruct him to prepare the necessary documents to transfer this property to you. The documents will be held in escrow until Ochoa is confirmed dead, at which time I will instruct my attorney to transfer the property to you." I paused and looked at Hollinberry. "And, lastly, I guarantee not to shoot you now."

Hollinberry pursed his lips and looked at me. "And how do I know you won't renege and come after me once Ochoa is dead?"

"The same way I know you won't do the same to me."

Hollinberry smiled for the first time in our conversation. "A gentlemen's agreement?"

"Exactly."

Hollinberry switched his coffee cup to his left hand and extended his right. "Done." He paused for a moment and looked at me. "Would you have really shot me?"

I smiled and pulled up my right pants leg. “Damn straight.”

At that moment, Wes and Buck walked into the kitchen. They could see my exposed ankle holster and Beretta.

Wes looked over his shoulder at the revelers. “Jesus, Hardin, there are still people all over the place.”

I let my trouser leg fall. “Relax, boys. Mr. Hollinberry and I have come to an understanding. Nobody’s going to get killed . . . except for Frederick Ochoa.”

Chapter 44

I'd been back in my office about two weeks when Wes called bright and early one morning.

"Hey, Wes. What's up?"

"Has Yazov's will been probated?"

"Not yet. Last I heard from Daltry, it'd be a couple more weeks. Why?"

Wes paused. "Well, pal, I heard a rumor that an attempt had been made on Ochoa's life."

"Damn. Hollinberry doesn't mess around, does he? Is Ochoa dead?"

"According to my source, it wasn't Hollinberry. Word is the Cubans were behind it. And no, they didn't get him."

"Cubans?"

"That's the word on the street. So let me ask you, pardner, what the hell happens to our deal with Hollinberry if somebody kills Ochoa before he does?"

I heard a beeping sound on my phone. "Hold on a sec, Wes. I got another call coming in."

I transferred to the incoming call. "Hardin Steel."

"Sheriff Steel, this is Johnathan Price, Tortola Immigration. I'm the officer you discussed Mr. Hollinberry with."

"Yes, sir, Officer Price. What can I do for you?"

"Well, I just wanted you to know I ran Mr. Hollinberry's passport information by Interpol."

"Find anything?"

"Yes. Turns out Mr. William Hollinberry was indeed born in Stockbridge on December 14th, 1970. And the passport is valid."

"I'll be damned."

"I hope not, Sheriff. But there's more."

"Always is," I mumbled.

"Yes, well, William Hollinberry died June 15th, 1971. He was six months old."

I laughed. "Pretty damn young to apply for a passport."

"Indeed. Interpol has issued an arrest warrant for this fellow passing himself off as William Hollinberry."

I couldn't very well tell Officer Price I'd made a deal with the international assassin. "Excellent work, sir. With Interpol looking for him, I doubt we'll see Mr. Hollinberry again."

"I hope you're right, Sheriff. Anyway, I just wanted you to know."

"Many thanks, Officer Price. Take care."

I managed to reconnect with Wes. "Sorry, Wes, that was the immigration officer we met in Tortola. He had some information on Hollinberry. Seems the passport he was using was issued to a guy who died about forty years ago."

"Damn, does that old scam still work?"

"Evidently."

"So what do you think?"

"About what?"

"Jeezus, Hardin . . . are you paying attention here? About goddamned Hollinberry, *that's* what."

I chuckled. "I think no matter who tags and bags Ochoa, I'm deeding Yazov's villa to Hollinberry."

"Wise choice, Stainless. I don't want that SOB dogging us the rest of our lives."

"Keep me posted if you hear anything else."

Wes exhaled softly. "How *the* hell did we get in such a mess?"

I laughed. "I think it had something to do with my second ex-wife."

"Uh-huh. Stay frosty, Stainless. And watch your six."

I closed my cell phone and dropped it back into my shirt pocket. Looking around for some matches, I reached across my desk and opened my humidor. The sweet smell of aged tobacco drifted toward me. There was one Cuban cigar left. I trimmed the end, walked over and opened a window, and fired it up.

I leaned against the window frame and watched two squirrels in an oak tree getting it on. The male had an impressive set of balls and was going for greatness. Nothing like a good cigar and watching two squirrels fornicate to get you right with the day.

Betty Filmore, the dispatcher, opened my door and leaned in.

"Sheriff, you've got a call on line one."

The way she said it, I knew something was up. "Who is it?"

Betty smiled and shook her head. "He says his name is Raúl Castro, and he sounds quite agitated."

The End

Made in United States
North Haven, CT
28 February 2025

66359094R00196